Replaying the Game

Emily Tudor

Copyright © 2023 Emily Tudor

All rights reserved

The characters and events portrayed in this book are fictitious. Any similarity to real persons, living or dead, is coincidental and not intended by the author.

No part of this book may be reproduced, or stored in a retrieval system, or transmitted in any form or by any means, electronic, mechanical, photocopying, recording, or otherwise, without express written permission of the publisher.

ISBN-13: 9798373873857

Cover design by: Hannah Nguyen
Edited by: Alexis Smith & Grayson Holmes
Printed in the United States of America

For Lexi, Hannah, and Grayson. Thank you for being the best friends a girl could ask for and for giving me the courage to write this book. I loved using our friendship as a guide for the characters we created. It's basically fanfiction about ourselves at this point, but it's fun, so who cares?

And for anyone who has dared to open themselves back up to love when it has shut you down before. I'm proud of you! The bravest thing you can do is allow someone to love you the way you deserve. Be patient. Be unapologetically yourself.

AUTHORS NOTE

Hi beautiful readers! I wanted to preface the book with a few things, so bear with me.

This is the first book I have ever entirely written, from thinking about the idea to drafting it and finally seeing it through to the end. I usually started an idea that I had and never finished them because I was too scared. Too scared to put my words into the world for others to read and judge. But then, I met some people who gave me so much love and support and pushed me to do this, and I took the leap. I wrote this book with their help and their love alongside me. These characters came together and were inspired by three people I love so dearly, and knowing that they helped me take the leap and were with me while writing and editing this book means the world.

That being said, in no way is this perfect. This book was written, edited, and created using four people. It will not be perfect, and I don't expect it to be perfect. There might be some typos we missed, among other things, so please do not judge us too harshly on that.

This book holds so many beautiful things in it, including romance, but at the core of this book, I hope the friendship between the girls shines as well. These girls all hold a special place in my heart, and I hope you love them as much as Hannah, Lexi, Grayson, and I loved creating them. The friendship between them is the center of this universe we created and I hope you love them all in their own way.

Writing this book helped me in so many ways, but I am glad that I can finally share my words with the world and hopefully make some of you feel seen and heard. I love you all! Thank you for taking a chance on this book. I hope you enjoy it!

PLAYLIST

Adore You - Harry Styles
All I Want - Olivia Rodrigo
August - Taylor Swift
Bad Habit - Steve Lacy
Bags - Clairo
Better - Gracie Abrams
Big Black Car - Gregory Alan Isakov
The Bottom - Gracie Abrams
Ceilings - Lizzy McAlpine
Daylight - Taylor Swift
Enchanted (Taylor's Version) - Taylor Swift
Friends - Chase Atlantic
Grace - Lewis Capaldi
Here With Me - d4vd
I Don't Wanna Know - Knox
I Wanna Be Yours - Arctic Monkeys
Jealous - Nick Jonas
Just a Little Bit of Your Heart - Ariana Grande
Like Real People Do - Hozier
Like the Movies - Laufey
People Watching - Conan Gray
Pool House - The Backseat Lovers
Until I Found You - Stephen Sanchez
The Way I Loved You (Taylor's Version) - Taylor Swift
Wildest Dreams (Taylor's Version) - Taylor Swift
You Don't Go To Parties - 5 Seconds of Summer

CONTENT WARNINGS:

This book contains references to the loss of a parent (off-book) and sexual touching without consent (not graphic but could still be triggering for some, especially some words used.)

"Let me tell you something about love. It does not knock often. And when it does you have to let it in." — Brooke Davis (One Tree Hill)

1

Hadleigh

"Is this book just a how-to get away with murder for dummies?"

Honestly, that's a valid question. It quite literally details how the main character got away with framing someone else for murder. Finishing up this series was a big highlight for the book club this week. One of my favorite parts of the week happens on Wednesday nights with the three other people next to me.

Book club—the Grand Mountain Book Club, with only four members. We meet weekly to discuss our pick of the month. Since we just got back to school, we've been taking the entire time to discuss what we read over break, even though we facetimed all the time and read together.

That's how attached we all are. From four corners of the United States, we still maintained our friendship. I was worried that I wasn't going to make any friends coming to college here, but the fact that I found these three people, I know we'll be in it for the long haul.

"I honestly think Paige could be the main character in this book. Being a criminal justice major herself, she could get away with murder and frame someone else." I say out loud to the group. On the outside, Paige Yarrow is the sweetest and most sunshiney person you will ever meet. With long, dirty blonde hair, she looks and acts like the sun. Her eyes are light green, and she's around 5'6" and pale. On the inside, though, she's insane. She watches true crime for fun and tries to solve cold cases when she can't sleep. Suffice it to say she has definitely chosen the right field of study.

"I am neither going to confirm or deny that statement."

"Confirm or deny all you want, we all know it's true. I always hear those murder documentaries on your laptop before you go to bed. One time I walked into the apartment, and you had fallen asleep in the middle of one. I had to turn it off before they started talking about cut-up body parts. Especially before I made a sandwich for dinner. I seriously don't know how you watch those."

That beautiful human being is Amelia Ellis. She and Paige have their own apartment on campus for the next two years. They're both juniors and have been inseparable since they were randomly assigned to be each other's roommates freshman year. A match made in heaven, or hell because they're a bit too similar, and it gets creepy sometimes. Amelia has short, curly brown hair and is around 5'9", with eyes the color of the ocean. They stand out against her olive skin.

"I definitely don't want to bail Paige, or honestly any of you, out of jail, but if I had to, I would. Only once, though, and only if you were innocent."

That was Ella Williams, our resident mom friend. With long, reddish-brown hair that she's wearing in her natural curls today, she's around 5'5". Ella has golden skin with huge, round brown eyes. She's a senior this year and is in her last semester here ta

Grand Mountain. She's the fiery one of our group. Did someone say something crass to you? Get Ella on the phone, and she'll make them regret it. She's always there when you need her. I'll be so sad to see her go, but I know I at least have another two years with Paige and Amelia. Though, it won't be the same without Ella. She's the founder of our little book club, after all. She saw Paige reading one of her favorite books in the library, and she immediately went up to her, and they chatted about it for an hour. Word spread about a book club being formed on campus, and I went to the informational meeting. Only the four of us showed up, and the rest is history.

Granted, it is a tiny campus. A nice liberal arts college in the middle of Virginia. The town of Grand Mountain, our campus, is named after it. It's more of a college town, with some bars and eateries around it. Our school only has around 5,000 people attending, and even that number might be shooting a bit high. I like it, though. You get mostly all four seasons here, and Virginia in the winter is stunning. We're currently in the second semester. which means we're right in the middle of winter. It makes for good book-reading weather. Since it's only the first week back in classes, we haven't picked a new book yet, but we've spent most of our time discussing the books we read over break. We all read this book over break and spent the whole time talking about it. I couldn't ask for anything better.

The spring semester has officially kicked off, with syllabus week in full swing. My sophomore year. It's weird to think I have been on this campus for a year and a half already. Coming back here didn't feel strange like last time. It felt like coming home a little bit. I'm excited to end year two here. Hadleigh Baker, that's me, back and better than ever. I'm the shortest one in the group, at 5'4", with short black hair, big round brown eyes, high cheekbones, and plump cheeks.

"So, what do you guys want to read this month? I could make a chart, and Paige could make her pros and cons list she so dearly loves," I say to the group.

"Harass me all you want. A good list is the key to a stable life."

"Paige, when have you ever described yourself as stable? Yesterday you burst into the living room with tears running down your face about that Romeo and Juliette retelling you're reading," Amelia laughs as she says that. That book is still a sore subject for Paige, I didn't think we would bring it up right now, but Amelia loves to play the emotional warfare game.

"Okay, fine. Maybe not stable, but organized. First, I get all my assignments done efficiently. Second, I told you not to bring that book up right now, or I will start crying again!" she shoots Amelia a death glare that ends up not looking that scary at all.

"Okay, before Paige starts babbling on and on about that book, let's change the subject. Hads, why don't you make a chart with three books and send it to the group chat, and maybe by Friday, we can vote? Sound good? I have to get back to my apartment. I have my stupid internship tomorrow."

"Oh, right, the one with Leo. How's that going? Are you guys still at each other's throats like always?" Since it is Ella's final semester, she grabbed an internship with this amazing marketing firm just around the corner from the school. Unfortunately, the person who got the only other spot is the person she despises the most. None of us know why she hates him —nobody dares to ask—but that's how the cards fell.

"Please do not dare use his first name around me. He is Zimmerman and Zimmerman only. We're not on a first-name basis because he infuriates me with his stupid face and even stupider British accent."

"Ah, yes, the classic enemies-to-lovers trope," Amelia says while standing up.

Ella shoots her a death glare. "That's not what's happening here. Also, enemies to lovers are saved for fantasy books. You don't see me threatening to kill him with a knife to his throat, do you? That's real enemies to lovers. We would be haters to lovers sans lovers because that will never happen!" Her voice got progressively louder as she exited the room, leaving the three of us behind in silence.

"Like I told you guys before, Zimmerman is a no-go topic right now. We don't even know what's happening with them, but I told you not to bring it up." I stare at Amelia, and she just smiles.

Damn her and her emotional warfare. I swear she gets off on this shit or something. She's practically giggling right now.

"I've tried to get her to stop, but she likes how it makes her feel when we react how we do. It is one of her favorite hobbies." Paige states as she grabs her tote bag.

We exit our tiny classroom and start on the cobblestone path toward our rooms. We catch up with Ella as she walks back to her car. It's a chilly night. A nice breeze blasts through the air, though I'm not cold because my cardigan and boots keep me warm, despite wearing a skirt and tights. Paige is probably okay since she wears sweatpants and a long-sleeve cropped shirt with a zip-up hanging off her arms. Ella has a graphic tee with a picture of Matt Healy, some black leggings, and chunky platform vans. Amelia has on some comfy jeans with a black hoodie and white sneakers. We all walk in silence for a minute, just listening to the breeze and bustle of the campus around us. It's a friendship like this that I never thought I would find, people with whom you can share the silence and not have to fill it with meaningless conversation. Sometimes their mere presence is enough. My three non-biological sisters.

"I might apply to be a tutor," I say to them just before Ella gets in her car.

"Oh, wow. Honestly, if any of us were to do that, it would be you. No offense to the rest of us, but Hads is definitely the smartest," Ella says.

"I agree," Paige and Amelia say simultaneously. That happens so much that we're all used to it at this point.

"Any specific subject, or just a tutor in general?" Paige asks.

"I think just in general if the school will let me, but helping someone succeed will make me feel good, so why not do it?" I say with slight confidence. Being a tutor is something I've wanted to do, but last year, they told me I couldn't until I took some more classes. Now that I have a few more under my belt, I can at least sign up for it—which I did the day I returned to campus.

Ella strolls across the parking lot to her car and says goodnight to us. "Welcome back, guys. I can't wait for all the books we'll read this semester! Text me when you guys get home safely, please. Love you all so much!"

We all say goodnight and head toward the apartments and dorms. It has been a chill first week so far. There aren't too many assignments, and I can still breathe normally, so this year is off to a good start.

Grand Mountain College is my unofficial home for the next two and a half years. With these three beside me, that doesn't seem so scary. Paige and Amelia split off and head toward their apartment.

"Bye, Hads! See you tomorrow!" Paige says as she scurries to catch up with Amelia, who's now unlocking their front door. She's always three steps ahead of P. I wave in her direction and walk back to my dorm, where my roommate—Taylor Finnegan—is probably already asleep. She goes to bed early every night, except Friday or Saturday when she's at some party or campus outing. Though I will say, she's one of the funniest people I've ever met. I have to be quiet coming in, though. I always hate when I wake her up, even though she says she doesn't care. Our relationship is solid since she got me out of my shell during freshman year, and I can't imagine having anyone else as my roommate.

I turn my key in the door and drop my bag. I quickly text the group chat, stating I am in my dorm and safe. I also write a quick note to myself to make a chart for the three options of books for book club, before sticking it onto my desk so I don't forget. I slip on my pajamas and crawl into bed. Setting my alarm for 8 AM tomorrow, and I mentally groan at having to get up early. I'll probably lay in bed for fifteen minutes contemplating my existence like I normally do and miss breakfast. I'm okay with that. Tomorrow morning I have statistics, which isn't that bad per se, but the fact that at 9 AM and I have to deal with equations and math makes my head hurt already. My class after that is criminology, which I have with Paige and my brother,

Oliver. Thankfully, I only have the two morning classes on Thursdays. I like having a free afternoon.

I just hope this semester goes smoothly. Taking as many credits as I am is already sending me into a spiral, and it's only week one. I don't think I could handle anything else on top of that.

I close my eyes and stare at my ceiling until my eyes are tired enough that they shut, and sleep consumes me.

2

Hadleigh

    I'm about to snooze my alarm for the third time when Taylor throws a pillow at me. "Good morning, sunshine! Please get up or shut your alarm off because it's driving me up a wall."
    "Taylor, I'm contemplating my existence right now. This is my time, please, you know my morning routine."
    "Does it involve waking up the entire hallway? Your alarm is louder than a car horn. What's up with that?" I push up off my bed and start to get ready. It's only 8:20, so I'm not going to be late. "Oh, I meant to ask. Have you seen or talked to your brother since you got here?"
    "We flew here separately, so I haven't. He did shoot me a text asking if I got here okay." Going to the same college as my grumpy older brother Oliver wasn't on my bucket list for life, but here we are—both at the same small college in Virginia. Him studying criminal justice, and me studying biology. What a world I live in. Paige probably sees my brother more than me since they have all the same classes.
    Don't get me wrong, I love my brother. He's one of my best friends. He even taught me how to drive. Going to the same schools for our entire life has been okay. He tends to keep to himself, but he's always there when I need him. We're quite different. I talk, and he

listens, occasionally grunting out a short answer. I like to read, and he prefers watching movies. I love him to death, though. We're close in age—he's only one year older than me—so I've come to find his comforting silence rather nice. However, we don't often cross paths on campus, which isn't bad. It still allows me to have a bit of freedom from my family.

"Are you free for lunch today? I have some time in the middle of the day if you want to grab a bite at the dining hall."

"Yeah, I can meet you at the one by Smith Hall. That's where my class at 1 is." Taylor is studying journalism at Grand Mountain. She wants to be a news reporter someday. I think she has a good shot too. Especially since she has an on-campus job reporting everything happening on campus, which is on the website daily at 9 am.

I throw on a black skirt, some tights, and a green off-the-shoulder sweater. I grab my Doc Martens and pack my bag for the day with my iPad and computer. Since my first class is statistics, I grab my giant textbook and throw that in my bag as well. I swear I don't ever have to work out again. The weight of carrying these textbooks is enough. I check the time and have 15 minutes before class starts, so I grab my stuff, lock the door, and head on my way.

✕

Trying to figure out probabilities this early should be a crime. I've never liked math, even though I'm good at it. I just don't enjoy doing it. I would rather read an ancient book than have to do equations ever again. Thankfully, my next class is a bit more exciting. It feels weird since I've never had a class with any of the book club girls, but Paige will be saving me a seat so I can sit next to her and not my grumpy brother, who most likely doesn't want to be seen with me.

I walk into Cranks, which is the name of a building and not a dive bar. I head to the third floor, enter room 358, and immediately spot Paige. She sits towards the middle of the classroom with her bookbag in a seat, and when she looks up from her kindle, she waves me over. Sometimes, I don't know how she does it. It's like she's never tired. Warmth radiates from her as if she's had three cups of coffee already, though I know she hasn't because she doesn't drink it—she gets panic attacks. Regardless, I'm always accepting of the happiness that radiates from her, spreading it to everyone she knows. Plus, it helps to have that in an early criminology class.

As students trickle in, I notice that there aren't a lot of female students studying criminal justice. It's us and two others in a class of 30 students. Paige and I look so out of place in this room. My brother walks through the door, and I give him a wave. He shoots one back and sits right behind me. Great. So much for not wanting to be seen with his little sister.

"Has your first week back been okay? Sorry I haven't texted much, but if you want to keep the tradition up, maybe we can go for a walk every Saturday morning like last semester?" Oh yeah, another thing we used to do. While I was trying to adjust to campus life and being away from home last year, my brother offered to keep up our tradition of going on walks. We do it a lot at home. Every Saturday morning, we walk around this park by our house and watch the sunrise. Oliver and I are from a small city in California. I loved growing up there, but it felt so loud at times. Being on this tiny campus makes the outside noise seem so much quieter. Sometimes I hate getting up that early—especially on the weekend—but it helped me feel more comfortable around campus. I also liked the idea of keeping some traditions from home. Bringing them here made me feel less lonely, as if a piece of home would always be with me. It also allows me to snap some photos. I love photography, but being here sometimes, I don't have enough time to do it.

"That sounds good, and you know how much I like rambling on while you grunt and stare off into space." It's free therapy. As I said, my brother is a good listener, but he always gives good advice when I require that too. I guess he's going into the right field. He's quiet but also good at putting the pieces together.

"Hads, why are you taking this class? This is far from what you want to do and doesn't make sense."

"It makes perfect sense. I'm trying to become well-rounded in my studies, and criminology interests me. Also, this is a liberal arts college, and being able to dip my toe in different fields will eventually make me more appealing to job applications. I'm not afraid to step out of my comfort zone and try new topics. Boom." I say as I spin back around and face the front, just as the professor walks in.

Paige leans over a bit. "This professor is really easy with grading, and there are usually only four chapter tests and a project throughout the year, so I think you'll be alright. Your poor brother just thinks you're trying to steal his thunder," with that, she turns around and winks at him. My brother responds with a cold stare at Paige's bright smiling face.

I'll be honest. It's weird to see her interacting with my brother. I knew they knew each other well and have had almost every class together since freshman year, but seeing them interact was like watching a puppy run into a boulder—my brother being the boulder.

"The contrast between your and my brother's personalities is such a dichotomy, I don't even have time to get into it because we'd be here all day."

Paige stares at me for a minute before speaking. "He's one of the only people I like in my classes. Yeah, he's quiet, but he always gets his work done whenever I've had a group project with him. I'd like to call us acquaintances, but sometimes I forget he's your brother. You're both so different."

I turn around and grab my iPad from my bag. We still have some stuff to go over regarding the assignments and such. This class is only once a week for an hour and a half, which is nice in retrospect; I should be able to get ahead on other things and not have to worry about this one.

"Paige, why was I not aware that most people studying criminal justice here are dudes?" I feel so out of place in this class. I don't know how Paige does it, but big props to her because I would not want to be in a field of study with all this testosterone.

"You get used to it. It sucks sometimes having to do the group projects all by myself since I don't trust them to do it right, but you also learn how to stand your ground, which I've never really been good at," she says the last part a bit quieter. Paige has always been a ball of positivity, but in the past, she has told me stories where people have treated her like a literal doormat. Thus, she has a hard time sticking up for herself. I'll hand it to her, though. She has been trying to be more outspoken in the last year. Maybe Ella will have to teach her a masterclass in not taking any shit from people, and I'd honestly enroll in that too.

The professor starts the lecture, and I open my iPad and start writing my notes down while Paige types aggressively on her computer. I look behind me and my brother writes with terrible handwriting in his notebook. Today's lecture is on the concepts of crime, and I know this class will be a breeze. Having a break from the difficult courses and a class with a friend is nice. Don't get me wrong, I've made acquaintances in my other courses, but none of them I would call friends.

Sophomore year, please don't throw me for any loops.

3

Grant

"How is it two weeks into the semester, and you're already failing a class? Is that even remotely possible?"

"Try taking Intro to Lit at 8 in the morning and see how you like it," I said that a bit meaner than I intended to. I'm just too worked up to be nice right now. I got an F on my Lit quiz yesterday. An F. It's only been two weeks, and I've already failed the first quiz, and now Coach is threatening to bench me when the season picks back up.

Thankfully, right now we're just conditioning, but being *benched*? That's something I can't afford. After practice, he wants to sit me in his office, and my nerves are on a high right now. Luckily we aren't too far into the season, but still, a sit down with the coach is one thing I do not want to be doing. I focus on doing the fucking sprints while simultaneously trying to figure out how the hell I am going to pass that fucking class.

Friday night conditioning sessions are usually crazy. First one of the semester, and I'm already in hot water. Great. Just fucking great.

✕

I take a seat across from the Coach's desk and

wait. He likes to do this thing where he waits for you to talk first. Some sort of psychological power trip shit or something. I'm sick of waiting to hear about this, so I bite and start talking. "You wanted to see me?"

"You're failing a class already, and it's the second week of the semester."

Of fucking course. Word travels fast around this tiny ass college, and I should have known one of my teammates would either speak a bit too loud or rat me out to Coach.

"Your scholarship could be at risk, boy. Get your grades up, or you're off the team," With that, he stands up and leaves me alone in his office.

Off the team? I'm failing one class! This is fucking ridiculous. I grab my bag and get up, heading toward the locker room. I burst through the door, the anger practically fuming off my body like I just stepped on hot coals.

"Yo, Grant, what the hell is going on with you?" my teammate Ryan says. I never really liked that kid. He's a sophomore like me, but his attitude sucks, and he goes through women like toilet paper. Typical jock asshole.

"Coach threatened to kick me off the team if I didn't get my grade up, so naturally, I'm pissed because I have no idea how to do that." I'm heading towards the shower when Jacks Moore—my best friend and roommate—chimes in and says, "You could get a tutor."

It's like he's speaking another language right now. I've never needed a tutor before. I'm smart enough to get decent grades by studying a minimal amount, but a tutor? It's like I'm admitting I'm a failure.

"I don't need a tutor, I *need* Professor Collins to

stop giving weekly chapter tests on that stupid fucking book."

"What book did he choose for this semester? We did *The Catcher in the Rye*, and let me tell you, that main character was weird as shit. Honestly, the whole book was strange as shit. The kid was talking about ducks, and apparently, it was supposed to be a metaphor for something."

"Why does Collins format his class like that anyway? A semester-long study of one book doesn't make any sense. What is that teaching me anyway?"

"How to sleep with your eyes open in class?" says Holt.

"How to bullshit your way through life?" says Rhodes.

"How to do the bare minimum so you can focus on pulling more chicks?" Ryan says.

"You're disgusting, Ryan," I scoff and head towards the showers. I might be going crazy, but I'm seriously not considering this tutor idea. There has to be some other way I can do better, right? My dad used to always pride himself on never asking for help for anything, not even asking my mom for help when he died of cancer. Even in his final days, he would still try to get up and change his socks or take a walk when he could barely function as is. I think that's why now —five years later—I'm deathly afraid of failure. Asking for help is my greatest fear because why would I need it when I have it myself? Maybe I need to try harder, hit the books more, and look up some stuff about it. I can do this. Right? Can't I? I'm having a hard time believing in myself lately.

I'm studying physical education with a minor in

sports management. I want to become a coach one day. I think I always knew this would be the route I would take. My dad was the best coach I ever had. One day I hope to have even a fraction of the heart he did.

I know that something has to change soon, or I'll be benched and failing in two aspects of my life. One of which I've known since I was a kid, and I sure as hell don't want to give that up now. My mom always told me that I could do anything I set my mind to. I know it was hard for her after my dad passed. I may have lost a father, but she lost her life partner, the man she was supposed to grow old with. I can't imagine what she went through. It made us grow a lot closer since she's all I have now. I'm an only child, and she always tells me I remind her of him. Seeing what my parents had always made me want to find that for myself. My mom tells me to be patient and that it will find me soon, and I believe her.

But, God, can't I get a break at some point?

※

Back at the dorm with Jacks, and he keeps staring at me while I sit at my desk. He's got blond hair and is only an inch taller than me, which he acts like it's a big deal. It isn't. He's tall and skinny, but he has some muscle on him. Part of playing hockey is working out, and we have both built up a bit of muscle over the years.

"You wanna take a picture? It might last longer. What's up? Why are you staring at me?"

He's silent for a second, pushes out of his chair, paces across the room, and then sits back down. What the fuck is he doing? Is he about to confess to a crime or something?

"You realize if you confess a crime to me right now, we don't have attorney-client privilege, and I would have to marry you to not testify against you, right? Spit it out, Jacks."

"There is this rumor about a girl who got an A in Collins class last year. According to Holt, she applied to be a tutor this year. He heard her talking about it in a class he had with her."

"Jacks, I told you I don't need a tutor, just more study time for this class." Why won't he listen? I don't need anybody else's help, but honestly, an A in Collins' class is nearly impossible to do. Maybe I should reconsider?

But then I would have to find this girl, and how would I do that? Ask around about this elusive genius, seek her out, and beg her to help me? I'm usually not one for begging, but this is an all-hands-on-deck situation here. If I don't get my grade up and get kicked off the hockey team, I might just throw myself off the roof of the student center.

It's a Friday night, and all the hockey guys are planning to go out to this bar near campus, but I've decided to stay in and study. I know I'll be made fun of at workouts next week, but I don't care. Plus sometimes, going out is too much work. Most of the guys just want to pick someone up and fuck them, but that isn't me. I would say I've sworn off relationships, but when you've been cheated on three times before, you tend not to believe in that commitment anymore. So I just don't do it anymore, and yes, I sleep very well every night.

Tonight, I study. Monday morning, the hunt for this girl begins. I *will* pass this class, our midterm is in a month and a half, and if I fail that, I can kiss my collegiate hockey career goodbye.

I woke up with a purpose this Monday morning. I'm out the door in ten minutes, ready to begin my search for this girl. It isn't much of a search anymore because Jacks has a class with her. Holt told him her name, and it was just dumb luck. So now, I'm waiting for her outside of her class. Now that I think about it, can be seen as creepy. I don't know this girl. What will she think if some random guy comes up to her and asks her for help? Man, I sound pathetic right now.

I start to leave just as the class gets out, and I accidentally bump into someone. I turn to apologize, but before I can, this girl sends me a stern look. "Watch where you're going, dude. You almost knocked me over."

"Okay, I was about to apologize, but now I kind of don't want to." She shoots me a glare that could cut some sort of window pane. Who the fuck is this girl? Has she heard of compassion every once in a while? When did everyone get so mean?

"Did you need something, or are you going to just keep staring at me like a wide-eyed puppy all day? Move along, hockey boy." She might as well have stabbed me. What did I do to elicit this behavior? And hockey boy? Where did that come from? I don't even know this girl. While I'm contemplating what to say next, Jacks comes out of the classroom and walks towards the pretentious girl who apparently has an affinity for nicknames now. He looks at me and waves me over.

Wait, what? I should be walking away from this

girl—who clearly hates me for no reason, I might add—not walking towards her. I might as well have a death wish.

"Grant, this is the girl I was telling you about, the one who can help you pass Intro to Lit this semester." My mouth hangs open a little, and I feel like I can see steam coming out of her ears. Christ, I haven't even properly met this girl yet, and I've already pissed her off.

I hold out my hand to introduce myself, yet it's clear by her stare that she will not be shaking it. I introduce myself anyway. "I'm Grant, and I would very much appreciate your help. That is if you're available and willing to tutor this *hockey boy*." I toss her a wink, and she rolls her eyes at me. So much for a second-first impression.

She's silent for a minute, and it feels like no answer will ever come. "Hadleigh."

Then she just turns and walks away.

Fuck, she's going to make me work for this, isn't she?

4

Hadleigh

    I wouldn't call what I'm doing running away per se, but when some random guy who's like a thousand feet tall almost knocks you over on a day that has already gone horribly, you tend not to want to stand around and make friends with him. Oh, and he plays hockey. I don't have anything against jocks. I find it admirable that one can even play a sport and probably keep their grades up while finding time to have a social life. But all of them are pretty much the same assholes I know from home. Typical, treating women like objects, being too cocky, and my favorite part—the violent tendencies. Seriously, is it like the adrenaline rush or something? Why do guys want to punch each other in the face during sports? Is it testosterone or something? Is it some sort of power trip? The world may never know.

    He wants me to tutor him? It's been two weeks of actual semester work. There's absolutely no way he's already failing something. Honestly, it's laughable if he is. I can't help but feel a tiny twinge of guilt and pity wrapped into one.

    I don't feel *that* bad, though. I'm walking to the lounge to do some studying before I notice that the tower is following me.

    "Listen, I understand that my first impression wasn't the best, but to be fair, you didn't give me any time to apologize before you started verbally assaulting me."

Is this guy serious? Verbal assault? Give me a break.

"I'm sorry, are you talking to me, or is there a five-foot-tall ghost standing behind me that you can see and I can't?" He stares at me, and you would think I was speaking another language or something. Maybe he isn't used to his fake niceties not working on women. He starts to talk, but I cut him off. "Look, you seem nice-ish, but there is no way you are looking for a tutor, so what is the real reason you are harassing me while I am trying to study?"

"I actually do need a tutor. Professor Collins' class. Rumor has it you got an A in his class, which is very hard to do, and I currently have an F. So yes, I need a tutor, and you seem to be my best option now."

I'm kind of stunned. Does he have an F? It's been *two weeks*. It takes a special kind of idiot to fail the first quiz, and they get progressively harder as the semester progresses.

"Well, the rumor was right. I got an A in the class. I also just signed up to tutor, but why should I tutor you? You have been rude and pushy since we met."

"Yeah, we met five minutes ago. Believe it or not, I was there."

"There's that attitude again."

"There is that joyful spirit I've come to love so much." with that sentence, he puts his hand to his chest, feigning admiration. I think I threw up in my mouth a little bit.

"I'm not interested, which you're obviously not used to hearing, so let me say that again a bit slower so you catch my drift. *I am not interested.*" I turned to sit back at the table, but he still hasn't moved from where he was standing. I guess he didn't understand what I was saying.

"Okay, listen, this was exactly like the scene from the book when Nick carried away meets Gatsby, I'm like Nick, and you're like Gatsby, right? Too stunned that I'm asking you for help as if I just revealed my identity with a bunch of fireworks in the background."

I stopped because I didn't think I heard him right. "Carried away?"

"Are you getting carried away by denying me so quickly? Yes. Yes, you are."

"No, you said, Nick carried away. Is that what you think his last name is?"

He looks frozen. He might've forgotten how to breathe. It must be way worse than I thought. I can't even believe I'm going to say the following words out of my mouth, but for some reason, they come tumbling out. It's probably the pity talking. "Okay fine, I'll help you."

His eyes almost light up, and he looks genuinely shocked. Honestly, I am genuinely shocked that I said that too, but he is worse off than I thought. I said yes out of the good nature of my heart.

"I take it the book you'll be studying all semester is *The Great Gatsby*?"

"You've guessed correctly. I'm all for rich people and parties, but these goddamn metaphors and the fact that Nick and Gatsby are in love just don't sit right with me."

"Wh—What did you just say?" I have to hold back my laughter because this kid needs my help. Just from the last couple minutes of conversation, I can tell he has no idea what's happening in the book.

"What, the part about metaphors?"

"Okay, never mind. I will help you. It's clear that you need it, and out of the kindness of my heart, I won't report you to the dean for stalking me."

"Woah, stalking you?"

"You've been following me for five minutes and wouldn't leave me alone, thus the phrase stalking." I wait a couple of seconds til his pulse starts racing and then say, "Just kidding, man, this might be fun. After all, you are super gullible."

"This has been one of the weirdest interactions I've had with another person ever, and I'm starting to rethink asking you to help me."

"Well, it's too late now. You're stuck with me." I give him a condescending smile and open my iPad to look at my notes. He still hasn't left the table. When did he start sitting across from me? "What are you doing?"

"Well, I have time right now. Let the tutoring commence!"

I shoot him a side-eye. "Okay, pretty boy, listen up. I'm not going to drop everything to help you right now. We can set a scheduled meeting time every week that works for both of our schedules, and we can meet for an hour or two, and I can help you then. I have some notes to review now, so please go away."

"Oh, so you think I'm pretty?"

"Wasn't a compliment."

"Doesn't matter, you called me pretty, and I think that means we're best friends now."

"Nope, considering we aren't even friends and probably never will be."

"Wow, that hurts, Hades. My pretty boy heart is sad."

What did he just call me? "Sorry, what was that? Hades?"

"You gave me a nickname and I decided to return the favor. Hades, short for Hadleigh, also known as the God of the underworld."

I stare at him from across the table, and apparently, this interaction is over because he gets up and leaves. As he walks away, he shouts, "I'll email my schedule with times I'm available, and we can go from there."

I sit dumbfounded in my chair. What the fuck just happened?

✕

"He almost knocks me over and then demands that I tutor him. Like seriously, what is that about? Have men not heard of decency in the 21st century?"

The book club started half an hour ago, except we have yet to talk about books. It has just consisted of me ranting about my encounter with Grant on Monday. I am starting to rethink my decision to help him because of two things. I hate jocks, and he has already crawled under my skin. I just know tutoring him will be more stupid jokes and headaches for me.

I turn to face my friends, and they stare at me when I do. "What did I burn a line into the carpet from all the pacing I have been doing?"

"I don't think I've ever seen anyone walk and talk at that speed before, and I'm honestly impressed." Amelia looks genuinely impressed. Did they hear any of what I said?

"Are you guys even listening? I am in full crisis mode!"

Paige looks between Amelia and Ella. "This is a crisis?"

I let out a frustrated sigh. "Guys, this is the stupidest thing I have ever done. Why would I agree to this? I don't even like this dude. We're not friends, nor will we ever be, yet I still said yes to his stupid favor. Now tomorrow, instead of having my entire afternoon free, I have to spend it with a dumb jock who doesn't even know that Nick's last name is Carraway and not carried away!"

They continue staring at me. "Have you ever considered getting a therapist? They're quite helpful." Paige says as she walks towards me.

"I don't need a therapist when I have friends. You guys combined can help me." Paige guides me back to the table we usually sit around, and I slump in my chair.

"Okay, look, I know I literally signed up for this, but I thought it would be easier. Maybe some nice girl would need help, and maybe we would become friends in the end. Not some stupid jock I already hate."

"I am still confused about why you hate him and jocks in general." Paige looks at me, feigning confusion.

"It's because all the athletes at her high school were major grade-A dickheads, and they used to be mean to her. She dated one of them, and he humiliated her in front of the entire school. He cheated on her the whole time with some cheerleader," Ella relayed that info to the two shining twins—my nickname for Amelia and Paige, and I was quite proud of that one.

"I can't back out now, so I'm officially stuck with Grant. This semester was supposed to go smoothly, and now I am worried he will be a distraction from my studies."

"Hads, I think you're overthinking this. Think of this tutoring thing as a stepping stone, maybe helping someone else succeed will help you. Focus on the good parts. Maybe you and he could eventually become good friends?" Paige smiles at that last part. What is she thinking?

"Yeah, you never know Hads. You guys could be the next Naley," Ella, my fellow *One Tree Hill* lover chimes in. She's laughing at my pain. Literally chuckling.

"No," I snap, "Shut that down now. We will never be friends."

"Acquaintances?" Paige suggests.

"No."

"Allies?"

"No."

"Work associates?"

"Paige."

"Ok, moving on then."

She might be right, though. If I focus enough on the positives, my brain can outweigh the horrible negatives that unfortunately exist. It'll be fine, right? I need to stop jumping to the worst-case scenario every time something unexpected happens.

"You could just ghost and run away. I find that usually does the trick." It doesn't surprise me that Amelia would say that. She sometimes goes through these periods where she disappears off the face of Earth, but we always know she will come back.

"Amelia, you can't run away from all your problems. It'll catch up to you eventually." I say, smirking at her. We tell her that all the time, but we know it will never get through to her.

"Watch me." She half laughs and smiles.

"Okay, guys, can we get back to the book? I have a lot of reactions that I need to get out." Paige scoots her chair in while saying this.

"Yes, I can't wait to watch Paige scream and yell when the love interest calls the main character love." Ella gives her a look.

"I just have a lot of feelings. Sue me."

"Someone might someday, Paige. Don't get your hopes down quite yet." Amelia grabs her book from her bag, as do the rest of us, and we finally sit down to discuss what we came here to.

5

Hadleigh

    I walked into class today with a grim expression. I feel a bit tired. Or maybe I'm sick? I should cancel today's tutoring session. I have the flu, a fever, or better yet, both. I barely slept last night. My thoughts just kept racing for some reason. Why does tutoring this kid bug me so severely? I had concluded the previous night that it was because he was just another one of those dude-bro hockey jocks.

    I have a bad track record with dating, and the only boyfriend I've ever had was a football player at my high school. We dated for six months because I found out he was dating the head cheerleader while he was dating me. He only strung me along to humiliate me. At least, that's what he told me at a pep rally, in front of the entire school. His name was Kyle and that alone should have been red flag number one.

    After that, I dived head first into my studies and swore off men as a whole. It just wasn't worth my time or energy. That is also where my underlying hatred of sports comes into play too. Getting your heart shattered by an athlete in front of your entire high school will do that to you. I loved him, or I thought I did. I haven't lost faith in love. It's just hidden beneath layers of doubt, anxiety, and unease. I don't want to actively give my heart to someone and then months later, when they're bored of me, say, *"nevermind, I was joking, oh, and I was using you the entire time, sorry! My bad!"* No. I'm putting myself and my happiness first. It's what I've done since then and will continue to do until someone proves they want me *and* my heart—no matter how cold it might be at the moment.

It's easier to tell myself that I'm afraid of it happening again, rather than tell myself that I feel wholly unloveable. Ever since then, nobody has really shown interest in me anyway. It's also difficult for me to believe that anyone would ever show interest in me. I come off as cold and bitchy. I'm not a warm person to new people. It takes me a while to get to know someone, and even then, it has always been friendship since I got to college. Paige, Ella, and Amelia are the only exception to that rule. With them, it felt so easy just molding into our friendship, as if it had always been that way, but with other people, I don't believe they would actually want to spend time with me without some other purpose.

It's been a week since Grant ran into me and asked me to tutor him. We emailed a bit back and forth and agreed that Thursday afternoons were easiest for us both.

Paige noticed that something was off. For one, I was twenty minutes early since my statistics class got canceled. Since I barely slept, I woke up pacing. I needed to get my mind off of the session later, so I decided to come here and stare at my iPad screen with notes hoping that they seep into my brain.

They don't.

Paige is always everywhere early, so I figured she would be here when I arrived; she knows what today is, and I'm glad she hasn't brought it up. She is about to start talking to me when someone walks into the room and says my name. "Hadleigh Baker, in the flesh."

I look up, confused. "Do I know you?"

"Ryan Barnes, I play hockey with Grant. I heard through a little bird that you're tutoring him. What made you decide to do that? I think it's quite honorable of you."

Great, this is just what I needed today. Another dumbass teammate of Grant's pestering me about this. As if I wasn't second-guessing this decision anyway. "Sorry, are you in this class? Or do you often chase after your teammate's tutors and harass them?" I just want him to go away. Honestly, I wish everyone would go away right now.

Paige speaks up before he can, "Unfortunately, Ryan, you have maxed out your talking quota for today, so why not just sit down and leave us be? Hads is clearly busy right now."

Paige and I silently trade looks. I whisper a *thank you* in my gaze, which I know she catches onto because she gives my hand a small pat under the table.

"Relax, ladies. I just wanted to introduce myself. I was the one who suggested Grant get a tutor since he was failing. Grant can be kind of an idiot, especially when it comes to books. He once told me his favorite Hunger Games character was the one with the bow and arrow."

"Oh God, he's worse off than I thought. Is he allergic to books or something?" That came out unintentionally, and I kind of regret it. What if he tells Grant? *Wait. Why do I care?*

"I think he might be. One time, he told me that he had thrown a book out. Like, just tossed it in the garbage. And I thought, why do that to a perfectly fine piece of literature?"

"It sounds like you like reading, then."

"I enjoy it. Usually, before a game, I like to re-read my favorite chapters from my favorite books. I like to think it brings me good luck."

"Dare I ask, what is your favorite book?"

"I don't want to tell you. It's kind of embarrassing."

"I'm not one to judge what others read. I promise you that." I'm curious now. I've never met a man who likes to read for fun. It's kind of refreshing.

"It's Lord of the Flies." Okay, that I was not expecting. I'm about to say something back, but he cuts me off. "Listen, I would love to continue this conversation when there isn't a classroom full of students filtering in and a professor about to talk to us about serial killers or blood spatter patterns."

I look around, and sure enough, more people have entered the class and have sat down. Paige is staring at me like a deer caught in headlights, and my brother just walked in. His stare is drilling holes in the back of Ryan's head at how far over my table he is leaning.

This isn't good.

"Maybe we could go for coffee sometime? Or maybe you could come to one of my games, and we can go out after? Only if you want to, obviously."

"Can I think about it? Your teammate might keep me too busy not knowing about metaphors and character names."

"Of course. Grant can give you my number, or I can be glad I come to class early every week and talk to you then."

He walks away, and I blush a bit. I can't help it. Nobody like him has felt glad to be in my presence for a long time. It feels nice.

I turn to Paige, and she *and* my brother stare at me like I just knifed someone. Paige talks first. "Before your brother grunts loudly and strangles Ryan, can you tell us what in the hell just happened? Was he *flirting* with you?"

"Oh, because someone can't be interested in me, right?" I snap, and immediately feel bad.

"No, no, Hads, you're a catch. I've told you that any man would be lucky to have you."

At that statement, my brother just makes a noise that sounds like he is being strangled. "Anything to say, big brother? Or are you just going to continue to make noises like a broken fan?"

"If he touches you, I get a free punch."

Paige's eyes light up. "I'm not one for violence, but can I be there for that?"

"Nobody is punching anyone unless it's me punching Grant later at our first session."

"Come on, and it's not going to be that bad. You're overthinking it again. Like I said, just take five deep breaths and count to ten if he makes you want to rip your hair out." Paige gives me a small smile and turns back. I look back at Oliver, whose face is saying everything he isn't: *"What have you gotten yourself into, Hads?"*

I sigh and face the front.

I have no goddamn idea.

"D-Day is upon me," I say as I set my plate down in the dining hall. Taylor and I are having lunch before I have to go tutor Grant.

"Hads, you are being so dramatic right now. It's a one-hour tutoring session. 60 minutes. 3600 seconds. You'll be alright."

She might be right. Am I being dramatic? Yes. I know that. But how can I tutor Grant when he doesn't know the main character's last name? I know that this is going to take a lot of work on my part, on top of all the assignments I have to do for my classes.

It's just until midterms, Hads. You'll be fine.

"Anyway, you said Ryan Barnes introduced himself to you earlier? What was that about?" I told her briefly about how Ryan is apparently in my criminology class, and she almost screamed. She's found him attractive since we got here last year.

"I didn't even know he was in that class before today. He just strolled right on up to me. It was kind of weird, but he was funny." I won't lie, he was charming, but my guard was still up.

"Oh, funny, huh? You don't say." She shoots me a smirk. *Give me a break.*

"Taylor, you know I am not the friendly type with athletes. I don't tolerate them, remember?"

"Yes, you dated a guy in high school who embarrassed you. I know. Ryan is different, though. He has a reputation for being a bit of a douche, but despite the rumors, he can be just friends with a girl. He and I are friends, and he hasn't pulled anything funny when we study in the cafe. Well, not yet. At least, a girl can dream."

"Ew, Taylor, that's gross."

"I'm just saying. It can never hurt to have another friend. At least give him a chance. Maybe this will convince you to start going to school hockey games with me." She shoots me a huge smile.

"Don't get your hopes up."

I grab my plate and return it before I walk out the doors, heading for the library.

⚔

I walk into the library, one of my favorite places on campus. Every time I walk into the building, I feel instantly comforted. There are three floors, and each gets quieter as you ascend. The rows and rows of books on each floor bring me so much solace, especially when I'm having a rough day. I like to come in here, bring my music, and just sit and exist. Surrounded by so many books and words written on pages, everything will be okay. I get transported to another world here.

Also, the smell of books is one of my favorite smells ever. I'd bottle it up and spray it on myself if I could.

I venture to the second floor, where all the study rooms are. I rented out a study room every Thursday for an hour at 2 PM, so we have a quiet and consistent meeting place. The structure is good for me, especially when feeling like this entire situation is chaos. I look down at my phone, and it's currently 1:53 pm. I'm early. I fist the key to the room in my hand, only to walk over to the door, and it's already open.

Grant is already sitting at the table with his back against the door. Is it too late to run away? I pause in the doorway, thinking about if I could make a break for it. Before I can escape, he speaks. "I can hear your heavy breathing from here. Do I make you that stressed out, or is walking up a flight of stairs that hard for you?"

"No, I'm just practicing my deep breathing exercises for when you piss me off, which, wow! Happened in record time today. Should I catalog that for the future?"

"Aww, you already keep a journal about how dreamy and sweet I am? Make sure to add this one, and I want you to remember to tell everyone about how out of shape you are."

"The only entries about you in my journal are the ones detailing how I want to murder you and dispose of your body."

"You would never get away with that, plus, I would be missed too much. You would be better off killing someone like my teammate, Ryan. Nobody would miss that guy."

"Oh, speaking of Ryan, I have a class with him, and he introduced himself to me and suggested a coffee date soon. You wouldn't happen to have his number, would you?" I guess I decided to follow up with Ryan right then. I don't even know why I mentioned that to him. What is happening right now?

"Wait, Ryan Barnes? I didn't even know you knew him. What could you two possibly have to talk about?"

Is he mad? Why does he sound mad? And why do I care? "Are you sad you're not the only hockey boy I talk to? And also, we have lots to talk about, and none of that concerns you, so let's get to Gatsby, and then after we're done, you can give me his number. How about that?"

He doesn't say anything to that. He just shifts weirdly in his chair. I walk around the table and sit across from him, pulling out my personal copy of the book.

"So, Collins usually does the midterm on the book's first half and the final on the remaining half, so it's not cumulative."

"Yeah, we only have to know the first five chapters for the midterm. But every week we have a quiz on a chapter. The next one is chapter two, and I swear I get more allergic to words the longer I hold this book. I walked in here and felt like I had a heart attack. It's too stuffy in here."

I need an eye-roll counter. Of course, he thinks that. "Do you need me to bring Claritin next time, or are you fine with me letting you drop dead due to not liking to read?"

I've never talked this much about murder and death before. Maybe I need to stop hanging out with Paige...

"Sorry. That was a bit harsh. I can be civil for an hour every week, but outside of this bubble right here, don't expect me to smile and hang onto your every word like everyone else does."

I don't even know what it is about Grant that makes me extra on guard and mean. I'm not necessarily mean, but I usually say what I think. I can be intense sometimes, but it's dialed up tenfold with Grant. I need to learn to be civil and professional. I'm tutoring him. After all, a part of me wants him to succeed because that would mean I was doing my job well. He still hasn't said anything, so I continue talking. "So I'm thinking that we can do a breakdown of each chapter each week and hit on the main points I think Collins will bring up. The book overall is short, but there is a lot to unpack in a short amount of time. Does that sound okay?"

"Yeah, that sounds good. I hope you're good at this, so I don't fail the class and have to retake it."

"I don't want to oversell myself, but I think you came to the right person. Despite my hating your guts, I love this book. I know it like the back of my hand."

"Well, that sounds perfect. I knew you were good for something, Hades." He throws a condescending smile in my direction, and I roll my eyes. Seriously with that nickname?

※

Grant

I know she hates that nickname. That's why I'll be using it for the rest of the semester. It's just too easy to piss her off. It's quite a fun game, honestly. Every time she rolls her eyes at me, I think that this time will be when they get stuck and stay in that position forever.

Don't get me wrong, I'm grateful she even agreed to help me, but fuck, she's a fiery little thing. I never realized how short she is. I could stuff her into a locker and still have room for my hockey pads.

Hades is probably around 5'4", and she dresses like an art museum threw up on her. Black skirt, black boots, and a sweater that's dark blue. Is she wearing tights? Who the hell is this girl, and does she know that sweatpants exist? She has short black hair that's straight, which she probably maintains using hot tar. Her legs are shorter than her torso. No wonder she gets winded going up the stairs. She probably has to take each step two legs at a time.

And why the fuck is she talking to Ryan Barnes? That prick is a bigger asshole than me, and I'm not even an asshole. Hades just thinks I am. I bet he flashed that stupid grin and said some nice bullshit to her that is all lies. I'd spent all this time thinking this while she was talking about the book, and I didn't hear a word she said. "Sorry, I didn't catch any of that. Can you–"

I hear a loud thwack, and I look up at her, only to put it together that she just hit me with a ruler. Where did she get that? Did she bring that just to hit me with it?

"Hades, what the fuck? That hurt!"

She laughs. *Laughs* at that statement. Is she some sort of hidden masochist or something? "Every time you don't pay attention or you get a question wrong, I'm going to hit you with this ruler."

"Why the fuck are you going to do that?"

"Well, for one, it's really fun for me. Secondly, it will help you not want to get hurt, and you'll actually pay attention to the work, so you don't fail, remember?"

Right. Not failing the class, therefore not failing myself, therefore being able to play hockey still. The only thing that keeps me going. "Well, normally, someone slapping me with something comes with something fun after but hey, whatever works for you, right?"

With that, she throws me another eye roll. Unfortunately, her eyes didn't get stuck, and she continues. It's hard enough for me to focus knowing that Ryan fucking Barnes has talked to her. It's not like I'm being protective of her. It's just that she is *my* tutor, and what's Ryan's sudden interest in someone who isn't some sort of drunk girl that he can pick up in a bar? Fuck, I need to stop thinking about that and pay attention.

Hades smacks me with the ruler again. "Ow, fuck. Be careful with the hands. I still need to be able to hold a hockey stick after this!"

"What's your deal right now? I can tell you're not paying attention because your face looks constipated."

"Sorry, there's just a lot riding on this. Keep going, and I swear I will pay attention this time when you talk about those two eggs or whatever."

Another eye-roll. Only thirty-three minutes to go.

6

Grant

I can't get the fact that Ryan and Hades have exchanged communication out of my head. The first thing I thought about seeing that shit-eating grin at conditioning today was what he said to her to make her like *him* and not me. Why does that infuriate me so much? I think it's just the fact that it could have been anyone else on the team, and I would be fine with it. The fact that it was Ryan fucking Barnes angers me to my core.

Okay, maybe I'm being melodramatic, but still.

Today the team is in the weight room, and we are doing different types of workouts. One group is doing lunges with plates in their hands, another group is doing free weights, another is at the deadlift station, and I'm in the group that is doing overhead slams with the slam balls. It feels good to be able to let some of this frustration out. Between tutoring and my regular study load—on top of practice and conditioning—I feel so wiped out, and the semester just started.

Jacks is in my group and has been looking at me weirdly all afternoon.

"Can I help you?" I say as I slam a ball to the floor.

"How was your first tutoring session with Hadleigh? It was yesterday, right?"

"Yeah, it was. It went okay. We're both still alive, so she decided not to murder me, which I count as a win."

"When is your next quiz for Collins?"

"Tuesday."

"Are you ready for it?"

"I think so, she told me that the West Egg and East Egg are places and not a new type of breakfast food, so I feel more confident now that I actually know what is going on."

Holt motions for us to switch activities, and as I walk towards the free weights, Ryan comes up to me. What the fuck could he possibly want right now? "Barnes, if you need help with the slam balls, all you do is pick it up and throw it to the floor. It doesn't mean you should slam yours in a free weight, although maybe you could use it."

"That right there explains why Hadleigh doesn't like you. Now I know another topic of conversation we can use when we eventually go out for coffee, other than the fact that I like to read, and you don't."

"I've never seen you with a book in your hand, Barnes. Did you suddenly learn how to read in the past week?"

"Just a little embellishment, but Hadleigh sure enjoyed that fact when I talked to her yesterday."

"Yeah, and in the future, why don't you stay the fuck away from her? She isn't your type anyway." It technically doesn't count as threatening someone unless you punch them, so maybe just a verbal warning. This guy sucks. Have I said that before?

"Oh, I'm sorry. Have you laid your claim on her, or are you just worried she will pick me in the end?"

"I never said I wanted to date her. I'm just curious as to why you're interested in her suddenly. She never popped up on your radar before, or have you gone through all the girls at the school and don't want to go back around?"

"I'm actually not that interested, although she is hot. It's just fun pushing on you. I've never seen you get so defensive over someone you don't like." Damn, he's right. Why am I being so defensive over her? It doesn't matter. I'm doing her a favor by protecting her from Ryan anyway. She deserves better than him. Anyone deserves better than him. "Don't worry, bud, she's all yours, at least until I see what's up those skirts of hers. They just seem to be getting shorter every day."

I drop the weights I was curling, and Jacks puts a hand against my chest to stop me from doing something that would get me kicked off the team.

"Ryan, go the fuck away and get back to conditioning," Jacks says as I death stare at Ryan. This kid couldn't get worse if he tried. Why is he such a prick? Why does he think it's okay to talk about women like that? Does this kid have a mother, and did she drop him on his head a thousand times as a child?

Holt—our team captain that's graduating at the end of this year—signals the end of conditioning and tells us to huddle up. He talks about practices coming up and how we have our first game in February. It's the last week of January right now, so it's coming up soon. I barely hear him because I only think about how I can punch Ryan in the face when the season is over. He dismisses us, and we head to the locker room.

I play defense, as does Jacks. The two of us are pretty unstoppable in defending our goalie. I play right defense, and Jacks play left defense. Unlike many of these guys, I'm not looking to go pro in the future.

I really want to coach hockey, whether for a college team or just kids learning the ropes. My dad taught me everything I knew about hockey, and someday I hope to be half as good of a coach as he was. I always knew I wanted to do it, but that urge got stronger when he died.

Holt and Jacks are talking about going out tonight. I don't normally go out with the team on weekends, but tonight I need to clear my head, and one drink can't hurt, right?

"Hey, are you guys still going to the Hidden Bear tonight?"

"Yeah, Carter, why? You finally going to join and get laid for once?" Holt throws a casual smirk my way. I shrug that comment off. I just need to let loose a little. I've been working hard and deserve a night out with the boys.

"I'll be there." I say to him. Holt smacks me on the back and heads toward his locker.

"Damn, Hadleigh must be doing a number on you. You haven't needed a drink in a while."

"Jesus, why does everyone keep mentioning her today? We've had one study session, we hate each other, and everyone thinks we're going to get married."

"Yeah, dude, it's classic haters to lovers. You actually don't read, do you?" Jacks asks me.

Now I *really* need a drink. "Are we pre-gaming before we get to the Hidden Bear or what?"

He smiles and nods. "Absolutely we are. There's vodka back at the dorm. Let's go." I shut my locker as he says that and we head on our way.

7

Hadleigh

It's Friday night, and I'm going out.
For once.

Ella and I are at Paige and Amelia's apartment getting ready to go out on the town, which I don't ever do, so I feel very out of my element. But if the girls are there, then I am too. They can make anywhere feel safe.

"Guys, what do I wear to a bar? The only clothes I have are my day-to-day and pajamas. I don't think I own any going out clothes." This is my main problem right now. What do you wear to a bar when you don't want to get hit on by drunk men and just want to look cute with your friends? "Can you wear a sweater vest to a bar?" I ask, and the room goes quiet.

Ella looks at me. "Absolutely not, Hads. Let's go raid Amelia's closet for a dress or something."

"A dress? I don't know…I don't go out, ever. Why can't I just wear what I normally do?"

"It's girl's night out, and Ella told us we must dress accordingly. Trust me. I would rather be wearing sweats and a t-shirt right now."

Paige does look amazing. It's weird to see her in anything other than comfy clothes. She's wearing ripped black mom jeans and some heeled boots, with a brown cropped tanktop.

"Guys, I really need a night out. My internship has been killing me, and I swear I almost stabbed

Zimmerman in the face with a letter opener the other day. We're going out, and we will look hot doing it."

Paige, Amelia, and I all share a glance because we still don't know why Ella gets so worked up over Zimmerman. We only know a few things—they both got the same internship, and they hate each other. That's it, and usually, if you're on Ella's shit list, you're there for life. I worry that one day she might text the group chat and ask Paige what the best way to get rid of blood is, but that hasn't happened.

Yet.

(*The answer is hydrogen peroxide, though!*)

"I think I'll just stick with my skirt, but Amelia, this top is cute. Can I borrow it for the night?" I pull out this pink, cropped, backless sweater.

"Yeah, go for it. I haven't worn that in forever. The last time I did, I was headed to Monaco for a peace treaty signing."

"When did you go to Monaco?" Ella asks.

"I've never been to Monaco."

"Wait, then why did you just say that?" I stare at her, puzzled.

"Say what?"

"Guys, this is classic Amelia doing one of her bits. Yesterday when she left the apartment, she said she was off to DC to go start a marital affair with a senator. I swear she just uses movie plots as exit strategies." Paige says.

Amelia chuckles and sits down on the loveseat in their living area. She's wearing a pair of blue jeans, a black top, and some white sneakers. A very classic Amelia outfit.

Paige and Amelia's apartment is cute and cozy.

It's very them. The front door opens to an open floor plan. The kitchen is off to the right, with a small dining table that can seat four people. We play card games there sometimes or rant about books. To the left is a bookshelf that stands against the wall. Straight ahead is the living area, with a couch and a loveseat, a cute rug in the center, with a TV directly facing the couch. Hanging over the couch are a few art prints with their favorite book/movie quotes, and a shelf above the TV houses the Funko Pops of characters they love—such as Paul Atreides and Tony Stark. Amelia's room door is to the apartment's right, and Paige's is to the left. They each have their own bathrooms.

Paige's room has white walls, and the school doesn't allow residents to paint rooms, but filling those walls are shelves with comic books, a neon light shaped like a sun, white fairy lights, and a letter board with her favorite book quote of all time on it. She has two big white shelves filled with books and cute trinkets of things that her friends have given her. She has an entire hook station for her tote bags. Her closet has purple curtains hanging on the front of it, and her bed has lavender sheets and a comforter with sunflowers on it, her favorite. Her bedside table has a signed edition of her favorite book. It's basically a shrine at this point and another signed picture of one of her favorite actors. She has a small gray rug on the floor because she sometimes likes to sprawl out while doing homework. Amelia said that Paige fell asleep on the floor one time when she walked into her room at like 7 AM. She took a picture and sent it to the group chat. It was funny.

Amelia's room is a bit more neutral-toned. She stacks her books in towers on the floor rather than use a bookshelf in here. Her closet has light pink curtains hanging down the front. The walls are filled with pictures from National Geographic, and she even has some copies on her bedside table. Her desk is very organized, and there are more stacks of books on it. Her dresser houses a bunch of knick-knacks from her travels, she has been all over the place, and always buys a cute little something to remember that trip. Amelia loves encapsulating her travels down to one tiny thing that she can always have to remember. She says it's because her memory is so terrible she often forgets, but I think it's a sentimental thing that she doesn't want to admit.

Paige and Amelia are so different, but somehow their dynamic just works. Paige shows off her moods through her tote bags and when Amelia starts showing off her moods, let me and Ella know because we have a bet going on to see how long until Amelia starts letting more people in. She said two years, and I give it five.

Ella turned on her music and connected it to Amelia's speaker so we could listen to it while getting ready. I don't have any more getting ready to do, but then Ella walks out of the bathroom, and I swear all of our mouths drop open.

"Damn, girl!" Paige said, and her voice jumped up two octaves.

"Holy shit," I say.

"You look hot." That was Amelia in the most dead-panned voice ever.

"Please, hold the applause. I know, I know. No man or woman is going to stand a chance tonight," Ella beams at us. She wears black pants, a black crop top that leaves little to the imagination, and black sneakers. Red lipstick adorns her lips, and she looks really good.

"Now, guys, don't forget to drink water if you are going to drink alcohol tonight. The rule is you have a drink with alcohol in it. The next drink you order is water. We're not getting plastered. Except for Hads, this doesn't apply to you because you can't legally drink yet."

"Yes, I'm aware. Alcohol is disgusting anyway." I've never been the biggest fan of it. I wasn't much of a rule breaker in high school, and even if I did drink, it was at home with my brother—who doesn't drink alcohol.

"Is everyone ready to go? Let's paint the town red!" Ella says as she yells that walking out of Amelia and Paige's front door.

"Wait, red? As in blood?" Paige practically beams. Seriously, you would never think this girl—who's the living embodiment of the sun—likes murder so much. It's a weird dichotomy.

"Never change, Paige, truly never change." I throw my arm around her shoulder, and away we go.

"Here we come, Hidden Bear, here we come," Amelia says as she locks the door.

※

We grab a booth in a far corner of the Hidden Bear—a bar within walking distance of Grand Mountain. It's a Friday night, so it's a bit packed with people, but not too bad that we couldn't get a booth. We all sit, and Ella and Paige go to get drinks while Amelia and I stay behind. Paige's birthday is in June, so she legally can't drink but she has a fake ID. Amelia turned 21 over break in December.

"None for you tonight? I thought you guys were letting loose?" I ask her.

"Not in the mood, plus someone has to keep an eye on those two in case they wind up doing karaoke again," Amelia tells me.

The last time we all came out, Paige and Ella started singing the song *All Too Well* by Taylor Swift. The ten-minute version. In a bar that doesn't do karaoke.

And honestly, they sounded pretty good.

They return to the table, and Paige giggles at something Ella said. Those two are the troublemakers of our little group. Amelia and I tend to mellow them out.

"What's so funny?" Amelia says.

"Paige and I were just betting on if Hads is going to quit tutoring Grant before the next session or after it," Ella says a bit too loud for my taste, but whatever.

"I said before, and Ella said after. We bet twenty bucks." Paige smiles.

"Oh God, I totally forgot that was yesterday. How did it go Hads?"

"Fine?"

They don't look too convinced. Dammit, I'm going to have to tell them everything. I tell them about how we spent the first fifteen minutes insulting each other and how he kept zoning out the entire time. I get to the part with the ruler, and Ella practically shrieks.

"Are you telling me you slap him with a ruler every time he zones out or gets a question you ask wrong? Damn, Hads, when did you get so kinky?"

"Oh my God, Ella, it's not like that. It's classical conditioning! I'm teaching his brain to focus so he doesn't want to get hurt. Simple and effective for idiots like Grant."

"Speak of the devil," Amelia says, moving her eyes toward the door.

"Oh, this is about to get real fun," Paige says, already drunk. Man, one drink, that's really all it takes for her.

Sure enough, Grant and a bunch of his hockey friends waltz through the door, and he must sense me staring at him because his eyes catch mine. We're playing a hidden game here. Whoever looks away first admits defeat. I hold his gaze until he lets mine go because a friend asks him what he wants to drink. One point for me.

"Did you guys see that? It's like they're eye-fucking right now."

"Ella! Oh my God, stop. I will never like Grant. It's just this power trip thing we do, I guess. Our entire relationship is based on us either insulting or challenging one another."

"So, are you saying you have a relationship?" Ella raises both her eyebrows and winks. Fuck, she trapped me, and she knows it. I slide out of the booth and excuse myself, saying I have to pee when everyone knows I barely touched my water. I'm looking down, and then I run into someone.

Thankfully it's not Grant. It's Ryan. "Woah, where is the fire? Are you okay?"

"Hi Ryan, and yes, I'm fine. I just need to run to the bathroom quickly. If you'll excuse me." I try to brush past him, and he reaches out and grabs my wrist. "What are you doing?"

"If you wanna get up and dance later, let me

know. I would gladly be your partner." He winked at me and walked away. What the fuck is happening? I beeline for the bathroom. Thankfully, nobody's in here. I just need a minute. Why does his presence seem to follow me everywhere? Why does it annoy me so much just to know he is in this building right now? I wish I could leave, but I should be able to hang out with my friends and have fun for once without a stupid boy getting under my skin. So, fuck it, that's what I'm going to do. I splash some cold water on my face and step out of the bathroom when I run into another person.

This time it's Grant. He looks drunk already. Fuck. "Why were you talking to Ryan?"

Not this again. What is his issue? "It's called human interaction. You should try it sometime."

"Hades, he is bad news. You shouldn't be around him."

"And what does that make you then? Go away, Grant. It's bad enough I have to see you once a week. I'm trying to enjoy a night out with my friends, and you're ruining it."

"Hades, Ryan does not care about you. He just wants to fuck you and dump you as he does with the rest of the girls he preys on."

"Grant, enough! You can't dictate who I talk to. We're not even friends. Why should I listen to you?"

"Because I know him. I hear the way he talks about people when they aren't around. Plus, I didn't like how he grabbed your wrist earlier."

"Are you watching me now? Grant, I don't need a babysitter—especially you—watching my life play out like a movie. Just go back to your friends and leave me the hell alone."

"I forbid you from talking to Ryan."

"You forbid me?"

"Trust me. It's for your own good."

"Pardon me, Grant, but I can decide what is best for me. You don't even know me and are trying to bar me from talking to someone I think is genuinely nice? Fuck off and leave me alone."

"Hades, wait."

"Just stop, Grant! You are so goddamn infuriating. Why don't we just cancel next week's session? I can't stand breathing the same air as you anymore."

I push past him and return to my table, where all the girls are sitting except Ella. I sulk down in the booth, hoping that the entire bar didn't just hear that conversation, but knowing they probably did.

"Where's Ella?"

Paige's gaze shifts to the corner of the bar where Ella and some random dude are face to face screaming at each other. What the hell is going on tonight? Is it like Friday night scream fest in here?

"Who is that?"

"Zimmerman." Oh God. That makes sense now. I don't think anybody else could get Ella as worked up as he does. We have never seen them interact before—this is the first time we've seen him in person, even though we've all heard of him on campus. He's tall and towering over Ella right now, but her rage somehow gives her more height. He's got curly brown hair and lean muscles. Simply put, he's a specimen. I don't know how Ella resists him because he looks like every girl's fantasy. I don't think words alone could do him justice.

"I ship them."

"Who, Paige?"

"Ella and Leo."

"They look like they're going to claw each other's throats off." I say back to her.

"Oh, right, we're supposed to hate him because Ella does too. I hope he loses his favorite pen." Paige makes a face that she probably thinks is scary, but I don't think she's capable of that emotion.

"Paige, you're drunk," Amelia says.

"Sorry, I'll stop talking now."

"Why is he even here anyway?" Amelia looks around at us.

"He's friends with Holt—the captain of the hockey team—so he must've invited him to go out with them tonight," Paige says.

These fucking hockey players are the worst. "I wonder what they're arguing about now," I say.

"Maybe he put her stapler in jello, and she was mad because that was what she was going to murder him with," Amelia says while she giggles. Paige and I just look at her. "What, have you guys not seen that show?"

"Someone remind Ella that she owes me twenty bucks. I might be too hungover to remind her tomorrow," Paige looks like she is about to burst into tears.

"Why?" I say, and then I remember. They bet when I would fold and stop tutoring Grant earlier. Fuck. Maybe I should rescind my offer to cancel next week's session. He may be annoying, but I'd feel bad if he failed when I could have helped him.

"Paige, you have had two drinks. How are you already this drunk?" Amelia sounds like her mom right now.

"You guys know I'm a lightweight."

"Well, this night has turned into a shitshow." Amelia shrugs as she sips her water.

"I'm having fun," Paige says, but her voice sounds defeated.

"Paige, are you crying?" Yeah, she is. I don't even know why I asked.

"I just, love you guys so much." Oh great, we've hit the kind of drunk where Paige lets out all her sad girl feelings.

While that's happening, Ella storms back over to the table and announces that we are leaving. We get up out of the booth and head to the exit. I don't dare look in the direction of a certain someone, but from how my neck feels right now—heat blistering down it—I just know his stare is drilling into the back of my head.

Fuck, what have I gotten myself into?

And how do I get out of it?

※

We walk back towards campus in silence. Paige is blubbering some nonsense about some movie she watched the other day, but nobody is listening or responding. My head is a jumbled mess right now, and Ella has never been this quiet, so something obviously has her pretty torn up.

We get outside Paige and Amelia's apartment. Amelia is practically holding Paige up right now. In fact, Paige might be asleep, her mouth is wide open, and her eyes are closed.

"Do you want help getting her into bed?" I ask. Normally, Ella would, but she's staring off into the distance right now. I'm kind of worried about her.

"No, I'll be fine. Paige will curl up in a ball on her floor, most likely. Good night, guys. See you Wednesday?"

"Yeah, sounds good." Their door shuts, and Ella and I continue walking. She parked outside of my dorm hall. We are silent for a few moments. It's a comfortable silence. That is the one thing about all of our friendships that I adore. We can be loud and quiet together, but most of the time, we all just like being in each other's presence. Even if we say nothing at all, quality time is still some of my favorite memories with these girls.

"I saw you and Zimmerman going at it tonight. Do you want to talk about it?"

"I saw you and Grant going at it tonight too, so I'll ask you the same question."

"Got it. Just know I'm always here to talk." I flash her a quick smile.

"Why don't you like him, Hads? I know the story from high school, but he really doesn't seem that bad...."

I take a moment to ponder her question, and I can't think of an answer. "I honestly don't know. Just something about him has always pushed my buttons. I can't quite put my finger on it." I shrug as we reach her car.

She unlocks it and climbs in. "Hads, I say this with all the love in my heart. Sometimes hate and love are close emotions, and the only thing that gets in the way of one or the other is what *you* put in front of it."

"Are you speaking from personal experience?"

She pauses for a beat, and I can't read her right

now.

"All I'm saying is, keep yourself open to the possibility of love. You can never have too much of it. Goodnight." She shuts her car door and drives off, probably listening to The 1975.

I walk on the path toward my building and pull out my phone. I swipe to my brother's contact.

Hads: Tomorrow morning, 7 AM? The usual spot?
Sous Chef: Yup.

It's always been a running joke between us that he's my sous chef because of our last name, and I like to think of myself as being the better Baker sibling. I called him that once when I was little and it just carried into our adult lives. Maybe my brother can give me some advice that doesn't involve falling in love with someone who I don't dare falling in love with. Ella's smart, but sometimes she leads with her heart and not her head. I have to protect my heart like I've always done. But my head is so scrambled, and my brother knows how to even me out.

I take a deep breath as I enter my room and hope to God I can get at least one hour of sleep tonight.

Ella: I'm home safe! Is everyone else?
Hads: Yes!
Amelia: *one attachment*
Ella: Glad to see Paige is in her usual spot on the floor.
Hads: Is she alright? What is in her hands?
Amelia: She has water and that's just her scarlet witch squishmallow.
Paige: I LOVE YOU GUYS!!!!!!!!!!!
Ella: Yeah, that sounds about right.
Hads: Love you guys! Goodnight!

Amelia: Nighty night xoxo
Ella: Goodnight cuties! Love you
Paige: GOODNIGHT!!!!!!! DON'T LET THE SERIAL KILLERS BITE!!!!

8

Grant

Well, that could have gone better.

To be truthful, I didn't mean to sound like an overprotective piece of shit. It just came out that way. For some reason, whenever she's around, my voice gets more dickish, and it's goddamn annoying. It also doesn't help my being drunk. I pre-gamed too much before coming here since I'm underage and technically can't buy drinks. I went a bit too hard so I tossed my water bottle filled with lukewarm vodka into the trash. I need water.

She fucking left. She had one conversation with me, and *left*. Guess the whole friendship thing has gone out the window. I'm shuffling back over to Jacks' booth and notice he's all alone. Where is everyone?

Oh, right, they came out to pick up someone. Jacks and I did not. This scene seems about right. I still have a hard time wrapping my head around why she likes talking to Ryan so fucking much. That kid is about as interesting as a fucking brick wall. I sit in the booth, and Jacks gives me a weird look. "What the fuck is up with the color pink?"

"Sorry, what?" Jacks asks me, clearly confused.

"Pink. Why is it even a color."

"You have a sudden bone to pick with a color? Is that what you think about in the bathroom, G?"

"No, it's not. I'm just saying the color pink just

shouldn't exist."

"It *shouldn't exist*?"

"Yeah, why are you stressing the words like that, though?"

"Why do you hate the color pink so suddenly?"

"I don't hate it. I just think it shouldn't exist." He stares at me like I have two heads, and fuck, maybe I do. "I'm just saying, pink tries so fucking hard not to be white, but it will never get to the caliber red is at."

"What the fuck is going on right now?"

"It's just an observation I had. Geez, you act like I am speaking another language."

"Are you?" He asks me.

"NO, I JUST HATE THE COLOR PINK JACKS, GOD!" I'm yelling now, and I'm not sure why.

"Woah, calm down. This obviously wouldn't have anything to do with Hadleigh wearing a pink sweater tonight, would it?"

"Oh, she was? I didn't notice what she was wearing. The two events are unrelated, actually, so just drop it." My palms are sweating right now. When did that start happening?

"You were the one who started a war on a color just now, not me."

"And what is up with wearing a sweater if it's just going to be backless? Doesn't that defeat the purpose of a *sweater*?"

"I thought you hadn't noticed what she was wearing."

"LIKE I SAID, JACKS, THE TWO EVENTS ARE UNRELATED! You know what, you don't get it." I get up from the booth, shove the door open, and walk toward our dorm. That conversation pissed me off. I am obviously not thinking about her and what she was wearing. The two things are completely unrelated and have no connection to one another.

    I just hate the color pink.

    That's all.

9

Hadleigh

    I wake up to my alarm, and no pillow gets thrown at me. I realize that I forget Taylor went home for the weekend.
    I'm all alone.
    Like usual.
    I grab some leggings and a comfy sweater, put on my favorite sneakers, and slowly make my way to the bench we always meet. This is one of my favorite traditions of ours. Even though I'm not a great early riser, sometimes the fresh morning air can do some good for me. It takes me around five minutes to walk to the bench underneath a big pine tree, which is usually the one the college lights around Christmas time. Oliver isn't here yet, so I sit on the bench and wait for him. It was a bit cold this morning, so I grabbed my jacket. January in Virginia is no joke, the morning could be thirty degrees, and by the afternoon, it's seventy and sunny.
    I can't stop thinking about last night. I barely got any sleep. I don't understand why Grant's mere presence makes me so on edge. I might have overreacted when canceling the next tutoring session, but he was the one who tried to forbid me from talking to someone when we aren't even friends. His behavior doesn't make any sense, and it's making my head all jumbled. I see something moving in the distance, heading my way.

My brother comes into view, wearing his usual all-black running gear.

Oliver is one of the few people on Earth who runs for fun. I do not share that sentiment, however. I enjoy running only when running away from other people and my emotions. That's about it. Oliver is way taller than me. He stands at 6'1", and has round brown eyes like me. His jet-black hair complements his sharp cheekbones well. He has a runner's body and the most serious face I've ever seen. He doesn't have smile lines because he rarely smiles, and his face is weirdly smooth.

"Trying to up your endurance to chase after murderers, are you?"

He slows before me. "That's funny, Hads."

He didn't laugh. My brother is a man of few words. I have never heard him speak more than five sentences at once before, but regardless, he gives good advice. I enjoy his company, too, no matter how silent he may be.

I stand up, and we start on our usual walking path. We usually only walk a mile or so, that's nothing to Oliver, because my brother likes to run three miles before 7 AM.

"Have you talked to mom or dad since you got here?"

Shit. I just realized I haven't. I keep meaning to call them back, but I've been so tired I keep forgetting. "No, but I will tonight. I've been too busy or tired to get back to them."

"Mom wants us to go home soon and celebrate the Lunar new year with her family. It's in February, so make a note of it on your calendar."

"Ol, it's already on my calendar. Who do you

think I am?" That earns a grunt.

Oliver and I are half-Vietnamese. Our mom is Vietnamese, and our dad is White, but we still celebrate most of the holidays and traditions. Mom likes to celebrate as a family, but with school, it's tough. Our schedules often don't match up, and flying to California on the weekend is also difficult.

"I'll get back to her soon when I am less busy."

To that, he just looks at me. "Too busy fighting with Carter, huh?"

"Oh my God, how did you hear about that? Please don't tell me this is going around school now. That's the last thing I need right now."

"Paige told me."

What? "The bar argument happened less than 12 hours ago, and Paige was drunk last night. How did she tell you already?"

"She texted me while you guys were at the bar."

"I didn't realize you two talked so much, care to comment on that?"

He sends a glare my way. "Look, I know you can handle yourself, but Paige was worried that your argument would get out of hand. She knows I'm protective of you."

"Oh. Okay."

We walk in silence for a couple of minutes. Since Oliver and I are so close in age, he has always been protective of me. Once in high school, this guy spread a gross rumor about me all over school, so Oliver punched him. I love how close we are. I trust my brother. He's one of the only people besides my friends I go to when I need advice or a quiet presence.

"So what's the deal with you and Carter

anyway?"

Always right to the point he is. "Yikes, you can't even say his first name. I'm tutoring him," I say, as if he should know this already.

"I know that."

"Okay? So what?"

"Why do you hate him so much?"

"Why does everyone keep asking me that question? I just do!" We stop walking, and he turns and looks at me. This look is more of an *I know you're bullshitting me right now, so cut the crap.* "I honestly don't know my feelings about him. Everything in my head is so jumbled. I feel like I could be friends with him, but for some reason, when I am around him, I just get so—"

"Confused? Annoyed?"

"Yeah, I guess. I've never been good at talking to boys or making friends with them. Since Kyle happened in high school, I've wanted to stay away from them altogether."

"Good, I wouldn't want to have to punch any more of them who break your heart. It hurts my knuckles after a while." My brother chuckles for about two seconds and then returns to his normal stare. People often think he doesn't show emotions or feelings, but his shell starts to break when you get close enough to him. He and I laugh all the time. He just has a harder time than I do opening up to people. I think he's scared of leaning on people too much only for them to leave in the future.

I don't blame him. His high school girlfriend, with whom he had been dating for three years, died in a car crash. It was sudden. He was devastated. Since then, he hasn't really dated or even looked at the opposite gender. He worries it could happen again, so he stays away from love all together. It sucks, though. I really miss happy Oliver, this cold, grumpy version of him is nice, but I miss his laugh—the real one. The one Mia used to bring out of him. If Ol laughed, you couldn't help but laugh along with him. I'm also the only person he lets use that nickname. Sometimes I call him Ollie just to really mess with him, he hates when I call him that, but I do it anyway.

"You've only done that for me twice, plus I didn't ask you to. You just did it."

"You're my family, Hads. Nobody messes with my family."

I smile back at him as we make our way back to the bench. The sun is rising now, and we sit to watch it. I feel a bit better now, my mind still feels jumbled, but I feel like I have a solid plan for going forward. "Ol, what should I do? About this whole thing."

"I can't tell you what to do, Hads."

"I know, but please just give me some advice, anything. I think I'll email him and tell him to show up to Thursday's session, but I don't know what to say to him. I don't know what to feel about him."

He's still looking straight ahead at the sunrise. We both are. "Sometimes something good can be right in front of you, and you don't notice it until it hits you in the face."

"Wow, that's very poetic."

"I'm just saying Hads. It wouldn't hurt to become friends with this guy. Maybe it'll even get you out of your dorm room on the weekends."

"I occasionally get out of my dorm with you and the girls." He grunts. "Rude. I have a social life, you know."

"Sure you do. Your life is studying, reading, and apparently slandering Grant."

"I do not *slander* him. We just butt heads."

"Mhm."

"Okay, what would you do going forward if you were me?"

He seems to ponder this for a moment. Neither of us has turned to face one another. We're just sitting on the bench, staring ahead at the sunrise. Talking to one another. Mornings like these are my favorite. When Ol graduates next year, I'm going to miss this. "Show up."

"What?" I hate when he does this. Sometimes he doesn't elaborate, and I have to press him for more. It's like he talks in code sometimes.

"I think you should show up to the tutoring session on Thursday."

"I was thinking of doing that already, but why? I don't know if he will accept my apology. I said some pretty harsh things." I regret some of the things I said to him. I hate that in anger, I could say some mean things, but I can't take it back. I said them, and that's that.

"He said some harsh things to you too." True. He did try to forbid me from talking to someone, and that goddamn nickname... "But you did agree to tutor him, and you hate backing down from challenges."

"Okay, so I just show up and hope he does too? What if he doesn't."

"Then show up the next week."

"You make this sound so easy, but why?"

"Sometimes all you can do is show up and be there for someone when they need it. Show up, apologize, hope he does too, and maybe forge ahead on a path to becoming friends. Even acquaintances, for God sake. Don't waste time being angry at someone for no reason. It won't help anything."

"I think that's the most words I've heard you string together in two years." I say to him

"I know. I sound like a talk show host." We face each other for the first time in minutes, and then we both burst out laughing.

"Thank you, Ol. I needed this. Believe it or not, you were helpful."

"I'm always helpful. Thank you very much." He elbows me in the side before getting up. "Same time next week?"

"You bet."

"Good luck, Hads."

I smile at him, and he runs off back to his apartment. I stay on the bench for a while. It's peaceful over here. I think about the future and what it holds for me in the next two years. I feel a bit better about it. I think it will work out.

I just have to show up and be ready for whatever life has in store for me.

That I can do.

10

Hadleigh

"Okay, now that all of the book talk is out of the way, who wants to start our debrief about last Friday? I need to hear every version of everyone's point of view."

Wow, Amelia really gets down and to the point. Everyone's silent, I don't want to keep rehashing this, but the girls haven't fully talked about everything that happened that night. I guess it was bound to happen eventually.

"I got drunk and slept on my floor all night!" Paige says, a bit too enthusiastically.

"Yes, I know, P. I was the one who put you there." Amelia says.

"On my floor?"

"On your bed, but you must have fallen off. Or crawled off. All your blankets were on the floor with you."

"Oh, that's weird," Paige says.

"Seems like a normal night to me at the Paige and Amelia residence," Ella states. She has been far too quiet this evening. But then again, so have I. Schoolwork has taken up much of my time this week, but now I have to recap everything that happened all over again.

"Sorry, is this book club or group therapy now?" I say, a bit harsher than I mean to.

"Hads, you can go last. There's a lot to unpack with you," Amelia shifts her gaze to Ella. "Tell us what's going on with you and Zimmerman because Paige seems to ship you two, and we have no information to say otherwise if you guys love each other or want to kill each other. So start talking, and don't leave anything out." Amelia grabs four small popcorn bags out of her bag and hands them around as if this was community theater or something.

"Really Ames?" I say.

She just shrugs with a smirk on her face and looks at Ella, waiting for her to begin speaking. "Nothing really has happened between us. It's just his cocky, better than everyone else attitude that really annoys the shit out of me."

We all wait for her to continue. We know there's more to the story.

"You guys know I was one of two to get a really coveted internship with that marketing firm. What you don't know is how hard it was to get into. I worked my ass off for it. I was one of the only women applying for it, and the interview and intake process was grueling. I had two separate interviews, one with a board of people and another with the head of the firm, and I obviously got the internship position. After all that work, I assumed the process was the same for everybody. It wasn't. Zimmerman had one phone call with the head of the company and immediately got the placement. He kept bragging to me about how easy it was getting in here. Meanwhile, I worked my ass off to prove to these people that I could do good work for them. During the first week of our internship, I was sent out for coffee while Zimmerman was allowed to sit in on meetings and take notes. It was humiliating, and he won't let me live it down. He also keeps messing with my desk and is just overall an ass."

"Jesus," I say.

"Oh my God," Amelia says, looking a bit sad for her.

"Yeah. I work part-time, go to school full-time, and now I have this internship two days a week, where I have to eavesdrop to actually learn things. Meanwhile, Zimmerman gets everything handed to him simply because he has a penis. It's not fair. But that's how the world works, and if I have to prove everyone wrong and that I'm capable of making a name for myself, then I will. And I will do it in heels with a goddamn smile."

I take a deep breath, "Ella, I think you might be my hero."

She smiles at that, but not a full one.

"I didn't realize it was like that for you. I'm so sorry." Paige looks like she is about to cry. I love how deeply she cares for us. It's sweet.

"Ella, I will gladly punch Zimmerman in the dick for you. Just name a time and place." Amelia says with a bright smile. I didn't know she was prone to violence. Maybe Paige has corrupted her a tiny bit.

"Thank you, guys, but I can handle him from here. I don't think he was expecting me to bite back when he first started this rivalry with me."

"Yeah, that was a loss on his part. I definitely would not want to be on your bad side." I say, and I fully mean that. Ella as a friend, is one of the strongest, most caring people you will ever meet, but get on her bad side? You don't fuck with her. She might literally bite your head off and not lose any sleep over it. I aspire to be like her when I grow up.

"Well, on a lighter note, I joined the criminal

justice club on campus! I forced Oliver to join me because we get extra credit for a class we are both taking. I told him, 'you always take or do any extra credit. You can never have too many points!' He grunted at me. But he showed up to the meeting, so I count that as a win!"

"Paige, what exactly does the criminal justice club entail? It sounds like a bunch of you guys just sit around and talk about cases, and isn't that what you do in class?" Amelia and, frankly, all of us look genuinely confused.

"I'm actually a bit shocked that you got my brother, of all people, to join a club on campus that requires him to be social." I'm a bit stunned, I didn't think my brother was the club type of person, but yet again, I am surprised by the musings of Oliver Baker. Quite an enigma he is. Maybe I don't know him as well as I thought...

"He barely talks during club, but he did introduce himself and not just grunt. As I said, a win is a win." She smiles and sinks into her chair.

"Now, moving on to Hads. What the hell is going on with not only you and Ryan, but you and Grant?" Amelia asks me.

"Oh, right," Ella says as she slips Paige 20$. She chuckles as she grabs it and puts it in her tote bag.

"Okay, first of all, that bet is null and void because I did not quit tutoring him. I momentarily called it off. Second of all, I'm going to tomorrow's session. Regardless if he's there, the only thing I can do is show up and hope he comes too." I sigh heavily. Indeed, he might not show up tomorrow, but if I do, at least I can say I tried.

"You're deflecting, and don't say you're not because I'm the queen of deflecting when people ask me questions I don't want to answer. Start talking, or I'll make Paige torture you for information." Amelia says.

"I never agreed to that!" Paige practically jumps out of her seat.

"Damn, Amelia, fine." I'm pacing at this point. "There's no deal with Ryan and me. I think he just wants to be friends. He seems nice even though I haven't talked to him much. He's in the same class I have with Paige and my brother. That's it. Null and void. And as for Grant, for some reason he thinks he carries authority over me and can tell me who I can and can't talk to. He apparently saw my conversation with Ryan at the Hidden Bear Friday night and got mad about it. Or mad at the fact that Ryan grabbed my wrist when I tried to walk away. I actually don't know what he was mad about, come to think of it. He tried to forbid me from talking to Ryan, and I told him he wasn't allowed to do that, canceled the session, and returned to the table we were at, wanting to sink into the Earth and stay there."

I stop pacing and turn to look at them. They are all wide-eyed. I'm not surprised. The specifics of it sound pretty bad.

"He told you he didn't like how Ryan grabbed your wrist?" Paige says.

"That's the one thing you took away from all that? Really? As a criminal justice major, I expected more from you. You know, seeing the bigger picture kind of thing?"

"I'm just pointing out something obvious."

"And what would that be?" Ella asks.

"Yes, Paige, please enlighten us!" Again, Amelia

giggles, I think we all know where Paige is going with this, and she couldn't be more wrong.

"Your trope is haters to friends to possibly lovers. I can see it all playing out in my head right now. Obviously, he was feeling jealous and overprotective of you because he cares about you. He thinks Ryan is a bad guy. Therefore, seeing Ryan aggressively grab your wrist was something that popped his cork, right? That's why he blew up on you, and said all that stupid stuff that guys say when they get jealous!" Paige looks around as if she had just made some grand declaration or discovered a new water source on a different planet.

"Popped his cork?" Ella says, confused, as are the rest of us.

"What? It's a phrase that people use."

"Maybe old ladies at bingo." Amelia giggles. What's she so happy about tonight?

"Amelia, this is the most I've heard you laugh, and the fact that it's about everyone else's misery says more about you than me." I say while shooting her a sharp glare, and she shrugs.

"So what are your next steps, Hads?" Ella steers the conversation back.

"Well, I'm going to show up in our study room tomorrow, and if he doesn't come, then I guess it's over. If he shows up, we can continue as normal. I'm going to apologize for what I said, and maybe he will too. I don't know. I know I gave up too easily, which is unlike me. There might still be some animosity between us, but it wouldn't be us without a bit of that now, would it? Not that Grant and I are an us. My brother gave me some good advice, and I will try to keep my mouth shut and help this kid pass Intro to Lit, even if it kills me." I end that statement a bit louder than I intended, but I'm determined to see this through.

"Well, that is good to know, Hads. I fully believe in you. Though, don't stop the banter between you two. It's funny hearing it, even from a distance, when it can be muddled. Paige, are you ready to go? I want to finish that documentary before bed tonight."

Her eyes jump out of her head, and she leaps out of her seat, "I *knew* you were into it. You kept hovering in the kitchen while I was watching it!"

"The killer murdered a bunch of dudes. Of course, I found it interesting." She eye rolls and gets up while Paige grabs her tote bag.

"Good luck tomorrow, Hads! I bet he shows up." she throws a wink my way. Sometimes her optimism can be a bit much, especially when she's shipping me with a guy I barely know and can't exactly tolerate.

After Paige and Amelia leave, Ella and I stay seated for a few moments. "I'm sorry about the internship. I didn't realize it was so difficult for you. I remember how excited you were when you got the spot." I reach over, grab her hand, and squeeze it.

"Part of me wishes I told you guys sooner. Keeping all that bottled up for so long has not been fun."

"I bet." I heavy sigh.

"I get it, you know."

"What?"

"Hating someone. It can be exhausting."

"I guess I never realized how similar our situations were. I mean, yours is a lot more annoying than mine but still."

"It's nice to talk it out sometimes." She says.

"I know. Sometimes it's hard to formulate words

about how I am feeling. We just got off to a rocky start because of my bias against men and the fact that he ran into me when we first met."

"I know, but Hads in the future, if your head feels jumbled, you can always come to me. We're in a similar situation, believe it or not, but yours might actually end well." She says that one with a laugh at the end. I think she could be right. I also know I don't want to continue hating Grant forever. He seems...okay sometimes.

"I will, I promise. I've never had an older sister to talk to about boys before. Sure, I have Oliver, but it's not the same. He just threatens to punch any guy that comes near me." I love how protective my brother is, but sometimes it's nice to be able to rant to the girls.

"Well, now you have three older sisters to come to." She smiles and squeezes my hand back. "But I would come to me first. The shining twins are wise, but since we're in a similar situation, we could use a bit of comfort from each other."

"Maybe we could get coffee every week. Would you like a little weekly rant session about everything bugging us? Only if you're down for that."

"Coffee and ranting? Count me the fuck in. We can also go over our One Tree Hill rewatch. Season 3 is coming, and you know that's my fave."

"Oh my God, yes! Things are about to get wild, and my Naley heart will be healed. We can figure out a time to meet next week."

"Sounds good to me! I'm also proud of you. I don't know if I mentioned that." My heart constricts a bit when she says that, but I keep my face neutral.

"Proud of me for what?"

"For not quitting. And for showing up tomorrow.

Your brother might be silent 85% of the time, but he can give good advice when needed."

"Thanks, El."

"Yeah, and even if he doesn't show up tomorrow, there's always next week. It'll all work out how it's supposed to." She gets up out of her chair and heads for the door.

"Drive safe, and text me when you're home!" I tell her.

"I will. Don't stay up too late doing homework!" She half-shouts across the building.

"No promises!" I smile. I feel a lot better about tomorrow now. Even if he doesn't show up, I will not give up hope. I will see this tutoring through, and maybe there is a small chance we can become friends. I just hope I don't fuck it up.

11

Grant

    We've been practicing for a couple of weeks now, but today for some reason, I can't focus. We're supposed to be doing shooting drills right now, but not only have I missed every single shot I've taken—the irony is not lost on me there—but I actually fell over onto my ass after I shot one. We have a game coming up, and the team looks good. I, however, do not look good. Normally, hockey is where I go to escape the anxieties of everyday life, but now it's just causing more. I don't know what to do to relax. Nothing seems to be working.

    Coach hasn't pulled me aside again, thankfully. I have another quiz next Tuesday, and I'm hoping to study by myself tomorrow and get a good grade. Hades canceled our session tomorrow, but the study room is still rented for that time, so I might make good use of it. It is a quiet room where I can focus.

    I'm next in line to shoot again. I grab the puck, and I skate toward the goal. I guess I could've just snapped it, but I'm taking a more strategic route this time. I skate fast, coming up on Holt, who's currently in the goal. He's the best on the team, so it makes sense why none of my previous shots have made it. That just proves Holt is doing his job. I come up on the right of the goal and try to sneak it into the left.

    It worked.

    Huh. That felt good.

Coach blows the whistle, and we circle up around the bench area.

"We have our first game against South Valley next Monday. You boys are looking good but not great. Conditioning Friday will now be an on-ice practice to prepare for it. South Valley is looking strong this year, and we have to come at them with everything we got. And it's our first home game, so we don't want to let the school down at home, do we?"

"No, Coach!" We all say in unison.

"Good. Now go shower. You all smell terrible."

Always a truthful one, he is. I like him as a coach, but as a person, he sometimes scares me. He is around 6' 3", with bulky arms and a thick mustache that matches his jet-black hair. He has an entire sleeve of miscellaneous tattoos.

All the boys head to the locker room. It's nice that the rink is on-campus. The crowds for home games are electric here, too. That's another perk. I love feeling the hum of the crowd when I'm on the ice. It's where I feel the most alive. I open my locker and shove my equipment inside, grabbing the shampoo, conditioner, and my loofa and body wash. I am not the type of guy to use 5-in-1 shit on my hair and body. With flow as nice as mine, you have to keep it well-maintained. Plus, it's weird that some people use the same shit on their hair and body. It seems kind of fucked to me. I quickly shower and change into fresh clothes.

"Hey, G. I won't be walking back with you tonight. I'm going over to Beeson's apartment for a movie." Jacks informs me.

"You're going to watch a movie, on a Wednesday night after practice?" I ask, feeling skeptical.

"Yeah, so?"

"Will Claire be there?" His face flushes, and I have my answer. Jacks has had a crush on her since freshman year when he first laid eyes on her. But he has been too scared to do anything about it. It's cute, honestly. "I hope you have fun, man. Maybe tonight will be the night." I nudge him over a little bit, and he looks embarrassed.

"Shut up."

"Never." I throw a huge smile at him, and he flips me off and walks away. God, I love that kid. I shut my locker and grab my bookbag, heading for the exit.

As I walk across campus, I notice how quiet it is. It's around nine on a weeknight, so that doesn't surprise me. This campus basically shuts down after 7:30 on weeknights. I see a few students walking around, but only one catches my eye.

She has short black hair, is wearing a skirt, and carrying a book. I swear I could spot her from a mile away. I debate about going up to her if she is still mad at me, but what's the worst that could happen?

You could say something stupid and mess it all up.

Right. Me and my big mouth. I decide to go up to her anyway. I match her pace as she walks.

"Hades, you're out late for a school night. Shouldn't you be studying down in the underworld?"

"I just came up to steal more souls. Are you volunteering? I'll gladly take yours. Oh wait, you don't have one. It looks like you're safe this time."

There's the banter I missed.

I grab her arms, about to apologize, when she looks down at where my hands are touching her. I removed them for fear of getting kicked in the balls or something, and now I am just standing here awkwardly.

What do I do with my hands?

Have I always been this awkward?

What is wrong with me?

Say something, idiot. She is looking at you like you're insane. "I just wanted to apologize properly for the way I acted Friday night."

"Okay?"

"So, uh, I'm sorry, Hadleigh. I had no right to tell you who you could talk to. I don't really even know why I said that. What I really wanted to say wasn't coming across right, and I should never have said those things. I feel really bad about it, and I hope you can forgive me." She's looking at me, and I can't read her face. She's quiet, a bit too quiet. I'm having a strange moment of deja vu, to the first time we met a couple of weeks ago. It's strange all that has happened between us in a short time, but I hope that we can be something other than mean to each other—maybe even friends.

"I'm sorry too. I overreacted and said some mean things that I feel bad about. For some reason, I can't control my tongue around you." She looks me in the eyes when saying that, so I know it's sincere. Her voice is so whispered right now. I don't think I have ever heard her this quiet before. I can't say I like it.

"I accept your apology," I say.

"I accept yours, too."

"Cool."

"Great."

"Wonderful." *Really Grant? Wonderful? What's next, exquisite?*

We stand awkwardly on the sidewalk for a beat too long, and she clears her throat, gives an awkward wave, and begins to walk away. "Uh, have a good rest of your night, Hades."

Her back is to me, but I faintly hear her say, "See you tomorrow."

Maybe there's more hope than I thought. I walk back to my dorm with a smile on my face and a bit more pep in my step than before.

12

Hadleigh

I walk out of stats, my brain feeling scrambled. I'm walking to Criminology right now, and I don't know why I feel so nervous today. I mean, I saw Grant last night, and he apologized. It seemed sincere, but I wasn't sure he heard me when I told him I would see him today. To be fair, I said it kind of quietly. I tried to say it louder, but the whisper was all I could get out.

I feel marginally better today now that we have seen each other and cleared the air. He must have just come from practice or something because he had a gym bag with him, and it looked like he had just showered. His hair was wet, and falling all in front of his face—not like I was staring at his hair or anything.

I walk into class and notice Paige isn't here yet, which is odd because she's always early to everything. My brother's in his seat, though. I walk over and plant myself in my seat when all of a sudden, Paige comes bolting into the room and sits in her seat. Was she running here?

"Sorry." She's out of breath. "I got wrapped up reading this mafia book and completely forgot what time it was." She says this through a lot of huffs and puffs.

"Paige, you realize you're not late, right? Class starts in ten minutes."

"I know, but my philosophy has always been if

you're on time, you're late. If you're early, you're on time." She says, still catching her breath.

"That doesn't make any sense," Oliver says deadpanned.

"It doesn't have to make sense to you, Mr. Grinch. It's my philosophy."

"Was that mafia book good? It seems like you lost yourself a little bit, huh?"

"Oh yeah, it's definitely going to be a favorite. It's a *Beauty and the Beast* retelling." She smiles at that.

"You girls and your books." Oliver sounds less than enthused. I turn a bit to say something snarky at him when someone taps me on the shoulder. I turn around, and it's Ryan.

"Hey, Hads."

"Uh, h—hi Ryan, what's up?" This is only the second time we've interacted, and it still makes me slightly uncomfortable. I'm just not used to talking to the male species that much.

"I just wanted to chat, and I was wondering if you were busy Monday night?"

"Uhm, no, I think I'm free. Why?" Paige is almost laughing right now. What's going on?

"Well, I have a hockey game on Monday night—the first one—and I was wondering if maybe you wanted to come watch?"

"Come watch the hockey team with you?" *I'm so confused.*

"I mean, I'll be on the ice, so I can't watch with you, but maybe you can bring the book club or something?" He smiles—now he knows I'm clueless about hockey.

"Oh, right, because you'll be playing. Uh, yeah,

sure, that sounds fun, I guess."

"Maybe after we can grab a bite or something?" I hear Oliver grunt behind me. *What's his deal?*

"Yeah, that sounds good!" *Why is my voice so high-pitched?*

"Alright, cool," he slides a piece of paper across the table, "There's my number. Text me?"

"Yeah, okay."

He tilts his chin up and walks away back to his seat. I turn to face Paige and my brother, ready with my snarky comment from earlier when I meet Oliver's face, which looks sharp. His ears could be on fire right now. Paige looks confused and maybe even a bit scared. "Why are you both looking at me so weirdly right now?"

"Uhhhhhh." Is she speechless right now? I don't think I've ever heard Paige not have anything to say before. She goes on rants about how some serial killers were stupid and details how they couldn't have been caught, but to *this*, she's speechless.

"I'm going to kill that kid."

"Oliver, calm down. You can't threaten murder in a criminology class." I say to him.

"How dare he ask you out right in front of me. What kind of prick does that?"

"Wait, what? He didn't ask me out. He asked me to watch his hockey game. That just sounds like an invite to me." I look over at Paige, and she doesn't meet my eyes.

Shit, did he ask me out? Did I not pick up on that?

"This all seems very fishy. Ryan grinds my gears. My gut says not to trust him." Paige is still looking at the floor.

"Fuck, wait, did he ask me out?"

"Yes. And now he's going to die." Oliver moves to get up, and Paige shoves him back down.

"I will not be an accomplice to this. Save your murderous tendencies for later. You don't want to go to prison, do you?" Paige asks him.

"I would never go to prison for someone, but for him, I'd think about it." Oliver sounds pissed.

The professor walks into class, and we have to drop the topic for now. Why would Ryan ask me out? On a date? The lecture starts, but I can barely think. How did I get roped into this alternate universe where a guy on the hockey team just asked me on a date? None of this makes sense. Ryan and I barely know each other.

I start getting notifications on my iPad from our group chat.

Paige: Guys! Ryan Barnes just asked Hads out! ON A DATE! It was super awkward, and I don't like him.
Ella: Ew, what? When did this happen?
Amelia: Who?
Paige: Just now! Before our class started
Hads: It's not a big deal. My brother only threatened to kill him twice. But what do I do? Going to a hockey game alone sounds lame, and I don't date? How do you do that?
Ella: Are you guys thinking what I am?
Paige: OMG, WE CAN ALL GO! Ryan said she should invite us, but I still don't like him.
Ella: Yes, Paige! Don't worry, Hads, we'll be there with you <3
Amelia: I'm still confused about who this man is, but okay, sure.
Hads: Thanks, guys :) Maybe it won't be too bad?
Ella: Our girls first date in a while. We can all get ready together. OMG, I am so excited.
Paige: I still don't like Ryan, but I'm still excited for

Hads!
Amelia: Is hockey the one with a puck?
Hads: Amelia...

  I chuckle as the conversation ends. I get another notification, though. It's from just Ella this time.

Ella: I know you have tutoring later.
Ella: Keep your head up. If he doesn't show, you didn't let him down.
Ella: Proud of you for showing up still.
Ella: Also, does Paige do background checks still? We should ask her to do one on Ryan, just in case...

  I look over at Paige and, judging by how she is vigorously typing on her computer. She might already be one step ahead of Ella.

Hads: Don't worry. She's already on the case.
Ella: I love you!
Hads: Love you too.

13

Grant

It has been a pretty chill week. Since I saw Hades, I feel much better about where we stand now. Even if she doesn't show up today, I still think I can pull something out of my ass about this book. I passed the last quiz I took for Collins, and since Hades started tutoring me, some of the metaphors she explains are beginning to make sense. I walk into the library, and this once stuffy place is growing on me a bit. I don't think I ever stopped to take in my surroundings when I was here. The floor-to-ceiling windows on each floor, the way that each floor gets quieter depending on which one you go to, the quietest at the top. I never even noticed we have a café in here either. What the fuck? I'm really starting to question my eyesight after not noticing all these things. Hades was right, it's nice here, but I'll never tell her that. Her ego is too high as is.

I walk up the stairs to the second floor and head toward the study room. I notice the light is on, and my heart starts to beat faster. Could she be in there already? Has she been waiting for me? I was around five minutes late to what would have been our normal time, but I didn't rush over here because I wasn't sure if she would be there. As I walk in, nobody is there.

I notice that I'm disappointed.

Regardless I take my usual spot at the table, open the book, put my headphones on, and dive in. I'm like this for around thirty seconds when something hits my hand. I look up, and Hades sits across from me with that damn ruler in her hand. "Did you just whack me with that?"

"You were late, so yes, I did." She smiles.

"Oh, I was late? I was under the impression that we were no longer doing this."

"Then why did you show up?"

"You said you had the study room rented for half the semester, so I figured a nice quiet room for a bit would help me focus."

She looks me up and down, and rolls her eyes. "That makes sense."

We're quiet for a moment, and then she starts to explain chapter 3 of Gatsby. "So, this is actually the chapter where Gatsby gets introduced. The enigma that surrounds him makes this introduction very important. Now, Gatsby throws these lavish parties all the time, and no invitations ever get sent out, but Nick gets one. This is a big deal. Everyone likes to speculate about Gatsby, but when Nick and Jordan sit at the same table and he introduces himself, they're quite stunned. The party is lavish, and it goes on all night. Gatsby calls everyone old sport, and Nick is attracted to Jordan even though he knows she's a cheat."

"Oh, wow, okay. There's lots to unpack in chapter three."

"Yup. Will you pay attention the whole time, or will I have to use my favorite ruler on you?" She smiles mischievously at me. This girl has to be a sadist or something. There's no other explanation for why she likes hitting me so much.

"Ha, ha, freak. I'll have you know I enjoyed being

smacked, just not in the way you're doing right now. Plus, paying attention has helped me because I passed the last quiz I took in Collins class. Aren't you proud of me?" Her cheeks look a bit flushed.

"Well, I'm proud of myself. You seemed like a lost cause before me. So, I guess I'm proud of you too, by association, of course."

This girl really doesn't make anything easy, does she? "Oh, of course."

We spend the next forty-five minutes talking about the metaphors and how Gatsby's parties are 'very American' because the West Egg members and the East Egg members are allowed at these parties he throws. She also talks about how Fitzy—F. Scott Fitzgerald—up until this point, has made the reader see Gatsby from a distance, but now we see him close up, and he still remains a mystery. I only got slapped with the ruler twice this time. It still stings when she does it. Hades always manages to hit a different spot on my hand.

We're just about finished when the most random question slips out of my mouth. "Why do you like to read romance books?"

She stares at me. I feel like I stepped over a line. "How do you know I read romance novels?"

"I saw one in your hand last night. It had a bunch of lipstick kisses on the cover, so I assumed romance."

She chuckles a bit and shakes her head. "Yeah, uh, that's our book club pick this month, and it actually was a romance, so one point for you, creeper."

"That feels good, but you never answered my question. Why do you like romance so much?"

She ponders it for a minute, then says, "I like watching two people fall in love. It's nice when you open a book and know that, hopefully, the two people will have found their way to each other when it's over. I have never really believed it could happen for me in reality after—"

She pauses, and it's like she cut herself off from saying something she didn't want to talk about. I wish she kept going, though. I want to know why she doesn't believe she could have what they do in books. Plus, why would people write about romance if it didn't exist in real life?

"I have a pretty messed up view of love and romance too, but I think it still exists out there. Somewhere, hopefully." I say with a slight chuckle.

She nods as if she agrees with me, and as she does, her timer goes off, indicating that our time is up today. We both gather our things, and as we leave, I ask her if she wants me to walk her back to her dorm.

"Uh, no, it's okay, I'll be alright. Thanks for the offer." She smiles as she hurriedly walks to the staircase and disappears from my eye line.

This semester may be looking up after all.

14

Hadleigh

  I'm out taking pictures all around campus on this cool Sunday morning. It's around 9 AM, and the campus is partially awake. Usually, I hate taking photos with other students around to see me, but I'm trying to get past that. Today I found this cute spot with a bunch of flowers. I finished all my homework on Friday, so I had a weekend free of homework, and it felt good. I was able to catch up on reading and take some more pictures, which I have been dying to do.
  Ella and I have a coffee date in half an hour. I'm very excited not only for the coffee, but for the company. Ella might be the oldest of our little group, and I might be the youngest, but her wisdom is helpful. I also want to get more out of her about Zimmerman, but she has been mostly a closed book about him. I'm taking photos of these cute lilies planted by the fountain on campus. When I heard someone calling my name, I looked around and saw Jacks Moore approaching me. I kind of know him. We have had some classes together. I also think he was there when I first met Grant. Yikes, he might hate me too. "Oh, hi Jacks, what's up?"
  "Hey, Hads, I was just wondering about the bio homework for Monday. Have you started it?"
  "I actually finished it on Friday. Did you need help with it? I don't mind."

"No, I think Grant would be mad and think I was trying to poach you from him or something."

"Yeah, he can be pretty territorial, but he doesn't matter. I can help."

"Grant is just like that because he likes you." He smirks at me as if I should have known that already.

"If how he is acting presently means that he likes me, then he's doing a bad job of showing it."

"Listen, Hadleigh—"

"Just Hads is fine."

"Hads, he's just misunderstood. Most people think of him as a typical hockey asshole, but he isn't like that. He wants something real. He's afraid of failing —believe it or not—and since his last three girlfriends cheated on him, he's afraid of getting too close to someone who could just decide that they don't want him one day."

"Oh. I didn't know all that. Grant still has no right to act all possessive and territorial, though. At the end of the day, I'm a person, and he doesn't own me."

"As I said, get a chance to know him, really know him, before you give up on him completely. Plus, his feelings about you are just really confused right now. He shouldn't act like he is, but he's an idiot."

"Okay. Thanks for this." My head is more confused now. "But I still don't mind helping you with your homework. Consider it a thank you for the clarity."

"It's alright. I give clarity free of charge. This might give me a chance to talk to Claire instead."

"Claire Canes? The girl who sits two rows in front of you in our bio lecture?"

"Yeah, Grant keeps making fun of me, saying that I'm too much of a wuss to talk to her and finally ask her out, which he's right, I am. I just wish it were that easy."

"Jacks, that is actually adorable, and I can't believe I am saying this, but I agree with Grant. You should just talk to her. Girls like it when you can be direct with your feelings."

"Got it, well thanks anyway. Also, about Grant."

"What about Grant?"

"I feel like I shouldn't be saying this, but fuck it. Grant is the type of person who cares fiercely about people when he cares about them. It's his nature, so go easy on him if he says some douchey shit. He just...cares about you, that's all."

I am so goddamn confused right now. I need to talk to anyone else about this. Thank God for Ella and our date soon. I need to fix my brain.

"Okay, well, thank you for this, and I'll see you in class on Monday." I start walking towards the library cafe, determined to escape this situation and my feelings.

"Yeah, no problem. Make sure you think about what I said!" He sort of shouted that across campus.

Don't worry, Jacks. I won't forget it. I can see how Grant *could* care about me, but in my mind, he doesn't. I try to think about the last time someone cared about me, only for them to be dragging me on the entire time. It's hard for me to look around, let someone take care of me, and believe they actually want to listen to my thoughts and feelings. I just don't see it happening to me ever again. After the last time, I don't trust anyone with stuff like that. It's easier to think that nobody wants to get close to me. That way, nobody gets hurt in the long run, and everyone is happy. But Jacks saying all that messed me up, so I turn off my camera and book it to the library.

※

I rush into the library cafe and quickly scan to see Ella sitting in one of the booths reading on her kindle. My mind is a mess. My face probably shows that because Ella looks wide-eyed at me when I sit at the table.

"Did you just see two squirrels having sex or something? Why does your face look like that?"

"No reason, just a friendly conversation with Grant's roommate about how Grant has confusing feelings for me and that he cares about me. Just another normal day." I say that a bit too fast and screechy for my liking, but Ella understands all the same.

"Wait, what? Back up a second. Grant's roommate just talked to you?"

I go over every detail from the past half hour, explaining how Jacks and I are acquainted through our class. I basically word vomit all over her for about ten minutes, and when I stop talking, she has no words. "Okay, wow, that is a lot to unpack this early when you're hungover. This just happened?"

"Yeah, right before I came here. I don't understand what he means by saying Grant cares about me. He sure has a funny way of showing it."

"Well, some guys are just like that. They tell you they feel one way and act entirely differently. It's not entirely uncommon. That's why women are sometimes better." Ella's pansexual and has had more experience than I have with relationships in general. I trust her opinions, especially when I'm this confused.

"I just, my brain feels so messed up. I didn't even like Grant a few days ago, and now I think he's tolerable?"

She slides a coffee over to me "Drink this. It's not alcohol, but it'll help."

"You ordered my coffee for me?"

"Triple shot latte with a pump of liquid sweetener. I figured you might need it." It is truly the little things in life. I love Ella so much.

"Thank you, Ells."

"Always, Hads. I have some advice for you if you want to hear it."

I take a large sip of my coffee. "Yes, please, I will take anything to de-puzzle my thoughts."

"First, *you* must figure out how you actually feel about Grant. I know you're tutoring him, but that doesn't mean you can't have at least a friendship. But you must figure out what you want, not what other people tell you. As soon as you figure that out, you'll probably feel better."

"What if I don't know what I want?"

"That's okay too, but you must make it clear to Grant. If you're confused about the whole situation, tell him that. I think he would understand."

"And what about Ryan?" I ask her.

"Ew, that creep? What about him?"

"We're just acquainted, but I don't know. Something with him seems off. Paige feels it too."

"Could you see yourself being friends with Ryan?" She asks me

"I think so. He seems to have similar interests with me, and he has only ever been sweet to me." It's just my gut that feels weird when I'm around him, but that's probably just me.

"Well, good. Then that's that."

"Ella, you make everything seem so easy." I tell her.

"I know, and that's why you guys love me so much. I'm the level-headed one in this group. It brings a nice balance." She winks at me and sips her coffee.

"Okay, figuring out my feelings. That seems easy enough, right? I can do that."

"You sound like you're trying to convince yourself. It won't happen overnight, babes, but I think you'll figure it out. Make a chart or something. Those seem to help."

How did I not think of that? Chart-making is one of my hobbies. I feel like I betrayed the chart Gods or something. "Yet again, you save the day. We should do this more often."

"I agree. Do you want to make it an every Sunday activity?"

"Absolutely." I raise my cup to cheer with her.

"To someday hoping you will spill the beans about Leo."

She shoots a death stare at me. "*Zimmerman.*"

"Right, yes, Zimmerman." I throw a coy smile her way. I will get more information. Maybe I should ask Paige about those torture techniques...

15

Hadleigh

"Okay, so that thing flying on the ice is called a puck?" Amelia is making me laugh. She has no clue about sports, and it shows.

"Yes, and right now Grant is playing right defense, which means he is trying to prevent the left winger dude from scoring." Paige is explaining this to her. Paige likes hockey and comes to games sometimes. The rest of us do not.

"I used to hate watching any kind of sport, but this is kind of interesting," I say as I watch them zoom around the ice. I wish I could skate like that, but I would definitely fall on my ass.

"Does anyone want a drink? Alcohol included. This seems like it would be really fun watching it drunk." Ella makes a point. However, I don't drink, and hockey is hard enough to follow sober.

"Do you guys see Ryan? I don't know what position he plays." I ask.

"Ryan is benched, but Grant's on the ice right now! He's number 11. Look, he just hip-checked that guy!" Paige says a bit too excitedly.

"Hip what? Is that illegal?" Amelia asks.

"No, it's when you slam the other guy up on the glass," I say.

"Doesn't that hurt? I'd feel all out of sorts after that." Amelia says, again clueless.

"That is the point. It throws the other person off their game, so you can swoop in and steal the puck." Paige knows quite a bit. I'm impressed.

"P, did you say Ryan was benched? Why? I assumed he would be playing if Grant is."

"Yeah, he's a goalie, but since Holt is a senior, he's on the ice first. Normally, he stays in the entire time unless we are up by a lot, then they switch, so the newbies get more playing time."

"Oh, I guess that makes sense, but why is Grant on the ice then? He's only a sophomore. I didn't think he would be a starter."

"Grant's actually really good. He starts most games," Ella shares that piece of information.

"How did you know that?" I say.

"He who shall not be named talks about hockey all the time. He thinks Grant and Jacks are really good defensemen or whatever. Plus, he's friends with a bunch of people on the team, so he goes out with them all the time."

We all stare at Ella. We have gone from Leo to Zimmerman, and now he who shall not be named. That's a bit frightening.

"Uh, anyways, he was right. Grant is the best right defense on the team, the senior who had that position last year graduated. He and Jacks work well together, on and off the ice. You can tell they have great chemistry." I think it is safe to say that Paige likes Grant, she has not stopped talking him up the entire game, and we're in period two.

"Paige, I know what you're doing." I caught her red-handed.

"If I am hyping up our hockey team, then yes,

that's what I'm doing. Anything else is pure conjecture." She throws a coy smile at me. She can deny all she wants, but I will never end up with Grant. A relationship is the last thing on my mind right now. I think. I switch my focus back on the game. Grand Mountain is winning 3-1.

"Okay, but like, why are the sticks shaped like that? It seems awkward to hold." Amelia is trying. I will give her that.

"I feel like they would be too. I've seen people break their sticks from slamming them too hard." Paige tells us.

"I could make a thousand jokes about the male species right now, but I'll refrain," Ella smirks as she takes a sip of her beer.

"So, Hads, are you going out with Ryan after this? Isn't that what he asked you in class?" Paige already knows what answer she wants out of my mouth, and luckily for her, on #TeamGrant, she gets it.

"No, I'm going back to the dorm. I asked for a rain check. It seems too soon. I don't even know him."

"Ah, okay." She says, a huge smile on her face.

The buzzer signals the end of the second period, and there's a small break before the last one. I see Ryan from the bench. He looks up at me, smiles and waves. I send a tiny wave back, suddenly feeling very on the spot. Grant's looking at Ryan, and he follows his eye line to where I am.

Grant just took off his helmet, and his hair is a mess. The brown curls are everywhere, even over his eyes. I don't know how he can see me through those. He's sweaty and gross, but he stares at me, and it heats me from the inside out. The cold rink no longer feels freezing. It feels like a goddamn sauna. I can't tell what he's feeling right now, and I don't know if I want to. How my stupid body reacts to him is just a coincidence, right? His gaze heats my body because of the hatred we used to have for each other. It has to be. Our eyes are still locked, and it seems like everything around me has disappeared. It's just us.

"Oh, they're definitely eye-fucking this time."

That sentence breaks me from my trance as I look over at Ella. I silently thank her for that. I excuse myself to go to the bathroom, and Amelia follows me. I just need to be alone for a second, but there's no way I can find my way back to our seats, so I say nothing as she silently walks next to me.

We enter the bathroom, and she tries to follow me into the stall. "Amelia, what are you doing? I know you know how bathrooms work, which is one aspect in life I don't need help in."

"I don't have to pee. I just wanted to talk to you."

"Okay, about what?" I ask.

"Hads, you cannot play this game with me. I'm the queen of deflecting and changing topics about things I don't want to discuss."

"I can't change the subject if I don't even know what we are talking about." I absolutely know what she wants to talk about, but I can't relive the past fifteen minutes. I will shove my feelings down until they make a semblance of sense—just like always.

"Hads."

"Okay, fine, what?"

"You guys were just staring at each other, and I could feel the tension coming off you."

"It has been a very busy semester so far. I have

a lot of tension around my neck area. That's what you must have felt." I say to her.

"Hads. You like him."

"I tolerate him."

"That stare looked locked and loaded with about a thousand different emotions. None of them were tolerable. It was mostly heated, and not the angry kind of heat."

"I—" I look her up and down and figure out what to say. "The truth is that my head is so jumbled, and I don't want to start a relationship and have it end like the last one or get in the way. My brain is so goddamn confused, and I can't seem to un-confuse it. But I'm trying."

Someone tries to enter the bathroom, and Amelia shoves the door closed and tells them to go to the other one. I laughed. "First off, I am proud of you for trying to unjumble your brain or whatever, but you can't ignore the stares. You both have had a very complicated relationship the past few weeks, but you clearly feel something for him. Just don't run away from that. It's okay to run towards it sometimes."

"Says you, Ames." With that, she laughs.

"Well, yes, but that is part of my brand, so I'm allowed to. I do, however, want my friends to be happy." She says with a soft smile. "Now go pee or splash water on your face or whatever. I'll be waiting outside."

"Thank you, Ames. I appreciate it."

"Of course."

I calm my running thoughts and meet Amelia by the stairs, and we return to our seats just in time for the third period to start.

The game finished, and Grand Mountain won. The fans are excited and rowdy while the four of us try to exit the stadium to beat the foot traffic. We get out of the stadium, and Ella starts yelling about how our team won and how our school is the best. She's drunk, and Amelia tries to corral her so she doesn't get hit by a car.

"Grant played well tonight. Don't you think?" Paige asks me.

"He did." She will not stop talking about him. It is pretty clear what point she is trying to make.

"So, it's like football on ice?" Amelia is still very confused. She is not a very sporty person, but neither am I.

"Yes, Ames, I told you that four times already." Paige interlocks our arms, and we continue on the sidewalk.

"P, you know my memory sucks, and ELLA GET OUT OF THE PARKING LOT I'M NOT SAVING YOU IF A CAR IS COMING!" She chases after Ella again. Maybe we need to get a drunk leash or something.

"Okay, maybe Ames and I should take Ella home and make sure she's okay. Hads, are you good to walk to your dorm, or do you want a ride?" Paige turns her head towards me.

"Yeah, I'll be alright. It's not that far of a walk, plus Ella drove here, and there's no way she's driving back home in her state."

"I know." She skips off towards where Amelia and Ella are resting on the sidewalk and looks back at me. "Text us when you're home safe! We love you, H!"

I smile and wave off after her, "I love you guys

too." I walk on the path toward my dorm, away from the loud noise of the excited fans. I had a lot of fun tonight with the girls, and watching the hockey team play definitely fulfilled my sports romance loving heart, but I still feel off for some reason. The talk I had with Amelia has been at the back of my mind for most of the night, and it's making my head swim. It's funny because Amelia is the queen running away from her feelings and is trying to tell me to stop doing that. I don't know if I can run toward someone, let alone run toward Grant and admit that I like him.

Which I don't.

I think.

I don't know. Everything feels so weird, which is why I don't do relationships anymore. It makes my head hurt. In another universe maybe I could like Grant, but in this one, I'm protecting my heart from any stupid jocks that could destroy it again. I nod to myself, noting that I am making the right decision and I continue on toward my dorm building. The winter Virginia air is blowing against my face as I get to my dorm. I take a deep breath before entering my building and breathe in the cold air, feeling it go into my lungs, and then I release it. I swipe into my building and quietly enter my room, careful to not wake up Taylor. I get ready for bed and grab my phone.

Hads: Congrats on keeping all of your teeth intact.
Grant: Uh, thanks? I think?
Hads: Congrats on the win tonight, it was more interesting to watch than I thought it would be.
Grant: Well I'm glad tonight has made you a future hockey fan.
Hads: I'm not buying season tickets, calm down.

Grant: It was nice seeing you in the stands. Hopefully you can catch another game before the season ends?
Hads: Maybe.
Grant: See you Thursday?
Hads: Sounds good.
Grant: Goodnight Hades.
Hads: Goodnight Grant.

16

Grant

I'm in my room about to head out to my next tutoring session with Hades when Jacks comes in.

"Off to tutoring today, are you?" Why does his face look like that? Since our game on Monday—which we won—he's been acting weird.

"Did you get lucky with Claire recently or what? Why have you been so weird lately?"

"Okay, when have you ever used that phrase in a sentence? And don't talk about Claire. We're in a bit of a rut right now." He looks a bit sad, and I feel like shit.

"You're right, and I'm sorry. What's going on with you and Claire?" I've been kind of a shitty friend when it comes to Jacks. Everything has been so busy lately, school, practice, and tutoring. I feel like we've barely had time to sit and talk. Friend to friend. Brother to brother.

"It's nothing, just a little argument. It doesn't matter. I came here to catch you before tutoring, not to talk about my life." He's deflecting, but I don't press.

"Okay, what did you want to talk about?"

"You."

"Me?" I ask.

"And Hadleigh."

"Me…and Hadleigh?"

"Yup."

"What about Hadleigh and me?"

"Oh, you know, just how you are in major denial about your feelings for her. Not a big deal."

"My major what about my what for her?" I practically shouted that. What the hell is he talking about? I don't have *feelings* for Hades. She is *just* my tutor. Although, I will admit seeing her at the hockey game the other day threw me for a loop. She came to watch Ryan, of all people, and for a split second, I wished she was there to watch me play. Not him.

"You heard me." He's smiling, and he kind of looks…giddy? What the fuck?

"You're out of your mind Jacks. She's my tutor. Plus, I barely know her!" I'm full-on shouting now. "No, Jacks, you may be right about most things, but you're wrong about this."

"Based on your reply to my statement, I will not concede just yet. You very clearly like this girl."

"Oh, I very clearly like her, sure, based on what?" I ask, a bit quieter now.

"Well—"

I cut him off. "Exactly, so you have no proof."

"If you let me finish, I can tell you."

I waved my hand and gestured to him to continue. I can't wait to hear what fake proof he conjures up.

"I only have one main point to make."

"Oh, just one, do you? I knew you had nothing." I say.

"It might be nothing to you, but to me, it showed everything I needed to see."

"And what would that be?"

"At the hockey game, you guys locked eyes with each other. It was only for like thirty seconds, but I watched it. Hell, I felt it. Not just from her side but yours too. You guys have it bad for each other. And you are both in denial about it."

"No, we don't. We started out hating each other, and frankly, I don't know where we stand now. According to her, we would just be acquaintances or maybe nothing. It was just a look. It didn't mean anything."

"You keep telling yourself that, G. Deny it all you want. I think deep down, maybe even into the depths of your charred black soul, you know I'm right about this. It's time to start trusting in people again." He looks at me as I open the door to our room and head toward the library.

I walk a bit slower than usual to the library because I can't get what Jacks said out of my head. He thinks I have feelings for Hades. Like feelings of love feelings? I could audibly laugh at the mere insinuation of that. Me and Hades? In a relationship? Yeah right. Never in a million years.

I push the double doors in, walk into the library, shuffle up the stairs, and make my way to our study room. I mean the study room Hades rented out for us. In no universe will Hades and I ever have an our, or an us. I'm almost through the doorway when I notice she's already there.

She doesn't even look up when she speaks. "You're late, were you too busy putting gel in your hair and forgot what time it was?"

Does she have a sixth sense where she can recognize my footsteps or something? How the hell does she do that? "No, I was actually...." Oh God, I can't think of a comeback right now. This has never happened before. Shit! *Say something, anything.* She cannot win this battle. She looks up at me as if she is waiting for me to say something, and I never noticed how pretty her eyes are. They're brown. Most people hate that they have brown eyes. Still, hers are like the color of this old leather journal my dad used to have. He used to write down daily musings and thoughts, and as I got older, he would write my hockey plays in them when we practiced together.

She slaps me with that damn ruler again. Fuck, how long was I zoned out?

"How is it possible you zoned out, and we haven't even started talking about the book yet? That has to be a new record." She smiles and motions for me to sit down, so I do.

She starts by talking about chapter four and highlights how in this chapter we dive deeper into who Gatsby is as a person and how he's in love with Daisy Buchanan. Apparently, they knew each other from before the war, and Daisy fell in love with Gatsby before she married Tom. They used to write letters to one another, but she still married Tom.

"I never understood why people write letters to one another," I say.

"I think it's beautiful." She says quietly.

"Why is that?" I find myself actually wanting to know her answer.

"I think it's far more personal than a text message. Being able to sit down and spend time writing the perfect words to say in a letter. And the anticipation of one being returned to you. There is a certain... romance to it." She smiles at the end, and it's like seeing a whole new side of her. It's different, and I want to see it more often.

"Anyways, this chapter also highlights the metaphor of the green light at the end of Daisy's dock and how Nick saw him reaching out to it one night. This is the object of his hope." She pauses and looks up at me, making sure it's clicking in my brain. Something in my stomach feels really weird. "Gatsby's love for Daisy is the source of his romantic hopefulness and the meaning of his yearning for the green light in Chapter one. That light, so mysterious in the first chapter, becomes the symbol of Gatsby's dream, his love for Daisy, and his attempt to make that love real. Does that make sense?"

"Yeah, it actually does. The green light is what keeps him hoping. It's what keeps him clinging onto the fact that he might be able to have her again one day." I say, hoping I finally understand something about this book.

"Exactly. It can be argued this metaphor also could be interpreted as the American dream, but I prefer the romance of it all. Gatsby really did just want to be with her, but in the end—well, best not to spoil it." She sighs and sits at the table rather silently.

"Is that it for today?" I feel very on the spot right now. When she gets quiet, no good thing can come after that. I feel like I'm waiting for a bomb to explode.

"Yeah, sorry. I'm trying to build the courage to ask you something."

"You want to ask me something?"

"Yes."

"Okay."

"Why don't you date anymore? I mean—fuck, that came out wrong." She sulks back in her chair.

"Why are you asking me that?"

"Grant, this is me trying to get to know you better, so just shut up and answer the question."

Does she want to get to know me? Maybe we weren't as far off as friends as I thought. "I don't date anymore because I don't want to. Plain and simple." I don't tell her that I don't date because I don't trust anybody anymore and that I am afraid every romantic partner I ever have will always want somebody better than me. I don't tell her I am so afraid of never being good enough for someone that I just gave up altogether.

"Oh, I guess that makes sense."

"Yeah."

The air feels thick, heavy, and awkward. My stupid mouth, which apparently has a mind of its own, decides to open up and speak. "So, Hades, why don't you date? Have you taken too many souls from people, and now you physically can't date anymore?" I sound like a dick. I *know* I sound like a dick, so why the fuck did those words come out of my mouth?

She looks a bit uncomfortable, fuck, why did I say that? I feel like an ass. The last thing I wanted to do was to make her feel like shit, yet I still said it.

"I don't know. I guess nobody has ever shown much interest. Plus, I'm a busy person." She says that super fast like she just said the first thing that popped into her head.

Nobody has ever shown much interest. Yeah, right, she's lying through her teeth. No interest? Is the rest of the world blind or something?

"So, next week, same time. I'll see you then!" She's halfway out the door before I turn around and watch her leave, feeling disappointed that I didn't ask her more questions.

Fuck.

Jacks was right.

I want every answer of hers to every question I ask.

I want to argue with her and play our stupid little back-and-forth game.

I want to let her hit me with that damn ruler anytime she wants.

I want it all.

Shit.

17

Hadleigh

It's a Tuesday night, and where am I? A booth in the library, with my coffee and a good book. I'm waiting for Paige and Amelia because we have a study date tonight. I got here early because I needed a change of scenery from my dorm room, and I just love it here. The library is the most soothing place on campus for me. I could sleep here, honestly. I put my book down and grab my laptop. I prop it open to the latest Google doc with the paper I'm working on for my biochemistry class. I check my email and compose one for my friend in class. Their name is Drew, and they're one of my favorite people in my major. I met them on the first day of classes freshman year, and they've helped me so much with these hard bio and chemistry classes. Some of the papers get too much sometimes, and I occasionally need their help. I type out my email with my questions and send it off.

I go to start my criminology paper when someone slides into the booth, I look up expecting Paige and Amelia, but instead, I am surprised. "Ryan."

"Ooh, what is with the cold shoulder, girl? Did I do something?" He asks.

"Well, you did just sit down in my booth uninvited."

"My deepest apologies."

"Did you need something?" I ask him.

"Well, no, not really. I was just wondering why you haven't used my phone number yet. That paper I gave you is probably burning a hole in your pocket."

Oh, this is a fun conversation. How can I burn a hole in that ugly shirt of his? Why do guys think that just because you hand your number out to girls means they will use it?

"Sorry, I've just been really busy and stuff. I haven't had much time to be able to hang out. Also, just because you gave me your number doesn't mean I will use it, Ryan. Plus, I don't date jocks."

"I never said date. To be fair, Hads, I'm okay with friends."

"Are you? That is not what Grant has been saying."

I look to the side, and Paige and Amelia choose to walk in right now. They make eye contact with me and sit at a different table, one with a direct eye line to where I am. Paige immediately takes out her phone, and I know what is happening when mine buzzes on my computer.

Paige: Guys! SOS!
Amelia: Paige, I'm sitting right next to you.
Paige: True. The SOS is just for Ella, then.
Ella: What's going on? Is someone hurt? Did Amelia trip someone again?
Amelia: That happened ONE TIME, and it was an accident.
Paige: Partially.
Amelia: He asked where ASIA WAS ON A MAP! I think my tripping him might have added more brain cells. I was doing him a favor.
Ella: Okay, is this what the SOS was about?
Paige: Oh, right. Ryan is sitting in a booth in the

library cafe talking to Hads!!! He took our spot.
Ella: Oh God, this sounds bad.

The messages keep coming, and my phone buzzes, but I ignore them. Ryan is talking about the game from the other night, and I'm zoning out. "Anyways, are you going to any more hockey games?"

"I might. It depends on, well, my interest. You guys did pretty well the other day, and I'll admit it was fun to watch."

"Yeah, you showed up with Paige and two other girls."

"Yup, my friends Amelia and Ella came too."

"How did you all become friends? Was it through your book club?"

"Ella and Paige started a book club, and I joined it. We meet every Wednesday night to discuss. They're some of my best friends because of that." My phone buzzes again.

Paige: Did he say my name? Is he talking about me?
Amelia: What is he asking you, Hads?
Ella: If he says some shit, let me know. I'll be at the campus in two minutes.
Paige: If he repeats my name, I'm coming over there.
Hads: Please DON'T. I'm trying to get rid of him.

"Listen, Ryan, it was nice talking about hockey and stuff, but I was waiting for some friends to study with tonight, and they're on their way here."

"Oh yeah, no problem."

He starts to slide out of the booth but pauses before walking away.

"Listen, Hads, we're friends, right?"

"Um, yeah, I guess. Why?"

Amelia: Why isn't he leaving? Did he forget his manual on how to dress appropriately?
Hads: I WAS THINKING THE SAME THING!
Amelia: His shirt is ugly.
Paige: Do I need to come over and kick his ass for you, Hads?
Ella: Paige, your punches feel like a feather hitting the ground. Soft and delicate.
Paige: At any given time, I have 12 murder scenarios in my head. TRY ME.
Amelia: Oh God.
Ella: Girl, what? You need to stop watching those true crime docs. You worry me.
Amelia: It's weird how someone so cheerful could be so murderous. Yesterday she told me she was feeling stabby, so I migrated to my room and stayed there.

"I just wanted to tell you I think what you're doing for Grant is nice. Tutoring and helping him even though he talks bad about you at practice."

"I'm sorry, he what?"

Amelia: H, why are you making that face? Did he say something stupid? Rude?
Paige: Amelia, remove your hand from holding me back, or I'll bite it.
Ella: Do I need to come to campus right now?
Paige: I can handle him if AMELIA LETS ME GO.
Amelia: P, enough with the empty threats.
Ella: Seriously, I will speed over to campus, Zimmerman made me furious today, so I have a lot of pent-up anger.
Amelia: Any threats of murder today?
Ella: Only four.
Paige: That's good!
Hads: I am going to murder all of you. Please STOP, just for a second.

"Yeah, he says some stuff about you when we practice. Something about being easy and how he just wants to befriend you to get up your skirt."

I don't know what to say right now. Grant and I were moving in the right direction yesterday. But can I trust Ryan? I don't think so. I just need him to go away and stop stirring the pot.

"Thanks for letting me know, but I can handle Grant myself. See you in class." He winks at me—gross—and leaves. Paige and Amelia scramble over and sit down.

"What the hell did he say to you? Your face looked a bit shocked at the end there." Amelia shuts my laptop for me, knowing we won't get much studying done. I tell them what he said, and Paige almost looks mean after I finish.

"Paige, are you okay? You look weird right now."

"No, I'm mad. He's lying. I bet he was the one who said all that stupid stuff. Grant doesn't seem like the type. He doesn't sleep around and hasn't dated in a while. Ryan's the one who is known to hump and dump."

Amelia almost spits her coffee out, and I laugh my ass off.

Ella: GUYS, UPDATE ME? WHAT IS GOING ON?

"Paige, what the fuck did you just say? Hump and dump? Oh my God, you sound like an 85-year-old grandma." Amelia says.

Hads: Paige just said the words hump and dump, and Ames and I are dying.

Ella: Oh God, another Paige phrase to make her sound like an old lady. I love her so much.

"Okay, whatever. My point is, I am still firmly on team Grant." Paige states.

"Of course you are. However, I am team me." I say. Amelia lifts her coffee, and we all clink our cups together and get to studying.

18

Hadleigh

Paige: Guys!!! I can't make it tonight! Huge paper to write due Friday :(I do, however, want to say that this book is AMAZING. I love a good YA mystery with a bunch of brothers.

"I knew she wasn't coming. She had articles sprawled all over her floor and her laptop in the center of it. Hurricane Paige strikes again." Amelia says.

"I don't understand why she loves the floor so damn much. The girl who loves being organized is the least organized when doing homework." Ella and I have always been confused about Paige and her love of being on the floor. It's quite odd for someone as in control as she is.

"Paige told me once that she likes to get different perspectives on things and calls it organized chaos. I think that's why she likes the floor so much. Not going to lie. The carpet in her room is super comfy." Amelia probably speaks from personal experience, I walked in after a night out, and both of them were asleep on Paige's floor. It was hilarious.

We talk about the book a bit more, this one has a love triangle, and we're all choosing who we like for the main character. After about half an hour of that, we switch topics.

"Ella, how's Zimmerman?"

"I met his sister the other day."

"Oh? And? How did that happen?" I'm shocked. This is an interesting new development.

"She was waiting for him outside the office."

"Ells, why do you sound so monotone right now? Did something happen with his sister?"

It sounds like she just saw the most boring play of her life, but instead, she met her rude coworker's sister. What the hell happened? "She's nice."

Amelia and I look at each other, confused as fuck. "This is bad because...."

"I'm not supposed to like her! She's related to my nemesis! I honestly don't know how their mother birthed one evil spawn and one super nice, gorgeous, and funny spawn!"

"What's her name?" I ask.

"Alissa."

"Does she go to school here?"

"No, she graduated before us. I think we are becoming friends. She gave me her number and asked if I ever needed to rant about Zimmerman to come to her and that we could go for drinks."

"She sounds fun. Does she like to read?" Of course, Amelia asks that books are very important for a friendship.

"Yes. She is sassy and sarcastic, and I was basically flirting with her before I knew she was related to him. I was a bit embarrassed, but she didn't mind."

"Are you going to text her?" I'm curious because how can she like one sibling and not the other?

"I already did. We're going out Friday night for drinks. She's only a year older than me, and she's British and funny, and UGH!" She sulks back.

"She sounds fun, and let's be honest, us book

club girls are a bit too chill for you. I think Alissa and you becoming friends will be good for you. You'll have someone to go out with when the rest of us are either too tired or don't feel like going out."

"You bring up a good point, Hads. Don't get me wrong, I love you guys, but sometimes I need to go out and play." She winks and shimmies her chest, and we all laugh. I think Ella and Alissa being friends will be good. Paige, Amelia, and I don't go out often, and Ella loves a good party. She's the most extroverted one in our friend group. Ella diverts the subject to Amelia. "Ames, what have you been up to lately?"

"Homework and a whole bunch of nothing."

"Are you planning your next trip yet?" Amelia is studying journalism—she recently switched her major to it—and she loves to travel. She goes all over the place and takes pictures. I think she wants to be a traveling journalist one day, though I am not sure.

"I have a few places in mind. None narrowed down yet."

That's all you'll get out of Amelia. She is about as open as a closed door.

"Hads, how's everything with you?" Ella looks over at me with a sympathetic smile. I should have known this was coming. Since Ryan crashed our study date yesterday, Ella has been relentless.

"Well, my brain is still confused, and I feel like I can't trust either of them, so I'm stuck in this weird gray area. I thought Grant and I were making progress, but I'm unsure now. Ryan is just this weird red herring. I don't really trust him, but he seems nice." I feel like my thoughts are playing tug of war. I have all these unanswered questions and feelings, and I don't know how to answer them. I am stuck in the purgatory of my thoughts.

Ella gives me a sympathetic pat on the shoulder and says, "You'll figure it out, Hads. You're a smart girl. Just trust yourself and try not to listen to any outside opinions."

"Except ours because we're always here for you, and we're usually right about things." Amelia says to me.

"That's true, which is why I love you guys, but I do have to get going. Taylor wanted to watch a movie when I got back."

"A little roomie movie night sounds fun! I have to get back home too." Ella says.

"Are you plotting out more ways to threaten Zimmerman tomorrow?" Amelia asks.

"Yes, but I also have to figure out what to wear for Friday night." Ella says to all of us.

We all get up and exit the classroom. Parting ways, I shift my bag to my other shoulder while I carry my book in my other hand. It's a fairly chilly night out, but with no breeze, it's not that bad. I didn't bring my sweatshirt, and I'm slightly regretting that right now, but my dorm isn't too far away from where we usually meet for book club.

Someone is walking the opposite way on the sidewalk I am on, so I shuffle over to the side so they have room. "How nice of you to make room for me on this huge ass sidewalk Hades."

Great. Just great. Of course.

"Yeah, I made room for your giant ass head. It must be that big because of the ego, right? I wouldn't want it to have to squeeze through anywhere." I say to him.

He looks me up and down. "There she is." *What does that mean?*

"I have a question, and I need you to be honest with me," I ask him.

"Hit me."

"If you wait long enough, I might."

"Hades, stop stalling and ask me."

"Do you like Ryan?" I don't know why I need to know, but I do.

He makes a weird face. I don't think he was expecting that question. "Do I like Ryan?"

"Yes, it's a fairly simple question. Do you need me to sound it out phonetically?"

"No, I don't need you to do that. The question just threw me off. I guess I don't like Ryan. Why do you ask?"

"He just has said some things to me. About you." I tell him.

"Ryan has talked to you? What did he tell you?"

"He told me not to trust you."

"He said that? To you? When?" His face is getting red.

"Yes, he did when I was at the library the other day."

"Oh, what? Were you guys on a date or something?"

"No, and even if we were, why do you care?" I ask him, a bit more sternly this time.

"I—I don't care." The vein in his neck is protruding now. "Has he kissed you, Hadleigh? Has he touched you?"

"What? Where did *that* come from, Grant?" Why is he being so weird right now? Why do our conversations always come to the same place—us fighting? It's getting frustrating.

"Please, I need to know." He says, a bit quieter now.

"No, we haven't kissed, he's just my friend, or we're friendly, I don't know. Why does it matter to you so much?" He doesn't answer me. "Are you jealous or something?"

"No, no, I'm not jealous. It's just that—"

I cut him off. "What then?"

"Hades, he isn't a good guy, and I don't like you being around him when you'realone."

"Grant, I can handle myself. I told you that."

"I know. I just have this urge to protect you from guys like him."

"Well, stop having that urge!" We're yelling at each other in the middle of the sidewalk. Thank God there's nobody around because I would be super embarrassed. Hell, I am super embarrassed.

"I CAN'T!" He screams. His face is all red and flushed.

I haven't ever heard him fully yell before. Oddly enough, it doesn't scare me. *He* doesn't scare me. I feel oddly safe out here at night, yelling at him in the middle of the sidewalk.

"Well, I can't fix that, so maybe you should see a doctor. I don't need you to protect me." I start walking towards my dorm when he grabs me by my upper arm, spins me around, and before I can register what is happening, he's kissing me.

Grant Carter is kissing me.

On the sidewalk.

When we were fighting ten seconds ago.

I should be pulling away. Why am I not pulling away?

My favorite book falls to the ground, and I could care less because this kiss is good. I haven't had physical contact like this in years, and I feel like my body just woke up from a coma. Every part of my body is on fire. I've never felt like this before with anyone.

Oh God, what's happening to me?

I pull away—his smile beaming at me—and out of reflex, I slap him.

"Oh my God, I—I'm so sorry." I'm flustered because I didn't *mean* to slap him. Shit, I just had a nice moment with Grant, and I ruined it. I need to get out of here before I embarrass myself more—if that's even possible. He was only the second guy I had ever kissed, and I *hit him*. Honestly, I blame him. He was the one who snuck up on me with his lips.

I turn around and hurry away.

Leaving him standing there on the sidewalk.

19

Grant

Today's tutoring session could only be described as awkward so far, and it's all my fault.

I was the one who kissed her last night.

I *kissed* Hadleigh. On the mouth. With my mouth. Why the fuck did I do that? Then she slapped me, which I deserved for attacking her with my mouth with no warning. I don't regret it at all, though. For a moment, she kissed me back. *She fucking kissed me back.*

I thought her slapping me would have knocked me out of my trance, but it didn't. In fact, I became more attracted to her because of that. I want to ask her about yesterday and see how she feels, but I can't. Her head is probably a mess—typical Hadleigh behavior—and she has barely looked me in the eye the entire time we've been together. She's super closed off, and I don't want to make it worse. I know she's on guard again, and I've been in the same position. It's been hard for me to open up to people, especially after being cheated on three times. But for some reason, it's so easy with her.

She slaps me with the ruler again. "Fuck, sorry, I got lost in my thoughts for a second."

"It's fine, but make sure you listen now because I don't like repeating myself."

"Yes, ma'am." She stares at me for too long and then continues to talk about the book. We have around fifteen minutes left of today's session, and I need to get her talking and break the ice. I hate the energy in this room right now. Should I ask her about the kiss? Talking about it seems like it's on a *DO NOT DO THIS* list of topics that I should never bring up again. She pauses for a moment, which is my moment to sneak some conversation in. "Listen, Hades–"

"No."

"What? You don't even know what I'm going to say." I argue.

"Yes, I do, and I don't want to talk about it."

"Isn't saying that talking about it, technically?"

"Grant. I'm serious. It was a mistake, and if I'm going to keep helping you, we must remain professional. What you did yesterday was anything but." She glares at me while saying that. I pause for a moment, thinking over my words carefully. She's right. We have to remain professional, but I think about that kiss whenever I look at her. I think about how she smelled like the rain, even though it hadn't rained in a couple of weeks. Her perfume has been in my head for the past 24 hours—all flowery and shit. I've got it bad for this girl.

"Okay, professional it is. That doesn't have to stop us from being friends, does it?"

"I guess not." She agrees.

"Okay, good. Is that all for the book today?"

"Yeah, I hit everything I wanted to talk about. We only have one more session until the midterm."

I check what time it is on my phone. "We still have ten minutes of this room reserved."

"Okay, what's your point?"

"Why do you never wear sweatpants?" I ask her.

"Why do I what?" She looks confused.

"I've never seen you in sweatpants. You're like the weirdest college student ever."

"I happen to like my style, thank you very much."

"I do too. It's very... academic or whatever. I was just wondering why you never wear sweats. You always look like you're on your way to an art museum, not a college lecture."

"It's just what I like to wear. I always feel like I am drowning in sweatpants, they make them too long, and I have short legs. It just looks weird, so I tend to stay away from them. Happy?"

"The happiest, actually." I throw a smile in her direction.

"If we're going to do this, why do you always wear that chain? You always have it on, and I didn't think guys were into necklaces."

"My dad gave it to me before he died. I wear it to always carry him with me, and it has my hockey number on it." My voice breaks a bit at the end. I look down at the gold chain around my neck. The chain's brand new because it broke last year. My mom had to get me a new one, but I couldn't part with the old one, so it's still at home hidden under my dad's old journal. I couldn't bear to part with it because it was the last thing he ever gave me, one of the last things he touched.

She's quiet for a moment. I didn't think she noticed the chain. It's usually hidden under my shirts and stuff. "I'm sorry. I didn't mean to make fun of it."

"I didn't think you were, but thanks."

Our eyes lock for the first time all day, and I have a flashback to when we were like this at my hockey game the other day. The room feels charged all of a sudden, and it's taking everything in me not to reach over the table, grab that cute sweater of hers, and kiss her until she falls over.

 But I can't.

 I want to. God, I want to.

 But I can't.

 I walk into the room, and Jacks sits on his bed most likely texting Claire. He looks up when I walk in, but I ignore him and go straight under my covers, creating a fort between us.

 Jacks sighs, and I can hear him getting up off his bed and walking towards mine. He yanks the covers off my head and stares down at me.

 "That was mean. I'm cold now," I say to him.

 "What's your deal?"

 "My deal? What are you talking about? My only deal right now is that I'm cold!" I say as I try to grab my sheets back from him, to which he stretches them further from my reach. "Rude."

 "Dude, you're sulking right now." He says to me.

 "I'm not sulking. Sulking is for sad people, and I'm not sad." After I tell him this, he rips my sheets clean off my bed.

 "That was for lying to me."

 "Dude! I just put those back on my bed! I'm making you put those back on."

 "No, not until you tell me what your deal is." He says, still holding my sheets hostage.

 "Hypothetically, I may have kissed Hadleigh, and she may or may not have slapped me for it."

 "You did what?"

 "This is all hypothetical, of course."

"So you didn't kiss Hadleigh, and she didn't slap you?"

"Well, no, those things did happen, but the situation I'm talking about is hypothetical." He pauses for a beat, releases my sheets, and leaves the room.

"Where are you going?"

"To sign up for therapy, just hearing about your life is making me want to speak to someone." He says to me as he walks out of our common area.

"You're totally putting my sheets back on for me later!" I yell to him, and I can see him shake his head as he walks away.

Grant: Do you know the fastest way to put sheets back on a bed?
Hads: Is this some sort of pickup line?
Grant: No, I have some better ones though, if you want to hear them.
Hads: I would rather stick my hand in a blender.
Grant: Do you believe in love at first sight, or should I walk by again?
Hads: Keep walking, preferably to Canada.
Grant: It's a good thing I have my library card, because I am totally checking you out.
Hads: Is the fact that you know what a library card is supposed to impress me?
Grant: Okay, I'm done. But seriously, any tips?
Hads: Google is your friend Grant.
Grant: You're like my own personal Google.
Hads: Goodbye.

20

Hadleigh

"He did what?!" Ella asks me, partially shouting.

"Yeah...my head has been in a constant state of what the fuck for the past few days."

"Okay, I need every minuscule detail again."

"Ella, I just told you what happened!"

"Tell me again." Ella and I are having our weekly Sunday coffee date, and I told her about how Grant kissed me on Wednesday night after book club. I still need clarification about it because on Thursday at our tutoring session, I could barely look at him. My face kept getting hot and beet red, so I avoided his gaze and said we shouldn't talk about it.

He looked slightly disappointed, but we should remain acquainted, or whatever we are. I'd rather dive into a literal can of worms before trying to figure out why he kissed me amidst an argument.

"I told you we were arguing, and he just kissed me. I slapped him and ran away." I say, quietly sipping my coffee.

"That is the part I can't wrap my head around."

"What?"

"The slap. Why did you do that?" She asks me.

"I don't know!" I almost spilled my coffee because I banged my hand on the table. Some people are staring at us now. Whoops.

"Okay, wow, Hads, you're very testy today, aren't

you? Too sexually charged?" She giggles after saying that.

"Very funny. It just threw me for a loop, and then at tutoring he was going to bring it up, and I banned him from talking about it because I didn't want to dive into it! It was *one kiss*, right? That isn't a big deal."

"Maybe to you..." Ella looks up at me while sipping her coffee. *What?*

"What's that look for?" She smirks and tilts her head at me. What the hell is she getting at right now? "Can we please just stop talking about this now? I need a subject change."

"I'm sorry, we can, but I'll be bringing this up at book club Wednesday, so be prepared to recount this for Paige and Ames. Paige is going to scream when she finds out you guys kissed."

"Yeah, well, you know how she is fully on team Hadleigh and Grant. She might make shirts."

We both laugh at that, I love Paige and her love for wanting her friends to be happy, but I don't think Grant and I will be friends anytime soon.

"In other news, Ryan and I are working on a project together for criminology. We have this case study, and I don't know where to start, so I'm thankful I have a good partner. We're meeting every Tuesday night to work on it." I'm excited about this project. We have to research a serial killer that was assigned to us. Paige is working with Oliver—as usual. Our professor knows they work well together, and he assigned the partners. The project is due at the end of the semester.

"Does Grant know about that partnership?" Ella asks me.

"Why would he? It's for a class."

"He just seemed very protective over you being around Ryan, and that was before you kissed."

"What are you getting at?"

"I'm not getting at anything. I'm just making an observation. Just be careful. Guys can be very territorial when it comes to a woman."

I almost choke on my coffee, fake a smile, and change the subject again. "So, have you finished season three of One Tree Hill yet?"

"Almost," Ella replies. "This semester has been insane, but this part of the season always gets me too deep in my feelings."

"I haven't finished either, but Naley is coming back together, so it's worth it in the end."

"I just can't wait for Brooke to say the most iconic line of all time…" she trails off, waiting for me to join her.

"He's on the damn door, under me!" we say loudly in unison. It catches us a couple of weird looks, but we're too busy giggling to care. We chat for a bit longer until our coffee is finished, and then I look at the time.

"As always, Ells, this was quite fun. I'll see you on Wednesday night."

"Absolutely, unless I'm in prison for murdering Zimmerman, then I fear you will never see me again. I'll plead guilty if it means that whore is dead."

"I thought you guys were semi-okay? Don't you like his sister more than him?"

"Yes, and it will forever stay that way." She wraps me in a tight hug, and when she lets go, she looks at me and smiles. "Next time he kisses you, let me know immediately. I want every sexy detail, including if there's tongue used!"

I roll my eyes, and she blows me an air kiss as she walks away.

21

Grant

Today's practice has gone smoothly so far. Jacks, a couple of other guys, and I have been working on defensive drills while the rest of the team is split into groups to work on offense. Our defense has been good, but we can continually improve. Our offense has been shit the past few games and during our scrimmages at practice.

Our puck gets away from us, and I go to retrieve it when Ryan bumps into my shoulder. "Watch it, Carter."

"You're the one who ran into me, Barnes. Chill, I just need my puck."

"That sweet girl of yours will be getting my puck soon." He jabs my shoulder again. What I would give to not be at practice right now. I remain composed and grab the puck. Our coach blows the whistle, and we all circle up, signaling the end of practice today.

"Good work today boys. On Wednesday, we'll continue doing what we have been doing except switching groups, so be prepared for that. Barnes and Holt, you guys will also be doing one-on-one goalie drills." The team murmurs, and we all skate towards the locker room.

As soon as I get in there, I rip my skates off and shove my practice gear into my locker. I'm about to grab my stuff for the showers when I overhear Ryan talking to some other guys.

"I swear her skirts just keep getting shorter. Do you think she wants me or not?"

"She'll be an easy pull for you, Ry. Why haven't you sealed the deal yet?"

"I'm taking my time with this one." I hear him say.

I walk around the corner and head for the showers. I don't say a word as I pass by Ryan and the other guys surrounding him. I just silently walk in between them, minding my own business. They murmur some 'heys,' and one of them even smiles at me and slaps my back like we're buddies. I get into the shower and hope this will erase the horrible practice I just had. The water falls around me, and I wash off the remains of the failure I have been feeling lately.

If only it worked like that.

※

I get back to my dorm and pull my phone out. I click on my mom's contact, and she picks up almost immediately.

"Hi, sweetie, how are you? How's school and everything? Is Jacks okay?" I missed hearing her voice. It's nice to hear when I'm feeling this shitty.

"Hey, mom, don't worry. Your other son is just fine. School's going okay. I'm actually getting tutored by this girl for a class I'm failing. Hockey is the same, still going alright." I'm not going into much detail right now because I feel so burnt out, but it's just comforting being on the phone with her.

"Tutored? Are you failing? Honey, what's going on?"

"It's nothing. I'll get my grade up in no time, don't worry. This girl is smart. I'm in good hands. How's work? Did you get that big promotion?" My mom works as a realtor for this big firm back in Vermont. She had a huge showing last week, and a promotion was in her future if it went well.

"I got it! The showing went great, and I had a bunch of offers on it. It sold to this lovely newlywed couple. I know they will put the house to good use, and I was very excited for them."

"That's great. I'm proud of you, mom." I really am. After all we've been through the past few years, she deserves every good thing that comes her way.

"Well, I won't keep you too long. I don't want to hinder any of your study time but don't forget to call your lovely mother, she misses you. I love you."

"I will mom, I promise. I love you too." I hang up and sit down in my desk chair. Even though we mostly talked about normal and mundane things, I feel a lot better than I did before. It feels like a weight has been lifted off my shoulders. I think just hearing her voice does that sometimes. It reminds me of the support system I still have and motivates me to keep going in the future. She's all I have left, and I want to make her proud.

But, what the hell am I supposed to do about Hades? This girl won't leave my head ever since I kissed her, but she couldn't be more clear about what she wants—not me. I don't want to push her too much, but I really feel like we could have something good together. I like the way she fights me on every turn. I like the way she constantly rolls her eyes at me when I say something stupid. I like how she challenges me.

But I don't think she feels the same way. *Think, Grant. What should you do?* I could pull a Gatsby and throw a party, hoping that she'll come. I doubt that would work, though.

I would throw in the towel, but the selfish part of me wants Hades all to myself. I want her smiles, her skirts, and her fucking ruler only for me. Ryan doesn't deserve them, and maybe I don't yet, but I'll spend the rest of the semester wrangling one smile or laugh out of her at a time, or die trying.

Let's fucking do this.

22

Hadleigh

Book club last night went a bit like this: Ella mentioned the kiss, I tried to hide in my sweater vest, Paige yelled at me for not telling us about it, and Amelia laughed.

So pretty smooth.

I walk out of stats and see Paige waiting for me outside my classroom. Her eyes light up when she sees me, and she comes up and interlocks our arms as we walk upstairs to class. We're almost up the stairs when my brother comes up next to us.

"Do you ever announce yourself, or do you always go up next to girls and stand there wordlessly?" I glance in his direction. He's straight-faced as usual, and then he walks faster.

"Paige, I don't know how you get him to talk more than three words when doing projects," I tell her.

"Honestly, he doesn't. I feel like I can speak the language of Oliver Baker. One grunt means yes, and a scowl usually means no. Have you started your case study yet? Your brother and I started researching the other day." We cross the threshold into the classroom and make our way to our seats.

"Yeah, Ryan and I meet every Tuesday night to work on it. We figure once a week is enough to ensure we finish it." I put my bag under the desk and pull my iPad out while Paige grabs her computer and opens it.

"Oh yeah, I forgot you were working with him. How is that?" She seems worried.

"It's been fine so far. Yesterday night went well. We got a lot of work done and talked a bit. I trust him a lot more. We have similar interests, and I can tell he wants to hear what I have to say when I'm talking. It's nice." I smile because it *is* nice. I haven't had someone look at me like that in a while. I would consider Ryan and I to be friends now. It's also nice that I can be friends with a guy without them wanting some other shit from me.

"Oh, that's good." She smiles, but it isn't a true one. I know she's a bit upset. Paige still doesn't trust him. Something about her gut feeling and how nobody with that sense of style could be a good guy, but I brush her off every time.

"To be fair, I don't like him either, Hads. In fact, you should stay away from the entire male population for the foreseeable future." My brother decides to pipe in.

"Even you, Oliver?" I ask him.

"Yup."

"Fine, but maybe I don't like that you always work with Paige on everything. She's my friend, and you can't have her."

"I don't want her, so fuck off." He practically bites at me. *What's up with him?*

"Okay, before this sibling spat gets out of hand, I'll intervene. Keep your eye on Ryan, and don't give in to his stupid charm. Once I overheard him say he doesn't like Disney movies. Disney movies!" She's whispering now.

"Easy, Paige. Not everyone looks and acts like

Rapunzel from Tangled like you do." Oliver motions for her to sit back down as more students filter into the classroom.

"Sorry, I don't understand how you don't like Disney movies. That's most definitely his serial killer trait." She says, without elaborating.

"Sorry, his what?" I ask.

"His serial killer trait, that when it turns out he's a serial killer, people will say it makes sense because what kind of monster doesn't like Disney movies?" Oliver and I look at Paige, confused but not that surprised. "What? It's a real thing. Besides that fact, Ryan looks like he could be Ted Bundy's son. He gives me the creeps, and Ted could lure many women in with his stupid smile and charm, so just be careful, Hads. That's all."

"Paige, I'll be fine," I reassure her.

"Yeah, Paige, she'll be fine because Ryan will die if he touches her," Oliver states.

"Oliver, the broody and murderous vibe fits your personality, but you realize it's okay to show feelings sometimes, right?" Paige smiles at him before turning back around and facing the front.

"I do smile, sometimes." Oliver grunts as he whips out his notebook as our professor begins his lecture.

"Okay, class, today's lecture is on the difference between manslaughter and homicide...."

I turn back around to Oliver. "You should *really* pay attention to this lecture."

He scowls at me, and I wink at him.

Love you, big brother!

"And that's all you need to know today. Make sure you've started your projects now and not the night before. I can tell! See you next week."

"Oliver, you must have found that lecture enlightening since you threaten murder all the time. That would be a homicide, and you would go down because I would testify against you, saying you had intended to murder whoever." Paige laughs as she jokes around with my brother. Their dynamic is so weird, but I have become used to it as this semester has progressed.

"Paige, I would never actually do it. Plus, who's to say you wouldn't be the person I was murdering?" He says to her.

"Aww, you would do that for me? How nice." She smiles at him.

Oliver scowls and leaves class quite quickly. What's up with him lately? He canceled our last Saturday morning walk because he was too busy, but something else seems to be bugging him. I doubt I will ever get it out of him, though. The Baker family is not fond of sharing our feelings. That has been alright with me, but maybe that is why I can't get my head straight about Grant.

Paige and I are about to leave the classroom when Ryan calls my name. "Hey, Ryan, what's up? Is it the project?"

"No, I just had a little gift for you."

"A gift?" What? I'm not used to accepting gifts from people I just became friends with. I also feel bad because I didn't get him anything. He hands me a box with wrapping paper on it.

"What is it?"

"Open it."

I rip off the paper and open the box to find a bag of salt and pepper crinkle-cut chips. "These are my favorite. How did you know that?"

"You kept snacking on them the other day, so I grabbed a bag for you from the dining hall and wrapped it for some fanfare." He smiles at me, and I can't help it, I smile back. The thought of it was lovely.

"Thanks, Ryan, you're a good friend." Paige coughs, and I almost forgot that she was standing right next to me the whole time.

"Sorry, I won't hold you guys any longer. I just wanted to make sure you got it. See you on Tuesday, Hads." Paige is blocking the exit with a stare that doesn't look that mean. "Paige." He half smiles and scoffs.

"Ryan."

"Excuse me." He says as he shuffles past her.

Paige watches him as he scoots by her and leaves. "Did I look mean? I was trying to look intimidating in front of Ted Bundy the Second."

"No, Paige, you couldn't look intimidating if you were covered in blood. You would still look like a ray of sunshine."

She looks down, "Damn." We start walking towards the stairs and get out of the building. It's a bit chilly today but sunny, so walking outside feels nice. Not too cold. Paige is wearing this giant red and black checkered sweater. It's super soft. She made me feel it a hundred times after she bought it. She pairs that with ripped jeans—a rarity—a black cropped long-sleeve shirt, and sneakers. I'm the opposite, with a black skirt, thick tights, boots, and a sweater with my winter coat over top of that.

"Do you want to get lunch before I have to tutor, P?"

"Yeah! Let me text Amelia. She can meet us at the dining hall."

"Sounds good. Ask Ella too."

"On it. Do you want me to burn that bag of snacks while I'm at it? He could've poisoned it for all we know."

"Paige, he didn't poison it."

"A lot of poison can be odorless and tasteless, just check the bag for tiny holes, and I'll shut up about it." She shoots a look at me. I tilt my head and look at her with my eyes widened. "Fine, die then. What do I care."

"You sound more and more like Amelia every day."

"She's trying to teach me to speak up more, but maybe I shouldn't listen to her as much."

"Yeah, Amelia likes to play emotional manipulation. I would go to Ella for those things."

"That's probably a good idea, but Ames and I agreed to swap specialties. She would teach me that while I taught her how to cyberstalk."

I take a deep breath and swallow my laughter. Of course, they agreed on that. "You and Amelia living together should sometimes be considered a state of emergency."

To that, she just smiles, and we continue walking to the dining hall.

✕

Amelia: Guys, give me five minutes for lunch, I'm at my favorite cafe by campus, and they made my coffee PERFECTLY.

Ella: The little things in life make it so much better.
Paige: Ames, can you get me an iced caramel latte?
Amelia: Why...are you okay?
Hads: Yeah, P, what? You're at the table right now. What could've happened in the five minutes I've been gone?
Paige: Nothing, I just have a long night ahead of me. Coffee might help.
Ella: Paige, we love you, but no.
Hads: Yeah, no way.
Paige: IT'S JUST COFFEE!
Amelia: Paige, I'm not getting you a panic attack with a side of caramel. Remember last time?
Ella: What happened last time?
Paige: I had a panic attack and hid in my closet until Amelia came home and found me in the fetal position.
Amelia: She looked like the apocalypse was coming. It was not good.
Hads: Yeah, no coffee is for the best, Paige.
Paige: You guys are right.
Ella: I just got here. Where are you guys sitting?
Ella: Nevermind, I found Paige. She just yelled my name across the dining hall.
Paige: What you asked where I was? It just seemed easier.
Amelia: Paige, this is why you don't need coffee. You're a walking energizer bunny.
Hads: True!
Amelia: *nine attachments*
Ella: Amelia is on her way, featuring about nine animal memes.
Paige: Does that pretzel have a phone?

23

Hadleigh

Since this is the last session before the midterm, we use almost the entire time going over all the chapters leading up to the halfway point in the book. Grant has been doing quite well this session, and it doesn't feel as awkward as last time. Everything is seemingly back to normal when he smacks *my* hand. "Hades, I've been talking to you for like five minutes, and you haven't said a word."

"You're not allowed to smack me with the ruler. Only I can do that."

"Now that you know how much it hurts, will you please stop hitting me with it?" He asks me.

I stay silent for a moment, pretending to mull it over, "No."

He smacks his lips together and shakes his head. "I can't say I didn't kind of enjoy it sometimes."

"Yes, I know you'll miss that after you pass the midterm because of me. You're welcome, by the way." I look up, and he's already looking at me. My heart starts to beat faster. What is happening to me? Heart attack? Stroke?

"Hades, I really can't thank you enough. You saved my ass. I'm very thankful you chose to do this for me."

I'm stunned. He seems genuinely thankful. "Yeah, of course, it was no problem. I didn't hate it as much as I thought I would." We sit there for a moment, staring at each other. What is up with us and the staring contests? I can't seem to look away from him, though. I had never studied his face this long. I want to run my hands through the sharp cheekbones and the fluffy brown hair for some reason.

Wait. Where did that come from? Okay, retreat, retreat. I clear my throat and look down at my notes, changing the subject. "Oh, also, I made you some flashcards to help you study before the exam. Just in case you needed a last-minute refresh on certain things." I grab the flashcards I made late last night and hand them over to him. He looks shocked. "What? Unbeknownst to you, I can be nice sometimes. Plus, if you fail, that means I failed as a tutor." I'm blabbering, but he still hasn't taken the cards from my hand.

He blinks a couple of times and grabs them, "Thank you, you really didn't have to do that. I think I'll be alright."

"Take them anyway, just for my peace of mind." I shove them at him again.

"I didn't hear a please, Hades."

I roll my eyes, of course. "*Please* take the damn flashcards, Grant."

He smiles. "I know that was hard for you, but I appreciate it either way."

"Whatever. Just don't fail. Got it?"

"I'll try my best not to. I don't want to be kicked off the team, so a lot is riding on this."

"That's why you needed a tutor? Besides the failing grade? I thought it was because you were dumb, not because you would get kicked off if you failed." I guess we really don't know each other if at the last session, we're finally opening up.

"Yeah, my coach threatened to do that if I didn't get my grade up, and well, here we are."

"I guess that makes sense. Would you really miss ice skating and slapping the puck that much?"

"Yeah, I would. It feels like it's the only thing I'm good at." Oh. Does he really feel that way? This conversation seems to be going heavier than normal, and I don't want it to end. I want to hear more about Grant and what makes him tick. This seems like the first real thing either of us has ever said. *Am I getting soft, or are we becoming friends?*

"I don't think that's true. You're already better at skating than me, so congrats, you're better at me in one thing," I tell him.

"Oh, just one thing?"

"Yup, and that's all you'll ever get."

"You can't be that bad at skating. You walk around as if you're not bad at anything. I'll believe it when I see it."

"I've never been ice skating, so you probably never will see it."

"Never?"

"Never." I don't know why I haven't, I just never had the time, and my balance sucks, so it never was number one on my list of things to do. Grant cocks his head and says nothing to that.

"Why did you hate me when you first met me?" He asks me.

"I didn't hate you, just heavily disliked. Plus, you ran into me and didn't apologize."

"You didn't give me a chance to! I was going to, I swear." *Yeah right.*

We both laugh at that. This conversation feels fun and different from previous ones. The banter we usually have—I'll find myself missing this now that our sessions are over. Are we going to talk after this? Do I want to keep in touch? Does he want to keep in touch? What if he doesn't pass and still needs my help? Would I say yes if he asked? I would, I think.

"I hated you because you reminded me of someone from my past." Oh God, why did I just blurt that out? I haven't really talked about this to anyone besides my friends. I don't know why it still hurts so much to talk about it. It was three years ago. It just makes me feel like an idiot. I trusted and loved someone, which was a lie the entire time. I never understood how people did that—lie to someone you love. I'll never get over the fact that he willingly hurt me. He knew what he was doing, yet he still strung me along like a tooth at the end of a string after it got pulled out of someone's mouth.

"Someone bad, I assume?"

"The worst."

"Well, I'm sorry. I assume an ex-boyfriend? Do you need me to get plastic surgery so I no longer remind you of him? Or do you want me to punch him? Because I will, just say the word."

"No, you don't need to go that far. He was a football player—"

"Ah, I get it. Football player and I play hockey. Hence the hatred of athletes."

"Wow, I guess I *am* that obvious. So, now you know. Feud over. Congratulations." That was the most monotone I have ever spoken, and I almost sounded like my brother. Grant looks at me almost apologetically.

This is why I don't tell people about this. I hate the look of pity that comes with it.

"Look, it really wasn't a big deal. He just... cheated on me the entire time, and I was in love with him. He told me he loved me too, but he was just dating me to use me because he knew he could. It was my fault. I didn't see through his bullshit, because I was so wrapped up in it. I swore off dating jocks after that—and all together—because all men are the same."

Grant hasn't said a word. He just looks at me and listens to everything I'm saying. "I'm sorry from all jocks and men in general. Hadleigh, really, I am. That guy didn't deserve you, and what he did was shitty and not your fault at all."

"Jacks told me you have a hard time trusting people too."

"Jacks has talked to you? About me? When?"

"A couple of weeks ago, he found me while I was taking photographs outside. He came and talked to me and told me your past relationships have been bad too. Care to share?"

"I didn't know tutoring was turning into therapy." He says as he leans back in his chair.

"Today it is. If you're comfortable, of course, but I shared my secrets. It's only fair I get one of yours."

He takes a deep breath. "All three of my girlfriends have cheated on me."

I try to act surprised since I already knew this, but it still hurts hearing him say it out loud. Jacks told me a while back about his relationship struggles, but hearing Grant admit it in a sad voice makes my heart hurt a bit for him. I know that feeling and how it sticks with you. "On behalf of all girls, I am sorry. You didn't deserve that either." I mean that. Nobody deserves to be cheated on or screwed with. It's just not fair.

"It's alright. It left me with major trust issues and a feeling of never being enough for someone I love. No big deal." He shrugs when he says that.

"You shouldn't say that. It is a big deal. You gave your heart to someone, and they abused it. Your feelings are valid, believe it or not. It's not your fault that they cheated on you."

"I could say the same to you, but you wouldn't believe me."

Damn, he's right. Back to the staring contest we are. He's looking at me. I'm looking at him. The room is charged and it feels like all the walls have come down between us. We both admitted our biggest faults and things that keep us up at night, and now here we are. What's next? I can't pull my eyes away from him. I trust him. I want to know more. I want to look deeper into those blue eyes of his. I kind of want to kiss him again. What is it about him that just makes me so... unguarded? This conversation we're having makes me feel safe and unjudged.

The door opens, and we come back to reality. "I'm sorry, guys, but I think I have this study room reserved for now...."

"Right! I'm sorry we were just leaving!" Grant says, practically jumping out of his seat.

"Apologies, let me clean up my stuff, and we will be out of your hair." I shove everything into my bag, annoyed that I'll have to reorganize it later. I just need to get out of here. That session was too confusing, and thankfully it was the last one because I don't know what I would do next time if I was alone with him in a room for an hour, with all the thoughts I was having. *I wanted to kisd him again. I wanted to feel his soft lips on mine.*

We leave the room and stand in the library awkwardly before I start walking.

I feel him start walking after me. "Well, good luck tomorrow, and let me know when you pass."

"When I pass? You have that much faith in me, Hades?"

"Faith in myself, yes. Plus, those flashcards are next level, so use them."

"You made them for me. Of course, I'm going to use them." He looks into my eyes when he says that, and my knees suddenly feel weak.

"Okay. This was fun. I guess I'll see you around."

"Yup, that sounds good, bestie." He throws a wink at me, and my heart flutters. I think I might be having a heart attack. Maybe I should go to the ER.

"Bestie? That's pushing it a little."

"Seriously, Hades. Can we? Be friends officially? I enjoy talking to you, even when you hit me with a ruler and say things that I don't understand." I stop at the bottom of the stairs for a minute and think. It has been nice talking to him these past few sessions. It's not like a relationship where he could break my heart at the end, right? It's worth a shot.

"Okay. Friends, it is."

"Great! Now, as your friend, the first order of business is to hit that guy who cheated on you. Name and address, please?" He follows me down the stairs and towards the front entrance.

"Grant. No."

"Why not?"

I lean in close next to him. "My brother already

beat you to it." I throw a coy smile at him and walk back to my dorm.

24

Grant
Two Weeks Later

I'm sitting in my room when Jacks races in like a bat out of hell. "Dude, the midterm grades are in!"

"Fuck!" I jump out of bed and rush to my computer. I log in and autofill all my information, and check.

"Did you pass?" He asks me.

"It's loading."

"Make it load faster."

"I'll refresh it. Hold on."

"GRANT, DID YOU PASS OR NOT?!"

"I'M LOOKING, JACKS. BE PATIENT, DAMN."

"LOOK FASTER!"

I scroll to the bottom, where the grade should be, and I see it. "I PASSED!" I jump from my desk chair, and Jacks throws his arms around me in a bro hug. We pat each other's backs, and man, it feels good.

"Thank God, you being kicked off would have killed our season. Not that I was worried about it." Jacks looks suspicious. He was worried. I can tell.

"B plus. I'll take it." I'm elated right now, and there's only one person I can't wait to tell. "Do you know where Hades is? I should probably go tell her I passed."

Jacks shakes his head. "You could try her dorm. It's not far from here. I think it's across the quad."

"Thank you. I'll see you later, okay?"

"Sounds good, loverboy." I throw him the finger as I close the door and run towards the quad. I don't know which dorm building she's in, so this plan kind of sucks. I go into one of the buildings in the quad, and I knock on the first door I get to. It opens in seconds.

"Um, hi? Who are you?" She asks me

"Hey, my name's Grant, and I was wondering if you know where Hadleigh Baker's room is. It's an emergency."

The girl smiles at me and motions to one down the hall. I thank her, and I'm about to knock on the door when it opens, and this random girl steps out.

"Who are you, and can you please move? You're very tall and in my way."

"I'm sorry, I must be in the wrong room. I thought this was Hadleigh Baker's room."

"It is. She is at the library right now. Why?"

"The library! Thank you…?" I don't know this girl's name.

"Taylor. I'm her roommate. You must be Grant. It's nice to meet you."

"You know me?" I ask her. *Does Hads talk about me?*

"She talks about you a lot. In both good and bad ways. It's mostly just ranting while I have my headphones in."

"Gotcha, well, thank you, Taylor. I'll be out of your way now." I run back out the door and head for the library. I'm full-on sprinting by this point. I'm too excited to tell Hades I passed. Will she be happy for me? Don't get me wrong, I'm happy I passed, but that means that now I won't be able to spend time with her unless she wants to. I'm kind of bummed. Besides hockey, seeing her every week was the most exciting part of this semester. I don't know what I'll do every Thursday now. Wallow? It's not like I can force her to spend time with me. Maybe I can find some excuses to keep hanging around her or something. Or maybe if my grades start to dip again, she can tutor me? I'm getting desperate for her presence at this point. I enjoy the way we argue and tease each other. It's been fun, and I haven't been able to trust anyone for a long time, but with her, it's so fucking easy.

I'm too in my head to notice the library inching up on me, and I basically ram into the door. I push the door when it's really a pull, and I'm finally inside. My eyes search for that short little underworld boss with black hair, and I find her sitting at a table with some other girls. I run towards her, and one of the girls looks up and gives me a weird look.

"Hades!" I whisper yell as soon as I get close enough to her.

"Grant, what are you doing h—" I pick her up and spin her around before she can finish that sentence. She wraps her legs around me and hugs me back. My heart is beating so fast. *I wonder if she can feel it.*

"I passed! We did it! We passed!" I'm still whispering in her ear while spinning her around. I could do this all day. It kills me when I have to set her down. I don't want her to get dizzy, but it felt so natural. We fit together like puzzle pieces.

"You did it! You really passed? I knew you could do it."

The short curly haired one speaks up. "Hads, you said five minutes ago you were worried that he wouldn't pass."

The blonde one interrupts her. "She's kidding. Hads had total faith in you." She throws me a smile, and I laugh a bit.

"Amelia, shut up." Am I assuming that's the curly-haired one? "Weren't you and P just leaving?" Hades shoots her a death glare, one I'm quite familiar with.

"Yeah, yeah, we'll go. Paige, let's go before you start playing the wedding march." *The what?*

"It was nice to finally meet you in person, Grant." The blonde one I'm assuming is Paige says to me.

"Hades talks about me a lot, does she? I'm assuming all bad stuff." I throw a coy smile at them.

"Well, you know how she is. See you guys later. Ella, send me that book you were talking about, please." *Do all these girls read?*

"Is this the infamous book club I'm always hearing about?" I ask them.

Another girl with long reddish black hair speaks up. "That would be us, yes." She looks me up and down, and I feel weirdly on the spot right now.

Hads practically shoves me over into a chair. "Grant, just sit down and tell me how it went. Did you use my flashcards like I told you to?"

"I did. They were actually really helpful, so thank you again."

"She made you flashcards?" The other girl—Ella, I think—pipes up and sounds a bit shocked.

"Ella, shut it." I need to write down all their names so I can remember them. I'm terrible with names.

"Sorry, it's just that you don't often make people study materials. Color me surprised, that's all." This conversation seems weirdly loaded with something I can't place yet. Does she know something I don't?

"Anyways, we did it! I passed and can continue playing hockey." I tell her.

"Grant, why do you keep saying we? You're the one who took the test. I didn't do anything" She's selling herself short. I can tell she feels awkward about it.

"Hades, I couldn't have done this without you. Therefore *we* did it. Together. I mean it when I say that." She looks down and smiles. Her face turns red too. God, she's so fucking cute. I would kiss her if we were alone.

"Well, thank you for saying that. I have to say tutoring you was quite fun in the end. I'm glad I could help." This feels like the end, and I don't want it to be. Fuck. *What do I do?*

"Let me teach you to ice skate as a thank you." Oh fuck, what am I doing? Did those words really just come out of my mouth?

"What?"

"At one of our sessions, you said you had never learned how. I'm good at skating. I can teach you—as a thank you for helping me."

"Grant, I don't know. You really don't have to. It's okay."

"She's just being nice. Hads, let him teach you to skate. That way, we can all go in the future, and you can skate with us rather than sit on the benches and watch." Ella says.

"It's too cold in there, and I'm always fine watching." She snaps back at her, speaking fairly quickly, she must be nervous.

"Grant, she would love for you to teach her." Ella tells me.

"Ella, stop." Hads snaps at her, clearly annoyed.

"What do you say, Hades? Please? It will make me feel better if I do something for you rather than just mooch off your brain power." To this, she smiles. *There it is.* I got her.

"Fine. We can go this weekend if that works for you."

"I would make any time work for you, Hades." Ella makes a weird choking sound, and I forgot she was here. Shit. Am I making a fool of myself? Fuck it. I want to spend more time with Hads, and I don't care who knows.

"Thanks, Grant. I, uh, appreciate it."

"Of course. Make sure you wear a jacket and gloves, it does get cold, and I know you're used to the underworld heat." I scoot back in my chair and stand up. I grab Hades' phone and swipe it open. "You should really put a password on this," I say as I punch my number into her messages and send myself one. I hand it back. "Text me when you're available this weekend." Ella shoots me a knowing look, and looks impressed. Hades looks a bit murderous, and I leave them before either of them has a chance to speak.

Was inviting her to go skating a good plan? Not really, but it gives me more time with her, which makes me glad I asked.

I just hope I don't fuck it up like I normally do.

※

Ella: PAIGE! AMELIA! SOS! HADS IS GOING ON A DATE THIS WEEKEND!
Hads: Ella, it's NOT a date. Calm down.

Paige: OH MY GOD, DID GRANT ASK YOU OUT?! I KNEW HE LIKED YOU. I COULD TELL FROM THAT SPIN!
Amelia: Paige almost fell out of her chair from excitement just now.
Ella: That spin/hug was very telling.
Amelia: I agree. It was a bit sensual. I wanted to throw up a bit.
Hads: Guys, shut it. He was just excited he passed.
Ella: No, you both passed. He kept saying "we." It was adorable.
Amelia: He gave you credit? Oh yeah, he likes you, Hads.
Paige: I'm so excited!!!! Hads, can we help you get ready? Where is he taking you?
Hads: Ice skating...
Amelia: But you don't know how to skate?
Ella: He offered to teach her as a thank you.
Paige: OHMYGODDDDD!
Hads: Paige, if you tell my brother about this, I'll make Amelia kill you in your sleep.
Amelia: I don't think so. Murder is more of Ella and Paige's territory.
Ella: I refuse to hurt Paigey. She's too cute to kill.
Paige: <3 Love you, guys!
Amelia: Paige just started crying.
Paige: No, I didn't! I got something in my eye.
Hads: Guys, it's really not a big deal. It's just skating.
Ella: Whatever you say...
Amelia: It's not too late to run away and change your name.
Paige: Hads, if you leave, I'll be very sad.
Hads: My God.
Amelia: *four attachments*
Ella: More bird reaction pics? Really?
Paige: It's her love language, and now she's laughing.
Hads: Fine, you guys can help me get ready.
Paige: YAY!

Amelia: Booking a plane ticket asap!
Ella: I'm bringing my entire closet!
Paige: Amelia, where are you going that needs a plane ticket?
Amelia: I'm off to a country with no extradition laws.
Ella: ???
Paige: China? Indonesia? Russia? Which one?
Hads: I'm disregarding this entire conversation.
Amelia: You'll never know! Xoxo!

25

Hadleigh

"Guys, I can't wear a tight dress to go ice skating!"

"Why not?" Ella is insisting I wear one of her *going-out* dresses.

"Ella, she's right. It's a bit too cheeky for skating." That would be Alissa—Zimmerman's sister and Ella's new friend. What a world we're living in now that Ella officially likes *one* of the Zimmerman's.

"What about some leggings and a crewneck? That's simple and warm." Paige pipes in. We're all crammed into my tiny dorm room. Taylor has gone out for the night, and before she left, she told me that she was excited I was getting out there, for once. I guess she's right, I prefer staying in over going out. I just didn't realize my going out of my dorm on the weekend was a big event that required four people to help me get dressed.

"Hads, I can have an Uber for you in five minutes. Just say the word." Amelia is lounging on the couch while Paige sits on the floor in front of her.

"Amelia, stop. She's going, and that's final." Ella shoots Amelia a death glare.

"Guys, don't overwhelm her. Hadleigh, babes, I think some cute jeans and a jumper would be adorable." Alissa's presence is oddly comforting. *Maybe it's the accent?* She's just the cutest. I can't imagine her brother being the he-devil Ella makes him out to be. Alissa is around 5'2"—short like me—with long brown hair with balayage. I've noticed that she wears a lot of neutral colors, and according to Paige's background check on her Instagram. She looks a lot like her brother—which is just painfully attractive—though she doesn't act like as much of an ass as Leo does, according to Ella.

I slip on the crew neck and leggings, put some thick socks on and put my boots by my bag. "Alissa's right. I think comfort over style is what will work today. I'll be uncomfortable as it is trying to learn how to ice skate."

"Ah! I'm so excited right now! I feel like a proud sister watching you get ready for a date, Hads! Someone take some pictures and document this moment." Paige says.

"Paige, don't overwhelm yourself too much, or you'll start crying again," Amelia tells her, grabbing the tissue box just in case.

"I just love you guys and these little moments together. Ella's graduating this year. It just feels like this era is coming to an end." Paige is tearing up. I can tell by her voice.

"Does Paige crying happen often?" Alissa looks around the room, and we all say yes in unison.

"Thank you for helping me get ready. I really appreciate it."

"Of course! We wouldn't miss this milestone for the world." Ella sweeps some brown matte eyeshadow on my lids and smiles down at me.

"Ells, I'm ready to go out whenever you're done, so I'll just meet you at the car?"

"Sounds good, Alissa. I'll be five minutes max. I'm almost done."

She stands in my doorway before leaving. "Good luck on the skating, Hadleigh, don't be too nervous. It's quite easy once you get the hang of it."

"Thank you for your help, Alissa. I hope to see you soon! Make sure Ella doesn't get too wild tonight!" I shoot Ella a look, and she smirks again.

"Don't worry, we both fire each other up. I'm the one she has to worry about." She closes my door and leaves.

"I like her. She's so nice." Paige says to the room.

"Same." Amelia agrees.

"Her presence is so comforting. Are you sure she's Zimmerman's sister? She at least might be adopted if he really is as bad as you say, Ells."

"I don't want to talk about him. But yes, they are blood siblings, and she's the better one." Ella finished applying the last of my makeup and picked up the mirror to show me.

"All done! I just spruced up your original routine with a bit of simple eyeshadow and eyeliner. What do you think?"

"I love it, Ells. Thank you." Seeing myself in the mirror isn't calming my nerves for tonight, but the girls being here has. I don't know why my stomach feels so weird. I've been on dates before. It's just been a while. I feel like I'm out of practice. Can you be out of practice from dating? I don't know. I think deep down I'm just scared. Scared that I'd put myself out there only to be humiliated again. To be betrayed again. I don't know if I could handle that a second time. It was just too much.

Also, I'm not even sure this *is* a date. Grant just wanted to repay the favor. Neither of us actually said the word date out loud or over text. It's just a regular

Saturday night skate session, and that's it. As friends and nothing more. The fact that I trust him enough near sharp skates and cold, hard ice says enough.

"Hads, did Oliver say anything this morning on your walk?"

"No, because he doesn't know, and we'll keep it that way. It's bad enough he wants to murder Ryan every time he glances in my direction in class. Grant shouldn't be on his radar too."

"Hads, your brother may be grumpy, but he would never actually do it. Trust me." Paige tells me, and she's probably right.

"Oh, Paige, please enlighten us more about what Hads' brother would do. Grunt? Stare? Ella and I have had a bet to see if he can speak more than three sentences at once." Amelia says.

"Really guys?" I say to them. "Oliver is very wise when he needs to be."

"Listen, twenty bucks is twenty bucks." Ella states rather nonchalantly. I roll my eyes at that, and everyone laughs until there are three knocks on the door.

"Is that him?" Paige's eyes light up.

"Shit, you guys were supposed to be gone before he got here. He's five minutes early."

"Maybe he thought you would slap him with that ruler if he was late again." Amelia chuckles as she says that.

"Okay, guys, get in my closet. He can't know that you're here." I say, swinging my arms toward my closet.

"Hads, really? The closet?" Ella looks like she would rather die.

"Yes, really, go. All of you. You can leave after we

get far enough away."

Paige hurries into the closet with a smile. Amelia throws me the finger, and Ella looks like she wants to kill me. As long as Grant doesn't see them, they can be mad at me all they want.

"I'm staying out here. Just to make sure it's actually him." Ella states, crossing her arms.

"Fine, there's no point in arguing with you because I won't win." I swing the door open, and Grant is standing there...with flowers? Ella snorts, and I stand there, not knowing what to do with my hands.

"Hi, Hades. These are for you. I didn't know what kind was your favorite, so I just got black roses to match your soul." He smirks. *Smirks at that.* Ella's laughing too.

"Thank you, Grant. I'll put them in a vase later. Let me just grab my boots, and we can go to the rink." He hands me the flowers and proceeds to lean against the doorframe, looking me up and down.

"Now, Grant, what are your intentions with my girl Hads tonight?" Ella asks him, and his face turns red.

"Ella, shut up."

"It's a valid question. Also, I'm the mom friend. I just want to make sure you'll be safe tonight."

"Ella." I threaten.

Grant is full-on smiling right now. Am I in the matrix? What is happening? "I intend to teach Miss Hades to skate and nothing more. But if she wants to make weekly skate lessons a thing, I will gladly oblige."

"Good. Just make sure she doesn't get hurt. I'll talk to you tomorrow, Hads." She throws me a wink, and Grant moves just enough for her to sneak by him. After that, she turns around and blows me a kiss, and tilts her head toward Grant. Good God, this is the worst night of my life.

I lace up my boots and look up at him. He meets my gaze, already looking at me. "You ready?"

"Ready as I'll ever be."

"Alright then, let's get skating." He smiles, and I walk past him in the doorway, shut my door, lock it, and we walk towards the rink. My phone buzzes in my pocket as we walk. I quickly look at it.

Paige: HE GOT YOU, FLOWERS. THAT'S SO CUTE
Amelia: Hads, can we leave the closet now?
Ella: This is definitely a date, Hads, whether you want it to be or not.
Hads: I'm putting my phone on do not disturb byeeeee.

※

Grant

Was getting her flowers too much? Neither of us actually stated that this was a date, but I want it to be, so flowers seemed like the right move. The fact that she didn't throw them back at me or burn them is a good sign, though. I'm not going to lie, I'm nervous. I don't think I've ever been this tense going on a date before. It just feels different this time. She opened the door, and I saw her in leggings and a crewneck and nearly fell over. I had to lean on the doorway for support because my legs felt like they were going to give out from under me. Not seeing her in her usual attire has thrown me for a loop. I wonder if she feels at least a tiny bit how I do. I wonder if her heart is beating so fast right now she might need to go to the hospital because that's what mine feels like.

Fuck.
I really like this girl, and I can't tell her.

It would be bad enough for her not to like me back--which I doubt she does in *that* way—but what would be worse is losing the friendship we barely have. We reach the rink after discussing odd topics like homework and classes. The walk to the rink was nice since it's not too chilly out. Usually, there are a ton of people here on Saturday nights because the college likes to do open skate night sometimes, but little does Hades know that I asked them not to do it tonight so we could have the whole rink to ourselves. I just told them Jacks and I wanted to get some defensive practice in for our game coming up, and they said yes. What the school doesn't know won't kill them, right?

I opened the door to the rink for her, and she thanks me. I lead her over to where the skates are. "Let me guess, a size seven and a half?" I ask her, knowing I'm right.

"How did you know that?"

"Hades, you have insanely small feet. It's not that hard to guess."

"I don't have small feet. You just have large feet."

"You're looking at my feet? Do you have a foot fetish or something?" I say, handing her the pair of skates.

"Don't be gross, Grant. For all I know, you could be the one with the foot fetish." I love the way she fires back at me. I could argue with her all day and never get tired of it.

"Come on, lace the skates up, and we can get started with some basic things." I shoot her a smile as I lace up my hockey skates. The ice is freshly resurfaced.

I slipped Greg—the guy who drives the Zamboni for the school—a fifty to make sure it was all set for tonight, and he pulled through. Hades looks like she is struggling to lace them up. "Do you need help?"

"No, I've got it. The strings are tangled."

"Hades, let me help you."

"Grant, it's fine. I got it."

"Asking for help is not a weakness. Just let me help you before you strain that big brain of yours." I tell her.

She looks at me for a moment. "It's simple laces, like sneakers, but fine."

I walk over to where she's sitting. I tower over her normally, but with my skates on, it's worse. I kneel on both knees—careful not to catch myself with the blades on my skates—and look at her laces. I carefully untangle them and look up at her. She's looking at me with a weird expression on her face. "What's that look for?"

"I'm trying to figure out if I could reach your throat with my skates from here."

"Hades, a simple thank you will suffice."

She whispers something I can't hear before standing up and almost falling back over. This is going to be fun. We get over to the door that leads out to the ice, and I glide on the ice effortlessly while she stays firmly planted at the door.

"It looks slippery. What if I fall and break my head open?" She asks me.

"It's ice, so it *is* slippery. That's the point. You're more likely to fall if there are cracks in the ice. This is fresh. You'll be fine. Plus, I would never let you fall and hurt that pretty head of yours. Even if you break your head open, your intelligence will still be intact, Hades. Come on, grab my hand. I'll steady you."

"Promise you won't let me fall."

I sigh. "I promise, Hadleigh, you're safe with me." My arm is still stretched out to her. "Come on. We don't have all night." She looks down at my hand, looks back up at me, and finally takes my hand. The contact is electric, and I know she felt it too because she jolts a little bit as we grasp hands.

"First things first, if you feel yourself losing your balance, bend your knees and try to recenter yourself. If you fall, try not to use your hands to break it, I don't want to end tonight at the ER with you having a broken wrist. Got it?"

"Got it." She smiles, and it hits me right in the chest. I should know this girl would never do anything halfway. She'll learn this and probably master it by the end of tonight.

"Now, to stop yourself, stand with your feet together and stick one skate out sideways. It's a bit weird initially, but you'll get the hang of it."

"I'm more of a visual learner. I like charts and stuff, so maybe you could demonstrate it, and I could try and copy what you do." Of course. The damn charts. I should've known.

"I don't know. I'm kind of a professional at this. Will you be okay standing on your own?" I ask her, just making sure.

"Don't underestimate me, Mr. Carter. I can do anything I put my mind to."

"I would never dream of underestimating you, Miss Baker. Okay, watch me." I show her some things: turn, glide, and stop. All the while, I feel her eyes on me, watching me do what I do best without the hockey stick and the puck. "Okay, try gliding on your own. Remember to switch feet and lift one and then the other."

"Alright, I got this." Watching her hype herself up is cute. God, I can't get enough of this girl.

She tries, and does it. It's like she's a natural at skating. She looks up at me when she stops and smiles. "I did it! That wasn't so bad."

"It's not that hard, I told you. That was good. I'm proud of you." I skate over beside her, and her cheeks get all red. I love being the one to do that to her. We take a few laps around the rink slowly. On the first lap, I skate backward and hold onto her hands. By the third lap, I let go and let her try a few laps by herself. "Okay, now try doing some swizzles."

"Swizzles? That's an actual word?" She's laughing now.

"Little Miss Dictionary didn't know that was a word? Wow. Someone call Channel 9. This is truly breaking news!" I yell, and it echoes in the rink.

"Grant, shut up. This skating terminology is new to me."

"Fine, fine. Let me show you." I show her how to put her heels out and in, and she copies me perfectly, of course. Why did I expect anything less from little miss 4.0 over here? She gets a bit too cocky at this point and falls over. "Hades!"

"Ow."

I quickly skate over to where she is on the ice and lean down to look at her. "Are you hurt?"

"I don't think so. I feel okay, just sore."

"Maybe we should stop for the night. Just in

case." I say, a bit panicked. I hope she didn't hurt herself too badly.

"Grant it's fine. I'm fine. Let's keep going."

"Hades, you don't have to perfect ice skating in one night. Skills like this take time. Let's go before you hurt yourself more." I stand up and look down at her.

"No, I'm staying here."

I groan. This girl is really fucking stubborn. "Listen, I'm not getting my ass kicked by Ella after you hurt yourself more. I promised I would keep you safe, come on." I offer her my hand, and she crosses her arms, still sitting on the ice. This girl is *challenging* me. And fuck if I don't love every second of it.

"Hadleigh, get up," I say to her.

"No."

"*Hadleigh.*"

"You don't scare me, Grant."

"Good, I don't want to scare you. I want to sweep you off your feet. How am I doing?"

"Considering I'm on my ass on the ice, not very well." She tilts her head down.

I kneel back down on the ice, lift her chin with my finger, and kiss her. She freezes for a moment and then kisses me back. My heart is going crazy right now. I swear it might beat out of my chest. She's fucking kissing me back. I break off for a second, still lingering close to her lips.

"How am I doing now?" I whisper against her lips.

"You're doing much better, but there's always room for improvement." She's whispering too, and not backing away from me. *Should I go for it?* I like seeing her like this—unguarded and not afraid to ask for my help.

"Do you want me to keep going?"

"Yes, please." She says, and I don't waste a second. I pick her up and get her to her feet, but she almost loses her balance.

"Fuck it." I pick her up. "Put your legs around my waist."

"Don't tell me what to do."

"Always fighting me even when I'm trying to kiss you. You're so damn stubborn."

"What if we fall? This can't be safe."

"I've got you, baby. Just trust me."

"I do." She looks at me, and I can tell she means it. *Motherfucker.* This girl is going to be my undoing if she keeps saying shit like that.

"Okay, then put your cute legs around me so I can kiss you again." She clears her throat and looks at me. *"Please."*

She smiles and does what I ask as I skate us towards the glass, so I'm not just free skating with her hanging onto me. I push her up against it and kiss her hard again. I could never get tired of this. She seemed a bit cautious at first, but now she has entirely given in to the moment. Her lips are soft, and they taste like strawberry chapstick. She parts her lips, and I push my tongue into her mouth, careful not to overwhelm her or anything, just enough to leave her wanting more. She whimpers against my mouth, and I almost lose it. "Christ, Hades, I'm never going to get that sound you just made out of my head."

She laughs, and I capture it in my mouth. Her tongue meets mine, and I lose myself in her. I know after this, all I'll be able to think about is how her legs feel wrapped around my torso and how her tongue feels against mine. This girl has slowly captured me in her aura, and I never want to leave it. I put my free hand through her hair, carefully leaving my other one where it is so I don't drop her. I grab a fistful of it and yank it gently to give me better access to her neck. She moans, and I can see her cheeks turn pink when she looks at me. Before she can speak, I capture her mouth again. God, she tastes so fucking good. I would gladly give up breathing if it meant I could kiss her for the rest of my life. I don't want to get too carried away because I still have to walk her back to her dorm, so I kiss her deeper and set her back down on the ice. "How am I doing now?"

She simply smiles at me.

"Speechless? I can't decide if that is good or bad." I throw a smile in her direction.

"I'm only speechless because my feet hurt from these skates."

"Do you want me to walk you back to your dorm?"

"I would love that. Let's get off the ice—" Before she can finish, I lean over and sweep her off her feet, carrying her off the ice. "What the hell are you doing?" She's laughing in my arms, and I feel drunk on this moment. I want to capture it in my mind and remember it for later.

"You said your feet hurt, so I thought I would help."

"Thank you."

I smile at her and skate toward the side of the rink. I don't put her down until I reach the small bench where her bag is. I set her down on it and plop down next to her. I unlace my skates, and she goes to undo hers. "Stop."

"What?" I take my skates off and kneel to unlace her skates for her. She looks down at me with a smile on her face. I did that. I put that there. If putting a smile on this girl's face was a full-time job, I would apply for it immediately. I return her skates while she puts her shoes back on.

"Ready?" I say as I return to where she is.

"Yup." I put my hand on the small of her back and guide her out of the building. I don't reach for her hand quite yet because I don't want to move too quickly. It's only about a ten minute walk across campus back to her dorm building. We don't really talk on the way back. I can't tell what is going on in her head, which kind of worries me. She seems a bit withdrawn. *Fuck, did I take it too far?* I know her history with her last boyfriend, and I don't know if she has even kissed anyone since then. I feel like she knows I wouldn't do that to her—kiss her only to break her heart later. I know how it feels to be duped during an entire relationship, and it doesn't feel good, but I also know it might take her a moment to truly open up to someone again. It took me a while to do that, but I always did it with the wrong people considering my track record. But I still believe I can find that person for me, and I feel like it could be her.

I'm so fucked. This girl has me hooked. I just hope she feels even slightly the same as I do. We reach her building, and stop just before the door. "Thank you for teaching me. I feel a lot better about skating, so thanks."

"It was my pleasure. Thank you for helping me pass my midterm so I can keep playing hockey. I don't know if you know how much I appreciate you helping me."

"I think I have some idea." We both laugh a bit. I lean in to kiss her goodnight, and she pulls away. Shit. "I—I'm sorry. I just—"

"Hades, you don't have to explain yourself to me. I get it."

"I just—I think we would be better off as friends."

Oh. This I was not expecting. Sure, she would need time to think. I didn't know this night would end with me getting friend-zoned. I don't care. As long as I can keep her in my life, I'll do pretty much anything, even if it kills me to do it or see her move on with someone else eventually. "Grant?"

"Sorry, I just got lost in my thoughts."

"So...friends?"

"Yeah. Friends." My chest hurts, my head hurts, this is killing me, but I can't lose her. As long as I have a piece of her, I'll be okay. I think. Or maybe I'm just gaslighting myself so this doesn't hurt as much later. It's probably the latter.

"Okay, um, good night then, Grant. Thank you again."

"Yeah, no problem. I'll see you around." She looks at me and nods, then turns around and walks inside—leaving me standing on the pavement feeling like I just failed in some way.

Fuck.

※

Paige: HADS, HOW DID IT GO!!! TELL US EVERYTHING!!!
Ella: djfndjoanfidanpg
Amelia: Ella's drunk

Hads: It was fine. Please don't ask for details.
Ella: ?????
Paige: What? That doesn't sound good.
Ella: dkd u gjsh kiss?
Amelia: Yeah, did he kiss you again?
Paige: I hope so!!
Hads has left the group chat
Amelia: Oh? That's my move usually...
Ella: WTF?
Paige: Oh, this isn't good.
Amelia: Paige, meet me in the living room.
Paige: On it!
Amelia: Ella, please be careful tonight.
Ella: Will do.
Paige: Should we add her back?
Amelia: Tomorrow. Just give her the night.
Paige: Okay :(

26

Hadleigh
Three Weeks Later

  I'm sitting in the library cafe at a table by myself, typing far too aggressively on my laptop trying to send this email to my friend Drew. We had to do a project together, and I'm sending them my section of it. My mind is elsewhere, though—it has been for weeks now. Spring break came and went, and I went home with my brother. We hung out with our family, and getting away from campus for a bit was nice. Paige and Amelia stayed on campus, opting not to go home, and Ella went home to visit her dad and sister. We all returned with not much to discuss since it was only a week, and we still had book club on Wednesday night.

  After Grant and I had our ice skating rendezvous and decided to stay friends, things have been weird. I feel like I'm just floating through the same routine. The past few weeks have blown by. I'm keeping myself busy so I don't start thinking about emotions and thoughts swirling around in my head. Grant and I grabbed coffee a few times, butu something still feels off. Our banter isn't as it was, and I find myself missing what we had before that night at the rink. We're finally sort of becoming actual friends, and it's been nice getting to know each other outside of tutoring. We actually have some things in common. It feels weird *relating* to Grant at all. There is a lot more to him than I originally thought.

Ryan and I have been meeting every Tuesday for our project, which has been nice. I consider him my friend now, too, and we sometimes talk before class, and even got lunch together once. He's nice to me, and I enjoy his company. The project has also been taking my mind off things, and book club has helped, although Paige wants to keep bringing it up.

The Wednesday after *it* happened, I told the girls everything. I didn't meet Ella for our usual Sunday coffee date because I knew I could only tell the story once. I told them everything. I told them he was being super respectful, and we practically made out against the glass around the rink. I also told them about how I told him we should remain friends. Paige was upset, and Ella and Amelia were just confused. I love them, but at the time, I just needed their presence, not advice—which they gave me.

What I didn't tell them was how much I regretted it. I didn't tell them how much fun I had with him at the rink that night. I didn't tell them how scared I was to open myself up to the possibility of a relationship again. God, why does this scare me so badly? That's what I have been trying to wrap my head around for the past few weeks. I had fun with him. Why did I have to do what I always do and pull away from someone when they made me happy? The self-sabotaging is real, and I just can't figure out what to do going forward. I've only seen him a handful of times since then, but our conversations have been cut short. He always has this look of longing on his face, that makes me feel bad, but I know I shouldn't feel bad for protecting myself and my heart.

I'm just scared and don't know how to get out of that feeling. It's so easy to do what I usually do and distance myself before things become too out of hand, but this time I didn't even see it coming. I just fell into it. It was so easy with Grant. Staying friends just seemed more manageable and less hurtful, but why do I still feel like this?

I slam my laptop closed and heavy sigh, putting my hands against my face. This is the first time I'm alone in three weeks with my feelings. It sucks. This is why I tend to steer clear of relationships, things get too confusing and everyone always ends up hurt.

"Taking out your frustrations on your laptop now? I didn't know this semester was going so terribly for you, Hades."

Fuck. My. Life. I look up, and there he is. The guy who's confusing my mind and heart. He looks good. He's wearing a purple hoodie and some jeans with sneakers. His hair is as messy as ever. He even has a bit of a shadow on his face. "Well, I can't hit you with a ruler any more, so I have to have something to fill that void."

"Yeah, I bet. I didn't know you missed me that much." His voice sounds sadder than usual. It doesn't have that normal Grant flair—the one he usually has when we do this ribbing back and forth.

"I never said I missed you." *Stop, Hads. You're being mean.*

"I know."

"I was under the impression you were allergic to the library. Do you want to sit down?"

"No, I just came in to get coffee. Jacks is meeting me here. We needed a change of scenery from our dorm, so we decided to come here."

"You won't catch a cold, will you?"

"Actually, someone once told me that I never really appreciated the library enough. I find it quite nice now."

Is he talking about me? I think he is. This conversation seems to be taking some kind of turn, and I need to get it back to friendly chatting, not whatever it is now.

He clears his throat. "So, how have you been recently? I haven't really seen you around much."

"I've been okay. Busy with projects and homework and stuff."

"Yeah, same here."

"Still passing Collins class?"

"Yeah, I am. Thanks to you." He throws a fake smile my way. This whole scene is awkward, and I want to run away. I need to retreat, but I can't. I knew I shouldn't have left my room.

"If you wanted, I could use your help prepping for the final he gives—only if you want to, of course. I just thought you might need to hit me with that ruler again or something."

"I'm not sure if that's the best idea."

"Why not? Just one friend helping another one with a final exam. One more session towards the end of the year. That's all. Do I need to beg you to make me more flashcards, or can I save my dignity for right now?"

I smirk at that. I would like to see that, but not in public. "Okay. But just one session when the final is."

"Good. I'll hold you to that."

"Okay."

He proceeds to stand there for an hour, or maybe

it's just a few awkward seconds. It's probably the latter, but it feels like forever. Is this how every interaction with him is going to be? Neither of us talked about the elephant in the room, how he clearly liked kissing me and how I also liked kissing him. God, this is so confusing. I can't put my feelings or thoughts in chart form, and that pisses me off.

"I should probably get going. Jacks is on his way now. I'll see you around, Hades."

"Bye, Grant." I smile at him and watch him walk toward the tables in the corner of the library. I immediately get up, grab all my stuff, throw it in my bag, and exit the library. I beeline for my dorm room, and pull my phone out to text my brother.

Hads: Are we still on for Saturday morning?
Sous Chef: Yeah.
Hads: See you then.
Sous Chef: Okay.

At least my brother hasn't found out about what happened with Grant. I'm looking on the bright side, right? I won't have to help Oliver bury his body when he finds out.

The bright side.
Right.
Beause I'm just a ray of fucking sunshine.

27

Hadleigh

    I'm up and at the bench under the tree in record time today. It doesn't help that I barely slept last night, but that's neither here nor there. I'm sitting down and shivering when Oliver jogs up to me and gives me his hoodie without saying a word.

    "Thanks." I smile at him while he takes his headphones out. Oliver still uses headphones that aren't Bluetooth. He grunts at me—which means you're welcome in Oliver language—and we start our usual route. Neither of us talks for the first fifteen minutes. It's just nice to be up before the rest of the world. Everything on campus is so quiet and peaceful. It feels nice to get out of my head for a bit too. "Why are you being so quiet?"

    I chuckle. "Isn't that what I am supposed to say to you, Ol?"

    "Yeah, but you always have something to say. I don't."

    "That's true."

    "What's going on Hads?"

    "Nothing! It's just been a weird few weeks!"

    "So tell me about it."

    "No!"

    "Why not? Are you scared I'm going to threaten to kill Grant?" I stop walking and stare at him with my mouth open. Paige must have told him. *Goddammit.*

I thought she was good at keeping secrets. She's practically a damn CIA officer. "No, Paige didn't tell me. I figured it out on my own. I'm not stupid Hads."

"I never said you were. How did you know then if Paige didn't tell you?"

"You've been really closed off for a few weeks. Before break, I was on a night run when I saw you walking with Grant to the ice rink. I later found out from Paige that he taught you how to ice skate that night—cute by the way."

"First of all, you're the only person I know who goes for night runs. That's weird, by the way. And why do you and Paige text so much? Your conversations can't be that interesting. You send me responses in emojis, and it's always the straight-faced one."

"Cut the bullshit and tell me what's happening."

I look at him and start walking up to where he is. "How did you know you were ready to start dating after what happened with..." I trail off. None of us say his last girlfriend's name, just in case.

"After Mia?" He looks at me with sad eyes. Damn, I hate that I brought this up right now. I know it still hurts him to talk about this, but I need clarity.

"Yeah, after Mia and what happened."

"Hads, you can say her name, you know. I won't be hurt."

"Sorry, I was being respectful."

"And I love you for that, but it's okay. I can talk about it."

"Okay." Oliver's first girlfriend—her name was Mia. She was super nice. Pretty too. She and my brother dated from sophomore year until the accident. Senior year she was in a horrible car accident. One of her friends was speeding down a busy road, racing this other car when they lost control and crashed into a tree. The driver—Mia's best friend—was in a coma for months, while Mia was pronounced dead on the scene. It was horrible. Our community mourned for months. My brother was a wreck after. He wouldn't come out of his room. He saw a therapist for months after, and eventually, things got better. It took a while, but then he went to college, and that was that. He has always been grumpy and quiet, but Mia brought out the other side of my brother. He smiled more and laughed so loud it was contagious. I miss that side of my brother, but I know it will come back in time.

"Well, Hads, I haven't dated since then."

"You haven't?"

"I thought you knew that."

"I don't keep a chart of your dating habits, Ol." He lightly laughs at that.

"I know. I know."

"So, how do you know when you'll be ready? To put yourself back out there after what happened?"

He ponders the question for a moment. I can see his brain working. "I think I've been ready for a while if I'm being honest. Don't get me wrong, I loved Mia and think part of me always will, but I can't change what happened. She's gone, and I know that my being sad she's gone is just the way love manifests after bad things happen. Grief and sadness remind you that what you once had was beautiful. I wouldn't change anything about what Mia and I had, but life continues. It has to go on, or else you're just stuck." I didn't realize my brother could be so poetic. He keeps going. "Hads, I know you're scared because of what happened with Kyle. I would be too. But don't close yourself off from something that could be great just because you're scared."

"I don't know how to feel any other way but scared when it comes to this. I just can't seem to take that leap into the unknown. It scares me—not knowing and feeling like he could turn out to be the same as Kyle was. I can't just turn that fear off."

"Grant isn't Kyle, you know."

"Wow, was that a compliment?" I ask him.

"No. Just an observation."

"What do you mean by that?"

"Grant taught you how to ice skate, Hads. He offered to do something for *you*. And according to Paige, he got you flowers before your little date. Kyle never even offered to drive you to school, let alone do something specifically for you."

I am never telling Paige anything ever again. I let what Oliver is saying sink in for a moment. He's right. Grant offered to teach me something on his own time. He did it for me. It never really clicked until now. I can't remember when someone did something just because they wanted to help me.

"I'm just saying, don't close yourself off like you always do in these situations, Hads. You deserve to be happy with someone who will treat you well."

"You deserve to be happy too, Ol. I mean it. Have you thought about getting back out there?"

"Yeah, maybe a little bit. With the right person, maybe."

"And who might that be?"

"Not sure yet. When I know, you will too."

"Good. I'm sorry I kept this from you. I know we usually tell each other things, but I was confused and didn't know what to do."

"It's okay. I get why you did it. Just don't make any rash decisions. Being friends first is usually the best thing you can do. That way, you have time to figure out your feelings, and it puts less pressure on things."

We're almost back at the bench again, and I didn't realize how much I really needed to hear this from my brother. He's right—in some respect—but the scared feeling will not go away over night, but maybe with time it will. I could see myself being friends with Grant first. Actual friends, not this weird monkey-in-the-middle shit we're doing right now.

"Damn, I owe Ella and Amelia twenty bucks," I say out loud, not necessarily to him.

"What?"

"You spoke more than three sentences today. They had a bet going. It's not important. Thank you, Ol. For being the best brother I could ask for."

"You're welcome Hads. I told you I can be wise when I want to be."

"Yeah, yeah, whatever. I'm going to sit on the bench for a bit, so feel free to go."

"Sounds good. Just remember what I said. And don't be afraid to text me if you need anything. I mean it, H. That's what big brothers are for."

"And here I thought it was your job to bully me as a kid."

"Yeah, well, I already accomplished that, didn't I?" He smirks at me.

"You sure did," I smirk back at him as he starts to jog away.

"I love you, idiot." He says while running away.

"I love you too," I say under my breath as my

phone buzzes. I pull it out, and it's from Ryan. I finally used his number because emailing him back and forth was a hassle for the project.

Ryan: Hey Hads. Got a second?
Hads: Yeah, what's up?
Ryan: I have a hockey game this Monday, and I wanted to know if you wanted to come. We do this thing every season where you give your jersey to a friend, and I wanted to know if you would wear mine to the game. If not, that's okay. I can ask someone else.
Hads: Uh, sure. Can I bring my friends too?
Ryan: Yeah, bring whoever you want. The more the merrier. And you'll wear my jersey?
Hads: Sure, just as friends, right?
Ryan: Yeah, of course.
Hads: Okay.
Ryan: Cool, I'll drop it off at your dorm later.
Hads: Sounds good!
Ryan: :)

It looks like the girls are going to another hockey game. This should be fun.

Hads: Are you guys free for a hockey game Monday night?
Ella: Yes, but I'm bringing my own drinks this time. Can Alissa come?
Hads: Of course!
Paige: EEEEE! I am totally free!
Amelia: If I say no, Paige will drag me anyway. So, no.
Paige: Amelia, shut up. You're going.
Hads: Great, see you guys then. Want to meet at P and A's apartment?
Ella: Sounds good to me!

I slip my phone back into my pocket and sit on the bench listening to the sound of the leaves rustling on the trees. It's the end of March, and spring is almost here. I couldn't be more thankful for that. It's my favorite season—a season of new beginnings. Which I hope remains true. I could really use one. I take a deep breath and continue to sit. I feel a sense of hope blossom in my chest.

Life continues, is what my brother said earlier. He's right. I feel like I've been so stuck in the past and what happened, that I never really had time to move on. I've just been stuck right where Kyle left me—in that feeling of humiliation and regret. I have to continue on before it eats me alive. I will not remain shackled to someone who never deserved me in the first place. Kyle does not deserve to move on so easily when I've been feeling like shit for the past few years. I bet he lost no sleep from what he did.

    I'm deciding right now to let him and the past go. I release it into the wind and watch it float away. I wish that's all it took, but I can feel myself becoming a bit lighter. *One step at a time Hads.* I have to move on, and starting now, I will.

    I smile and let the wind carry me away as I get up and walk back to my room—feeling lighter with every step I take.

28

Hadleigh

The hockey game is about to start, and our team has just gathered on the bench. They're in a huddle, and Ryan keeps making eye contact with me. He smiles, and I smile back, and it feels weird because he keeps doing it, and I don't know why. After the fifth smile, I start to ignore him.

"So, remind me again why you're wearing his jersey? I don't see many other people wearing a team member's jersey in the rink." Alissa has tagged along with our group and has been an excellent addition to tonight's festivities.

"I think Ryan has a thing for her, that's why."

"Amelia, you're wrong. Shut up." I cast her a glance and moved my gaze back to Alissa. "He asked me to wear it because it's a tradition or something. He didn't give me much of an explanation, but I agreed."

"Oh, that seems a bit odd. I guess it makes sense." Alissa smiles, and Ella hands her a drink as she comes back to sit down. "Thanks, babes. I don't think I could watch this without being at least tipsy." She says as she down most of her drink in one go.

"I said that last time too!" Ella is practically screeching. Who knew the sister of your nemesis could turn out to be a best friend? I certainly didn't. Paige keeps nudging my arm, and I turn to ask her to stop when she points down at the team. In the huddle, looking right back at me, is Grant. I've never seen his face like that. What's wrong with his face? He looks angrier than I've ever seen him.

"Is Grant mad at you or is he constipated? Why does he look like that, and why is it seemingly directed towards you, Hads?" Paige is asking me these questions, and I can't answer them because why *does* he look so mad? The game hasn't even started yet, but his stare is blaring into me that I might fall over if he keeps it up. He tears his gaze away from me and looks toward Ryan. He looks back at me and then back at Ryan. It's like he's watching a tennis match between the two of us.

"Oh, I am so glad I came out of the apartment tonight. I do not want to miss the show that's about to happen when Grant beats the shit out of Ryan." Amelia chuckles and grabs a snack from her bag. Seriously? Does she just walk around with snacks at the ready when shit goes down?

"This is like a jealousy scene from a romance novel come to life. I'm actually a little bit obsessed. Sorry, Hads." Alissa pats me on the shoulder as she says that.

"It's fine. Also, my life is not a romance novel. I'm sorry to disappoint, but Ryan and I are just friends, like Grant and I. Friends. Nothing more." I don't even think I believe what I'm saying to them. The only thing I know for sure is that Ryan and I are friends. Alissa looks back at me, a bit unsure.

"I don't think someone you are friends with looks at you the way Grant is right now," Alissa says to me.

"And how is he looking at me? Like he's trying to do 34 times 65 in his head?" I ask.

"No, he's looking like he wants to rip that jersey off you and give you his instead."

"Alissa—" I'm cut off by Ella.

"Hads, girl. He looks like he wants to cut that jersey off you, burn it, and then fuck you on the ashes. He doesn't like Ryan, right? He's probably seeing nothing but red right now." Ella smiles at the end of that. Why are all of my friend's sadists?

"No, you guys are wrong. Have Grant and I kissed before? Yes. Have we kissed on this very rink? Yes. Is he in love with me? No. Am I in love with him? No. Case closed."

"I've always been team HadsGrant in this love triangle," Paige says, smiling at me.

"This is not a love triangle. Men and women can be platonic friends with each other! It's not impossible!" I'm practically yelling at this point.

"Hads, love triangle or not, Grant clearly still likes you." Amelia points toward the bench, and Grant is *still* looking at me. Although his face changed, he looks a bit sadder now. Fuck. My friends might be right, but there's no way I'm admitting that to them.

"Can we just watch the game? It's starting?" I ask them, wanting to change the subject.

"Ah, deflection. I've taught you so well. My work here is done." Amelia puts her hand on her chest and hugs me from behind. She and Paige are sitting behind me, and I'm on the end seat next to Ella, who's between Alissa and me.

The referee blows the whistle, and the team gets on the ice. Ryan's benched, but Grant is playing. The face-off happens, and Grant isn't moving. He's stuck in his spot, still staring at me. His trance seems to break after a few seconds because he suddenly bursts into action as the game unfolds. This jersey seems itchy now, and it shouldn't. It's not like I betrayed him by wearing this. *Right?* We aren't together, and I shouldn't feel wrong about supporting a friend. I need to get out of my head right now, and Paige nudges me back into reality at the right time.

"Look!"

I look at where she's pointing, and the other team has the puck, and it looks like they're going to score. Jacks misses the interception, and Grant swoops in to try and protect the goalie from being scored on. I saw him do that move hundreds of times at the last game I went to. This time, he misses, and the other player soars by him, and they score. The other team scored in the first five minutes. It's now 1-0.

"Oof." Paige slumps in her seat.

"This is going to be a rough game," Ella says.

"What? Why? Do you guys know something I don't?"

"This is an easy team to beat, and Grant just fucked the play up. Even Jacks seemed confused, and normally they work well together."

Alissa smiles, "I'm sure it's just a rough start. There is still a lot of the game left." She stands up and yells, "LET'S GO, GRAND MOUNTAIN!" Ella joins her in cheering. This is going to be a long game.

Paige leans to my ear and says, "Grant always starts for the team. It might just be an off night for him, but I think you might've had a bigger effect on him than you think."

"Keep telling yourself that, Paige, even athletes have off days. I promise you my being here is not making him do bad."

She chuckles and then leans back and steals some of Amelia's snacks. It's not my fault Grant can't focus tonight. I'm just one person! Whatever. I'm pushing that thought to the back of my mind as I continue to watch the game.

One loss isn't going to kill the team. They'll be fine. Either way, it's not my fault. I'm simply a spectator watching a sport that Paige has to explain every time something happens. I grab Ella's drink and take a long sip before handing it back to her.

"Oh, absolutely." She smiles at me, and I wince, only slightly, not enough for her to see.

"Who puts straight tequila in a flask?" She only shrugs and smiles. It's going to be a long night.

✗

Grant

I got pulled by the final minute of period one. I am benched for the rest of the game. My head just is not in it tonight, and I know why. A certain black-haired girl sitting in the stands right now—wearing *his* jersey. *Ryan's fucking jersey.* I looked up in the stands tonight and saw that, and felt like my heart got thrown in a shredder. It shouldn't have pissed me off so much, but I couldn't help it. I've liked this girl for weeks, and remaining friends with her has been challenging. Every time I see her, I want to pick her up and never put her down. It took every ounce of self-preservation not to beat the shit out of Ryan. What kind of game is he playing with her?

Fuck.

Jacks skates up to me and just stares at me. "What?" I snap at him. I don't mean to, but my mood is shit tonight.

"What the fuck is up with you? You're missing blocks and playing like shit."

"Tell me something I don't know. I'm just having an off night. That's all."

"Grant, you don't have off nights, you have a few misses here and there, but you always come back stronger. Something is obviously wrong." I flash my eyes to where she is sitting out of habit, and Jacks follows my gaze. Her being here reminds me of the last time we were both in this building, and my brain remembers that very well, unfortunately. Shit. I'm busted.

"Oh." He says.

"Yeah."

"Why does she have—"

"I don't know, and I don't want to talk about it."

"Fine, just don't do anything stupid later."

"No promises. Go, the second period is starting." We're tied now, 1-1. Being benched has put my mood even further down. I've never been this in my head about a girl before, and it's fucking scaring me. I just can't help but look at her, she's directly across from our bench, and my eyes are magnets—so fucking attached to where she's sitting. I keep stealing glances hoping she'll catch my eyes like she always does, and we can do that staring game we love so much. Unfortunately, no matter how hard I try, she doesn't look at me. How am I supposed to tell her Ryan is a piece of shit when every time before she dismissed me? Granted, all those times I came across as an asshole. I don't know how to get her to listen to me. I can't just *tell* her. I would have to show her. Maybe that blonde friend could help me? She's a criminal justice major, I think. Could she help me with blackmail? Or perhaps extortion or something? No. I can't do that. Maybe I'll just politely tell her, fuck, I can't tell her what to do. She's stubborn and will do the opposite of what I say, and I don't want to seem controlling. I'll just have to think about it.

While watching the game, Ryan scoots up next to me on the bench. "Hey Carter, fancy seeing you here."

"Wow, do you use that line on all the women you pick up? I'm surprised it works so well for you." I want to slam his head into the side of the rink.

"Yeah, I bet it'll work really well on Hads later."

Don't punch him, do not punch him, Grant. "She's too smart to fall for that shit, trust me. If you knew her, you would know that."

"My lines seem to work just fine on Hadleigh." He says that with a stupid fucking smirk on his face. I want to wipe that shit off his face. Why is this kid such an asshole?

"What game are you playing with her?"

"Who says I'm playing with her?"

"Anyone could see it from a mile away. Stay the fuck away from her. She deserves better than you."

"Oh, and by better do you mean you? Is that what you're getting at?"

"Boys, watch the game and be ready, Barnes. You might be going in soon!" Our coach yells at us from the other end of the bench.

"Got it, Coach!" He yells back at him.

"Just go away, Ryan. I don't have time for this

right now."

"Fine. I'll leave you alone." He slaps me on the shoulder and returns to his original spot.

I've never wanted a game to be over as much as I do right now. I'll be okay if I can get through tonight without punching something. Hockey used to be the only thing I could count on not failing at, and now I'm sitting on the bench because the girl I like is wearing a jersey other than mine. I can't believe that's all it took for me to fail at what I do best. God, I can't stand this feeling. What would my dad say right now if he saw me? I look pathetic. He would probably tell me it's just a minor setback and always to look ahead but right now, I feel stagnant. I feel like a fucking mess. One girl has collapsed me in a few months, and the funny thing is I wouldn't change a thing. Not her snarky attitude, and the way she is so damn stubborn about some things. The problem is, I can't do anything to change my situation. If I tell her she's only going to retreat further. I have to keep our friendship going. If that's all I ever get of her, that's fine. It's better than not having her at all. Grand Mountain scores again, and I was barely paying attention. Shit.

Get your head in the game, Grant.

I pound on the side of our bench and sit back down.

Only one and a half periods left.

X

Grand Mountain wins in the final seconds of the last period. The score ended up being 2-1, and I sat on the bench for the last two periods. Today officially sucks, and I need a shower. Coach gives us a pep talk, and part of it is about players getting their heads together and not being distracted, and I know that shit is aimed at me. It makes me feel like a failure, unable to do the one thing the team counts on me for. I slam my locker shut, grab my towel and shower shit, and head to it. A voice stops me before I can fully enter where the showers are.

"I can't wait to see her in just my jersey later. I just know that bitch's pussy is tight." Ryan and the guys around him laugh.

"Who the fuck are you talking about, Barnes?" I don't remember turning the corner to confront him, but here we are.

"That sweet little thing that showed up wearing my jersey tonight, Carter. I can't wait to take it off her later. She'll be begging me to keep going."

I'm going to kick the shit out of this motherfucker. "Say one more thing about her, and I swear you won't like where this goes."

The fucker smiles at that. *Smiles.* Barnes looks to Rhodes. "Do you think that bitch can suck and fuck?"

I lose it. All I see is red before my fist connects to his face. I punch him square in the jaw, and fuck, it feels good. How dare he talk about someone like that? Let alone, Hadleigh. Jacks pulled me off of him and pushed me back. "Take a walk, Grant!" I push against him.

"Stay the fuck away from her. If you breathe in her direction, I'll kick the shit out of you. Consider that punch a warning." I don't wait for him to respond as I grab my stuff and get changed. Fuck the showers. I need to get out of here before I turn back and give Ryan what he truly deserves for talking like that. I studied my ass off to make sure I stayed on the team. I won't let Ryan be the reason I don't play another game this season. After I'm changed, I exit the locker room only to find the reason for me just punching Ryan standing outside the doors.

Was she waiting for him?

"Hey, Grant. Is Ryan in there? I wanted to give him his jersey back." She holds out his jersey, signaling for me to take it. She looks a bit off. How long has she been standing here?

"I'm not going back in there. Give it to him yourself." I don't know why I'm snapping at her when she did nothing wrong, but my sour mood continues to infect everything around me.

"Okay, what's wrong with you tonight? You were glaring at me the whole game, and now you're just being rude. Did I do something to you?"

"Yeah, actually, you did. You wore his fucking jersey in here. I'm glad you took it off because if I saw you in it now, I'd cut it off of you and throw it in the trash."

"Why does it bother you so much? Ryan is my friend! I'm allowed to support my friend, Grant! Just like I came here to support you too!"

"Oh, bullshit! You know how much I hate him, Hadleigh. I swear you're wearing this just to rub it in my face!"

The use of her full name jolts her back a bit. "Rub it in? What the fuck are you talking about?"

"A couple of weeks ago, we were here and I was kissing you. I thought nothing could top that, and you wanted to remain friends—which I was okay with. But then you show up here tonight, wearing his jersey, and

I could barely focus. Hadleigh, I was on the bench for the whole fucking game! That never happens! I'm not blaming you, but I'm blaming myself for getting too attached to you because you won't leave my fucking head, and I don't want you to." She's looking at me like I have four heads right now. I didn't mean to blurt all that out, but I can't fucking control myself around her. "Don't fucking trust Ryan either. I've told you this before, but Ryan is bad news. Please, just this once, trust me."

"What happened to your knuckles?" She asks me.

"What?"

"Why are your knuckles bleeding?"

I'm quiet for a second. What will she think of me if I tell her the truth? Fuck it, no lying to her. "I punched Ryan in the face."

She looks shocked, and rightfully so. "Why?"

"Why what?"

"Why did you punch him, Grant? What did he do?"

"Don't worry about it, Hades." I try to walk away, but she grabs my arm.

"I'm doing a project with him, and you're telling me to stay away? I'm getting deja vu and whiplash at the same time, Grant. You can't just punch someone in the face because you feel like it, and you definitely can't tell me who I can and can't be friends with. You don't have that right!"

"Just see him as little as possible. He doesn't care about you! He only wants to use you, Hads! You should hear how he talks about you in the locker room!"

"Grant, just leave me the fuck alone. You don't dictate my life!"

"Hads, I fucking care about you! I'm trying to tell you that Ryan doesn't, and you're dismissing me? Stop being so fucking scared of opening up to people and realize you have someone good right in front of you! I am right in front of you!"

The anger in her face breaks for a second and then returns just as quickly. "I'm so over this. Do you think you know me all of a sudden? Good luck with your final, Grant. I'm not helping you anymore!"

"Fine! Don't fucking help me anymore! Just keep what I said in the back of your mind." I storm past her and shove out the double doors.

I don't know why half of what I said came out of my mouth, but it did. God, I feel like a desperate son of a bitch when it comes to her. All I know is that when Ryan hurts her, I'll be there to pick up the pieces and show her how she deserves to be treated.

Hopefully, she'll let me.

29

Hadleigh

Paige and Amelia are arguing about something in this week's book section, and I'm completely zoned out. Ever since the hockey game on Monday, I've been so angry and confused. Primarily mad, though. I canceled Ryan and I's study session last night, under the guise of having too much else to do, but I didn't want to see him. After Grant stormed out of the rink the other night, I left Ryan's jersey by the door and bolted.

I was hurt.

I *am* hurt.

But I'm also confused. Grant said many things the other night that made me want to pull an Amelia and run away. I thought we could be friends first, but he doesn't want that.

"Hads?" Ella gently touches my shoulder and brings me back into the conversation.

"Sorry, I got lost in my thoughts for a second. What are we talking about?"

"Don't make me get the ruler. I'm not afraid to use it…" Amelia chuckles.

I roll my eyes. "I should never have told you guys about that."

"It's not a bad thing. I thought I was the kinkiest in this group, but you might give me a run for my money." Ella is trying to lighten my sour mood, and it's working a little. We're all silent for a minute until Paige breaks it.

"Okay, can we please talk about the elephant in the room? It's been killing me not to bring it up, and Ella I know you said not to, but I have to! Hads, what the hell is going on with Grant and Ryan?"

"Paige!" Ella shoots her a death glare. I love my friends for not wanting to provoke me right now, but I really need to talk this out, and there's nobody better to do that with than my girls.

"I don't even know where to start. I was waiting outside the locker room for Ryan to give him his jersey back, and I heard all this yelling. I moved forward to listen to what was happening, and Grant burst through the door looking pissed. I'd never seen him so mad. I asked him where Ryan was and if he could give it to him, and he just got mad at me! He snapped at me and was pissed at me for wearing Ryan's jersey!" I'm out of my chair and pacing at this point. "I told him that Ryan and I are friends, but he just—ugh! He brought up the kiss again, and I got pissed off at him. We were screaming at each other and then I saw his knuckles. They were bleeding, and he told me he punched Ryan! For no reason!" I tell them the rest of the story, sparing no details, and when I look up, Paige is on the floor in a star position, and Amelia and Ella are speechless.

"THIS IS THE BEST DAY EVER!"

"Is Paige having some sort of cardiac event or something? What is she doing?" I ask Amelia.

"He's down bad for you, Hads! Can't you see?" Paige looks like she's on drugs right now.

"Okay, hold on a minute—" Ella tries to diffuse the situation and then looks at me. "Why did he punch Ryan?"

"He wouldn't tell me when I asked him. He just told me not to worry about it." That part alone reignites my anger at Grant. Why couldn't he just tell me what happened?

"Grant isn't normally the punching type. That's more reserved for Oliver and Paige, who threatens it but never follows through." Amelia makes a good point, but I'm still angry.

"Hey! One day it might happen. You never know." Paige gets off the floor and sits in her chair again. "I think this just proves that he likes you. He wouldn't have punched Ryan unless he had a good reason."

"Or maybe he has always hated Ryan and used that as an excuse! Seriously, we're all back to hating him, right?"

"Aw, not this again. Can we skip these chapters and go to the end where you realize you're in love with him? Being mean takes too much effort." Paige says with a sad look.

"Not for me." Ella and Amelia say at the same time. They look at each other, smile, and fist bump.

"Really, you two? And no, Paige, I hate him so we all hate him. Those are the rules." I look around at the three of them, and they all nod. "Good. Can we please talk about this book because I truly believe these two characters are soulmates, and nobody can tell me otherwise."

"I agree!" Paige shouts, and that stumbles into a long-winded conversation about the book. In my head, I kick myself for not mentioning one little detail about something Grant said yesterday. I know I was supposed to tell them everything, but my brain can't wrap my head around this one thing he said.

I am right in front of you.

When he said that, everything around me froze and I forgot how to breathe. What did he mean by that? He has never outwardly expressed his interest in me, and then he goes and tells me that he's right in front of me. He was also right about one thing. I'm scared, but I'm also trying my hardest to do what my brother said —to move on, but it won't happen overnight. Time is everything, it heals all wounds or whatever, and I really need to focus on moving forward, but when Grant keeps punching people for no reason, it makes things difficult.

I zone back into the conversation and look at the girls around me. Even when we're passionately arguing about the books we read, I adore them. They tether me and my thoughts back to the ground. I smile and join the conversation, trying to dissolve the thoughts swirling around in my head when my phone buzzes, and the girls all look at me.

"What?"

"Is it him?" Ella asks me.

"It can't be the three of us because we're all sitting in front of you right now." Damn. Amelia makes a good point. I take my phone out and look at it.

"It's Ryan." I hear a few heavy sighs, knowing they are all coming from Paige, and I swipe my phone open and read what he said.

Ryan: Hey! Do you want to get coffee on Saturday? At the cafe in the library?
Hads: Sure! We can work on the project since I canceled on Tuesday :)
Ryan: Yeah, that sounds good!
Hads: Cool, see you then!
Ryan liked the message.

"He wanted to work on the project on Saturday. I said sure."

They all nod, and we continue to talk about the book. Was he asking me out? No, no, he knows we're just friends. I take a few steadying breaths and focus back in on book club.

30

Grant

    I'm a colossal failure and the stupidest man on the planet. Who goes on a date to try and get rid of a girl from their thoughts? Apparently, me, that's who. Jacks yelled at me before I left our room, but I needed to do this. I need to get her out of my damn head. I only fell for her because of the proximity, and I'll eventually be able to stop thinking about her every waking minute of every fucking day. At least that's what I keep telling myself.

    I asked out this girl named Jasmine from one of my education classes. She's pretty and has been flirting with me since we got to campus freshman year, but I was never really interested in her. She's not my type. She's tall, only a few inches shorter than me, and blonde. Very blonde, almost platinum—or whatever that hair color is. We're headed to this restaurant in town that serves only subpar Italian food. Making small talk on our walk over has been dull at best. I'm making jokes, and she laughs at them, but it all seems fake. I don't know. *Something* is just missing.

    We sit down at our table, and the waiter comes over and fills our glasses with water, and then leaves for a few minutes so we can decide what to eat. The silence is unbearable as we both look over the menu. I usually get the same thing, but I'm hiding in the menu so I don't have to start the conversation. Fortunately, she does.

"I'm so glad we're finally doing this. I've been dropping hints since we met. I didn't think you would ever pick up on them." She chuckles at that, and I fake a smile.

"Yeah, you're very persistent, Jas. You look great tonight, by the way."

"Aw, you're too sweet." She reaches over and touches my hand that's lying on the table. *Nothing.* I feel nothing. She does look good, which I didn't lie about. She's wearing dark jeans with a cropped black shirt that has some sort of logo on it. Her hair is long and curly, and she could probably stab me with her heels. The outfit I'm wearing tonight feels itchy. I'm wearing jeans, some nice dress shoes, and a button-down. It just all feels wrong. Everything about tonight feels wrong, but still, here I am.

The waiter comes by, and we order, the silence returning after. How do you talk to someone you have no interest in? God, this sucks, and it isn't fair to either of us, but I'm determined to see this dinner through.

"So, what made you decide you wanted to study education?" I ask her. She takes a minute to gather her thoughts before answering.

"I always loved teaching others how to learn and helping people achieve that. Eventually, I want to become a middle-school teacher. I think those years can be really formative, and I would love to help mold the minds of the younger generation."

"Wow, that's amazing. Most people don't seem as passionate as you, so props to you."

"Thank you. What do you want to do with your degree, Grant?"

"I want to become a hockey coach eventually.

That's the goal, at least. I don't really have an age preference." I leave the part out about my dad. I don't really tell people that unless I trust them. It's still hard for me to talk about him sometimes. I miss him every fucking day.

"That's awesome, though you might have to up your game. You didn't play too well the other day." I think she's trying to be funny, but that hits me right in the chest, and my heart sinks. I hate thinking about how I played and acted the other day, but it won't leave my mind.

"You saw that? Yeah, it was just an off night, I guess. Everyone has them once in a while." Why the fuck did she bring that up? Now I'm back to thinking about *her* in that stupid jersey that said Barnes on the back of it. Christ, this was going so well. Apparently, everyone saw how big of a failure I was the other night. The only thing I do regret is how I acted toward Hadleigh. I was a jerk, and I knew I was a jerk at the moment, but she got me so flustered I just spurted out random words. I wonder if she has mulled over any of what I said. It doesn't matter anyway, she's back to hating me, and I'm here on a date with someone else. I never wanted to admit that I wished she was there wearing my jersey. I wanted my name on her, not Ryan's.

That doesn't stop the regret from seeping in again. I hated myself after I walked out of the rink. When Jacks came home, we talked for hours about all of it. After that, he finally understood, and he's also on the hating Ryan train. He also thought I should tell Hads everything, but I don't think I can redeem myself. Even telling her everything he has been saying won't make her believe me, especially with my track record. All of a sudden, there's a hand waving in front of my face—Jasmine's.

"Grant? Are you okay? It looks like you zoned out for a second. The food is here."

"Oh, I'm sorry. I just have a lot on my mind tonight. What were you saying?" She goes on a rant about one of her classes and some girl that has been bothering her, and I nod—actively listen, but my mind is elsewhere. I wish I were here with her. In my head, I'm thinking about how Hadleigh used to hit me with her ruler when I zoned out. I'm thinking about how I wish it were her across from the table right now, smacking me with that ruler to get my attention back. God, what I would do to have her do that to me just one more time. I want her sitting across from me, fighting every stupid sound that comes from my mouth. I want the glares and the eye-rolls and all of it.

I want it all. I want her.

I continued the dinner and listened to Jasmine talk. It's fine. It really is. I wasn't just going to bail on her when I had this gigantic realization. So, we finish the date. I walk her back to her room and tell her that I had fun, but we should remain friends, and she agreed. It was amicable, she kissed me on the cheek, and I felt nothing. I know that the only sparks I'll feel are with a short, black-haired menace. A girl who's way smarter than me and who probably deserves better than me, but I'm determined now. I know what I want, and I'm going after it. Even if it ends with me being heartbroken, at least I can say I tried.

I text Jacks and one of my other friends named Brendan to meet me at my dorm.

Jacks: Did you forget I lived here? I'm already in the room.
Brendan: Is Grant having a mental breakdown right now? If so, I'm on the way.
Grant: Guys, just shut up. I need your help. Hurry.

I shove my phone back into my pocket and open the door to my building. Jacks is sitting in our lounge waiting for me with a sly look on his face.

"What's wrong with your face? Are you having an allergic reaction?"

"No, just excited. You've just had your moment of realization."

"What? How did you know that? And what's that?"

"I've been waiting for this to happen. You like her and are finally hatching a plan to go after her. I'm proud of you, buddy." He stands up and puts his hand on my shoulder. Is he for real right now? How did he know this way before I did?

"Are you guys about to kiss? Should I give you the room or something?" Brendan walks in and stops at the doors. He's not on the hockey team, but we all sat together at orientation and have been friends ever since. Brendan has wavy blonde hair and is about the same height as me. Good looking kid and an even better friend.

"No, nothing was happening. Just get in here." I say to him.

"Roger that." He salutes me and sits on the chair while I remain standing before them. I'm pacing slightly when I see Brendan hand Jacks a twenty.

"What was that for?" I ask, pointing between the

two of them.

"We had a bet going on how long it would take you to figure out your feelings. I said never, and Jacks said before the year was over. He won, so I owe him twenty bucks."

What is with the betting lately? What the actual fuck? "Great. Thanks for that, anyways that's why I called you both here. I need help. I don't know how to get this girl with my shitty track record. So, I need a plan."

Jacks takes a sip of water and points at me, "You know there's a Taylor Swift song for this. It's literally called *How You Get the Girl*. Maybe listen to that a few hundred times, and you'll be set."

"Yeah, that's a good idea. Plus, I'm not an expert in this field like Jacks is. He officially has Claire, and I have nobody at the moment. I would listen to him." They both high-five each other. Seriously? This has not been helpful at all.

"You guys are terrible at this," I tell them.

"Maybe just be there," Brendan says.

"Be where?"

"Wherever she is. That forced proximity bullshit in romance books that people love so much." Jacks and I both stare at him. "What? I have a sister. She goes on and on about this shit at family dinner every Sunday. That and the one-bed trope, or whatever. She goes crazy over those two. It's funny." Brendan commutes from about fifteen minutes away. I've met his family a few times. They're all hilarious. His little sister could give Hadleigh a run for her money in glares. The first time Jacks and I went over, she opened the door and greeted us with a stare that almost turned us to stone. It was hilarious. While Brendan is goofier, his little sister is all steel.

"What about a flash mob?" Brendan asks.

"No."

"Hold up a stereo in front of her dorm?" Jacks says.

"Absolutely not."

"Cover her room with flowers?" Brendan says.

"Maybe?"

"Buy her like a hundred new books?"

"Something more like getting her to forgive me and not breaking my bank account, please. Also, not something from a rom-com I've never seen." The two of them go silent.

"Well, clearly you have seen them if you know those suggestions are from rom-coms." Jacks counters.

I sigh heavily and slump down on the chairs. "This is not going to work."

"Come on. We have all night. Let's go to the whiteboard and draw up some ideas that aren't from Brendan's little sister."

"Fine, but we're ordering pizza. Especially if Grant is going to be pouting all night." He gets up and walks past me, and goes into our room.

"I'm not pouting," I say as I stand up and follow him in.

I should throw in the towel now, but I won't give up that easily. I want Hads, and I'll do whatever it takes to show her that I'm in it for the long haul. I just hope she'll eventually want me back. Because if that happens, my heart might be sealed and chained for the rest of my life.

31

Hadleigh

"Paige, I'm not going to get murdered in a public place during the day. You and Amelia can stay in your apartment." I had just returned from my morning walk with Oliver, when Paige called me saying I should cancel on Ryan.

"What if he slips something into your drink? I don't trust him!" She is shouting now and probably pacing in her apartment. I hear Amelia in the background telling her to chill out.

"Paige, it's going to be fine. Stop worrying so much about me. I can handle myself."

"I know, I know. Don't tell Ames, but I had a small latte this morning." She's whispering now. Shit. Paige having coffee just equals a panic attack. "Okay, I have to go. Text us an SOS if you need us!"

"Sounds good. Please don't show up in the library with wigs and—" She hung up. I send a quick text to Amelia and let her know that Paige had a coffee—just as a heads up—and I take a quick shower. After that, I don't take too long to decide what to wear. It's not a date, so I don't have to try that hard. I throw on a pair of ripped black jeans, a white crewneck, and my black boots. I'm grabbing my bag and my laptop when Taylor walks in.

"Hey, girl. Where are you off to right now? Do you want to grab some breakfast?"

"Hey, I'm off to the library cafe to work on a

project. Rain check? I could probably do dinner tonight." She's still wearing a dress and the heels I saw her put on last night. Good for her. At least someone is having the whole college experience.

"That sounds good. Are you hanging out with Ryan or Grant this time?" Taylor knows all about what has been going down. We tell each other pretty much everything, and I trust her. She tells me about her conquests, and I rant about mine. It's a win-win.

"Ryan, and shush. It's not a date. It's just for the project. And we hate Grant now, remember?" I stare at her, reminding her if I hate someone, we hate someone. Our first semester, she got into it with this girl, and she made me vow that I wouldn't talk to her either. It's girl code. If one of you hates someone, that means you both do.

"I'm just saying I wouldn't be mad at you if you decided to hit that."

"Taylor, ew. How many times do I have to say that we're just friends? Also, I know you like him, so I won't be hitting that out of respect for you and myself." I say that last part with a grimace. Do people actually talk like this?

"Fine, I'll text you later so we can have dinner, but I need a shower. See you!" She grabs her robe and shower gear and exits, heading to the community showers. I grab my bag, throw my keys, student ID card, and laptop with my notes into it, and walk to the library.

※

Ryan is already in a booth and has his coffee on

the table when I arrive. "Hey, I'll go order mine and meet you back here. Can you watch my laptop?"

"Yeah, of course. Does it do tricks?"

"Sorry, what?" I look at him, feeling quite puzzled about what he just said.

"That's actually my bad. I was trying to make a joke. You asked if I could watch your laptop, and I asked if it does any tricks, and I realize how stupid that sounds now. My bad."

I give him a weird look and go up to the counter to order. There aren't many people around, so it's made relatively quickly. I grab some napkins and head back to the table. Ryan's working away on his laptop, and I slide into the booth and set my coffee down.

Our project is simple, but it's a lot of work. Researching and putting together all the information we find has been the most challenging part. Each group got assigned a different serial killer. Paige and Oliver got the Unabomber—someone Paige was very excited to get. Apparently, she researched him a couple of years ago and has this obsession with him. That's super healthy of her, right? No wonder she has nightmares all the time. Ryan and I got Ted Bundy. Paige laughed when I told her. Hell, even Oliver laughed and he had to sit down because he was laughing so hard.

"So, I made this chart and put together all the things we have on Ted already if you want to look at it."

"Damn, Hads. You really do like making charts."

"Hey! Don't knock the charts, dude. They will be super helpful when we have to write this paper. Ten pages might not seem like a lot, but it is." He looks like he's judging me. I sink into the booth a bit. We had worked on the project for about fifteen minutes when

Ryan changed the subject.

"So, what has been your favorite book you have read this year?"

"Hmm, that's a good question, but a difficult one."

"I know, but if you had to pick a favorite so far, which one would you pick?"

I think hard about this one. I've read many good books in the book club and on my own. "I would probably say—"

"The one with all those kisses on the cover. I saw her holding it the most. She was practically attached at the hip to that one." Except it isn't Ryan or me who says that. It's Grant.

Did he install a tracking device in my mouth when we kissed? How does he always know where I am? It happens too much for it to be a coincidence. It also infuriates me that he's right. That *was* my favorite book so far this year. He's standing in front of our booth, wearing that classic Grant-asshole smile. "Grant, nice to see you as always," Ryan says, clearly trying to get him away from our booth.

"So, Hades, my favorite book this year—thank you for asking, by the way—has been Gatsby."

"I'm guessing that's the only book you've read this year? So, by default, it has to be your favorite." I say to him.

"Actually, I picked up a few more at the local bookstore. I'm trying to get into reading a bit more. I even picked up your favorite. I wanted to see what the hype was about." He smirks again and slides into the booth, forcing me to move over. I'm now sandwiched between Ryan and Grant. This might be my worst nightmare.

"Grant, leave," Ryan tells him—staring daggers at Grant right now.

"Why do you want me to leave? Unless this is a date, and I'm intruding? Am I?"

"Yes, you are—" Grant cuts Ryan's sentence off.

"Uh, Uh," he holds up his finger to shush Ryan. "I wanna hear it from Hadleigh." He turns his head to look at me. Heat rushes into my cheeks when he looks at me. Fuck.

"It's not a date, but—"

"Great! Now, Hades, I have a few questions about chapter seven of Gatsby."

"Grant, leave. We're working on something." Ryan insists this time.

"Ryan, she was my tutor and I have a couple of questions, don't get all in a tizzy."

Oh my God, what's happening? Is this some sort of dick-measuring contest? "I forgot my ruler. Should I get it? Are you two going to need it?" I look between them, and they stare at each other. I have half a mind to crawl under the table and leave them both here.

"I just have a couple of questions, and then I'll be out of your hair, I promise." Grant looks sincere.

"Fine. Ask away." I say to him, and I can feel Ryan tense next to me.

"Are you sure Gatsby and Nick aren't in love?"

"Grant, you've got to be kidding me right now. You really think—" Grant cuts Ryan off again.

"Yes, I really do think they are in love, sue me. Hadleigh? Confirm or deny."

"Grant, as I've said before, the book is about Gatsby's relationship with all these people, but Nick and

Gatsby's relationship is at the center in a way. Though many Tumblr users would say otherwise, they're not in love."

"Ha! I knew it! I knew there was at least a chance. Like I said before, love always wins." He looks at me when he says that, and for a beat too long. It makes me feel weird, but I can't say I hate how he looks at me.

No. No, Hads. We *hate* him, remember? My mind knows that, but the rest of my body hasn't caught up from the whiplash I have with him.

"Okay, Grant, goodbye. We have more work to do." I can tell Ryan is mad at the situation. Some part of me feels bad, but it feels good to help someone again.

"Is that all, Grant? We do have a paper to do." I ask him.

"Yes, that is all." He gets up from the booth and halts before walking fully away.

"Actually, one more thing Hades. I'm wondering where I could get some good pens and sticky notes."

"Uhhh, Amazon? Or Target? Why?"

"No reason. I just figured you know where the best ones are. Thank you!" He slaps the table before he walks through the library doors. That was one of the weirdest interactions I've ever had with these two. Ryan is silent for a moment before he speaks.

"Why does he call you that?"

"Call me what?"

"Hades. That seems kind of rude of him, in my opinion." Oh, that. Right. I think that was the first time he called me that in front of other people. It feels weirdly sentimental.

"Oh, it's just a nickname he has for me. When I first met him, I called him hockey boy, so he returned the favor by calling me Hades. We only used to do it during our sessions, but it kind of seeped out. So, back to good old Ted, okay?" I change the subject because I really don't want to talk about what Grant and I's stupid nicknames mean. It's not important. It's just another game we play to add to our weird ass relationship. The hatred game, as I've named it.

Ryan and I talk for another hour and then call it. He walks me back to my dorm, and that's that.

That was by far the weirdest, not date I have ever been on with two guys. Sophomore year is shaping up to be the craziest yet, and here I was hoping for a chill year.

I guess no matter what you plan for, the world usually has a different one.

32

Grant

"Great practice tonight, boys. We have playoffs next week, so get some sleep and keep those grades up!" Our coach has just dismissed us, and I'm heading into the locker room when Jacks stops me before I can grab my shower stuff.

"Have you had a chance to do what we talked about? Brendan keeps asking me, and I'm quite curious as well." He smiles at me, and I nod.

"I've started it, but I need to get into her room to steal some things. I just don't know how to do that. Maybe I could ask one of her friends."

"It is Wednesday, and they're all at book club right now. Maybe try asking Paige or Ella."

"Is that the blonde one?"

"You're horrible at this." He states, very plainly. "Just go to book club. I'm sure one of them will help you get the rest of the stuff you need." He slams his locker closed and heads for the showers. Okay, meet her friends at book club and beg them to help me. I can do that, right?

When I first met Hades, I wasn't one for begging.

But now I'd get on my fucking knees if it made her happy.

✗

I walk in to where they usually hold book club

and hope that I don't walk in on them discussing smut. I learned that word when I asked Brendan's little sister where I could get Hadleigh's favorite book. She told me the book was spicy, and I asked her what she meant, which led to this long, precise explanation. She told me I needed to tab my favorite parts of the book, which led to *another* long explanation. After she told me everything I needed to know, I purchased the book and some colored pens. Brendan's sister told me that certain people like a specific type of tabs, so I figured I would steal some of hers, so they match. The only problem is that I have to get into her room to retrieve them.

    This is where the book club girls come in. I knock on the door, and I don't see Hadleigh. I guess that's a good thing because I needed to ask the others for their help, but now my stomach feels weird. Something is wrong. I can feel it.

    "Hel—Hello book club. How's the reading going?" God, is my voice shaking? Why am I nervous right now? The blonde one's eyes are huge right now, and the curly-haired one is laughing. I really need to remember their names.

    "Is one of you named Ella? I'm sorry I am horrible with names, but I need a favor."

    "That would be me. It's nice to see you again." She stands up and crosses the room towards me. Damn, she's kind of scary. I hope she doesn't murder me right here in this classroom.

    "Don't worry. Paige is the one you have to worry about murdering you. She's the true crime junkie and could hide your body without getting caught." I realize now that I said the last part out loud. Whoops. The curly-haired one gets up and crosses to where we're standing. Damn, she kind of scares me too. What is with these girls? I thought people who read books were nerds. I need to rethink that frame of mind.

"Hi, Grant. Amelia. It's nice to see you again. I, for one, am excited to see where this will go." The blonde one—Paige, I assume—skips to where we are all standing. Is this some sort of group analysis or something? Why are we standing like we're in a cult?

"My name is Paige, and can I just say I've always been on your team." She smiles and holds her hand out for me to shake it.

"On my team?" I say as I grab it. I'm very confused right now.

"She's joking. Are you going to tell us why you're here, or will we have to guess?" Ella says, sitting back down.

Right. I explain to them the reason why I'm here, and by the time I'm done, Paige is crying—which apparently happens a lot. Amelia has a look on her face, and Ella looks like she wants to kill me slightly less than before.

"That is the cutest thing I've ever heard!" Paige says.

"I think Hads would really like that." Amelia agrees.

"We can get you what you need," Ella says finally.

"Speaking of Hades, where is she? Isn't she normally here with you guys?"

"Oh, right. She has been sick the past few days and isn't feeling well, so she stayed in tonight." Ella tells me.

"Oh, is she alright? Is someone taking care of her?" They all laugh at that.

"Hads would bite one of our hands off if we tried to take care of her. Trust us. We've tried." Ella grabs her bag, and the other girls look like they are heading out.

"Okay, well, thank you for your help. I really appreciate it." I smile. "What did she come down with? Flu? Fever? The common cold?" I'm just wondering, of course, as a friend would.

"The flu that's been going around on campus. Why?" Amelia questions me with a sly look on her face.

"No reason," I say as I walk fastly out the door, "Thanks, guys! See you around!" I shove out the doors and down the steps. I'm heading to the store, and then I'm heading to a certain stubborn girl's dorm room to nurse her back to health.

※

I stopped at a nearby pharmacy to grab a bunch of different things. I have an important paper I should be working on right now, but this takes precedence. I also got every variety of crackers that I saw because I wasn't sure which ones were her favorite, and I don't know if she can keep anything down.

So, I bought it all. Because why not?

I swipe into the building, and luckily, her door's unlocked. I DMed Taylor, her roommate, on Instagram, and she's staying with a friend so she doesn't catch the flu. I slip in, and I think she's sleeping, so it gives me time to unload all the stuff I have. I put all the medicine on her desk and quietly place the crackers on the floor. I turn on her kettle and grab a tea bag from her station. I go to her book cart and grab a few tabs off of it, not enough to make her notice they're gone, hopefully. I hope I don't scare her when she wakes up. The kettle starts making a noise, and I see her stirring. Fuck, is she going to throw something at me thinking I broke in?

Hadleigh

I've been sick for days. I've missed class, and I hate it. Usually, I don't get sick, but this year I've succumbed to the stupid college flu. I can barely move, but I've been keeping things down, and I have my emotional support water bottle, as Ella and Amelia have coined it. I woke up because I heard a noise that I assumed was Taylor who had forgotten something. Until someone comes up and sits on my bed, holding a glass of something, my vision is blurry from the dehydration, so I can't tell who it is.

"Ella, I told you, you don't have to take care of me. I even told Oliver to go away earlier. I'm fine."

"While Ella does seem like the one to take care of all you girls, it's just me." I know that voice. Why do I know that voice? "Here, baby, drink this. It'll help your stomach."

Oh my God, what is Grant doing here? My vision focuses, and there he is. The tall, curly haired asshole. How does he look good even when he's probably just come from practice?

"Grant, what are you doing here?"

"I stopped by the book club to ask you something after practice, but you weren't there. The girls told me you were sick, so I stopped at the pharmacy and got some stuff."

"Why?"

"Well, they told me you are stubborn and don't like when someone takes care of you. I know that already, so I figured if I just showed up here and did it, you would be too sick to be mean to someone who just wants to help you." He looks down and pauses for a minute. "Please, just let me help you."

I look at him for a minute, there are bags all over my floor, and he's still holding the cup with what is probably my tea. He did this for me? Or does he just feel bad? I grab the cup from his hands and drink it.

"I didn't want anyone else to get sick, so I sent everyone away," I lie. I hate when people make a fuss over me. It does feel nice being helped sometimes. I just have to let people in to be able to do that. It's too bad that I'll probably always push people away. It's just how I'm wired.

"I know you're lying right now. But I don't care if I get sick. As long as you get better, I'd succumb to the plague for all I care." He gets up and goes to do something at my desk. "How is the tea? Did I make it right? I wasn't sure how you liked it."

The tea tastes perfect, and now I hate tea. "It's good." More shuffling sounds lead me to speak again. "What are you doing over there? Did you ask Paige how to build a bomb, and this whole ruse was to blow me up?"

"I'm really glad being sick has not changed that damn attitude of yours. I have to say I missed it these past few weeks. Nobody on this campus can banter with me quite like you." More shuffling. Seriously, am I going to die soon? "Hades, what's your favorite type of cracker?"

"My favorite what?"

"Crackers, you know, saltines, ritz, et cetera."

"Well, for the flu, it's usually saltines. Plain and simple. I've kept a few down, but I ran out yesterday." He returns to my bed and hands me a box of them. "How did you know which ones I liked?"

He looks down again, "I didn't, so I bought pretty much every variety. Just in case."

Oh. I feel nauseous again, but it's not from my stomach bug. He bought every single kind of cracker.

For me. To take care of me while I'm sick. Is this a parallel universe? Am I having a fever dream right now? "Thank you. For the tea and the crackers, you can leave now. I'll be okay."

"Now, what kind of friend would I be if I left you here in your state? You look terrible, by the way. The flu does not look good on you."

"Okay, loser, I'd like to see you when you're sick. It's a proven fact that boys are horrible when they even have a sniffle. You guys are down for the count if your temperature goes up to 99." I think back to what he said again. "Also, we're not friends. I would compare you to a parasite or a demon. You've simply attached to me and will not let me go."

"Damn right. You'll never be able to get out of my reach, that I can promise you." He says that in a deep voice, and now I think he has some double meaning behind it, but I'm too sick to dive into that right now.

"Thank you for doing this. I appreciate it." He shifts a bit closer to me and hands me something. "What are these?"

"Oh, come on, seriously? Miss 4.0 GPA doesn't know what sweatpants are?"

"I know what they are, but why are you giving me

these?"

"Hades, you're wearing jeans right now while you're sick with the flu. How have you been sleeping in these? That's definitely your serial killer trait." Good God.

"So, you've talked to Paige, I see. Wonderful." I grab the sweatpants because I won't admit this out loud, but I have been uncomfortable. When I first came down with the flu, I fell asleep in the clothes I wore to my classes that day, and I haven't been back up since. Begrudgingly, I take the pants. "Turn around. I don't want you getting any ideas."

"You can blindfold me too, if you want. I don't mind." He turns and faces my closet as I take my jeans off and throw them on the ground.

"Gross."

"I'm kidding, Hades. Just put the fucking pants on."

"I am! Just give me a second!"

"I know sweatpants are foreign to you, so all you want to do is put one leg in first and then the other. It's really simple. Even I can do it."

"I'm done! You're lucky I don't throw this tea in your face." He turns around and makes a weird face. "Are these your sweatpants?"

"Yeah. You should keep them too. They look really good on you. I honestly don't even want them back after this. They belong on you. Also, I don't want your sick germs on me anyway." He looks me up and down as I crawl back into bed, not wanting to break down that sentence he just said. He grabs my laptop and joins me.

"What are you doing?"

"We're going to watch a show, and hopefully,

you'll fall asleep."

"I haven't slept in three days."

"I brought NyQuil for that reason. I'll grab it. Finish your tea. It should help you relax."

This dynamic is actually not bad. Why am I enjoying it all of a sudden? It must be the fever. It's making me lose my morals and sound judgments. "Thanks." He hands me the medicine, and I drink it. It tastes terrible. He has my laptop open, and starts playing One Tree Hill.

"This is my favorite show, but I'm assuming you already knew that." Grant is a sneaky fucker. Did he run a background check on me or something?

"I'm aware." He says, not elaborating on how he knew that fact.

"How do you know that?" Who is this man in front of me, and what has he done with Grant? "This is all very sweet, but you don't have to stay with me. I'll be okay. I'm almost through the worst of it." I don't want him getting sick when he shouldn't even be here in the first place. Regardless of what I say, he's not going to leave. He is as stubborn as I am. I get comfortable, and so does he. On my tiny twin XL bed, he looks enormous. It makes me giggle a bit.

"There's the laugh I missed. I've been trying to get that out of you all night. I asked the girls. Now shut up and watch the damn show." He looks serious right now, and then he starts laughing, which makes me laugh. We're both laughing while my favorite show plays in the background, and now I want to cry. I shove that feeling down because I can't stand crying in front of other people. This is fun. I'm having *fun* with Grant. Again. The show keeps playing, and we both keep our eyes trained on the screen. Every so often, I see him move his head to watch me while I keep my eyes trained forward. Eventually, my eyes get so droopy that I drift off to sleep, feeling a sense of peace as my eyes close.

Grant

She fell asleep on my shoulder, and I want to capture this moment in a bottle and remember it. Hads looks so peaceful that I know I'll be here all night, and I don't care. I kiss her on the forehead and turn off the show we're watching—which was surprisingly good—and now I'm invested. It's quiet in her room. I can hear her breathing. In and out.

I think I'm in love with this girl.

33

Grant

Hadleigh fell asleep on my shoulder last night, and I didn't want to leave her, but I had to at some point. She would've punched me in the face if she had woken up and seen me gathered on her floor beside her bed, or maybe she would've stepped on me and carried on with her morning routine. Thankfully, I feel fine. I don't think she passed her germs on me, but I could care less if she did. I would take all her germs if it meant getting something from her. I loved taking care of her. It felt like she was finally letting her walls down and allowing someone to help her for once. Maybe I should check in on her, just in case.

Grant: Hey, just checking in. Are you feeling okay?
Hads: I think today is my last day of wearing sweatpants. I'm feeling happy about that already.
Grant: Good, I'm glad.
Hads: Thank you, again. For what you did last night.
Grant: It was my pleasure.
Hads: I don't think I will run out of crackers anytime soon.
Grant: Good. Think of me when you eat them.
Hads: Brb, I have to throw up again because you just said that.
Grant: Haha, I'm glad you're feeling better! Let me know if you need anything else.

It's Thursday night, and the team just finished

playing. A Thursday night home game that we won, I might add. I showered and put all my stuff in my locker and am now going to spend my Thursday night reading and annotating a book.

I, the guy who used to hate the library, am now reading a book.

For a girl that I like.

Possibly love.

I'm doing this so I can see the smile on her face.

Jacks would call me whipped. Actually, he did call me that earlier. Only because I refused to go out with some of the guys and opted to read a fucking book instead. I guess that was warranted, but I don't care.

I'm walking out of the rink when Holt catches up to me.

"Come on, Grant, just one drink? We have to celebrate, especially since you had the most blocks tonight. You can have one drink and be home by 10. Sound good?"

He makes a good point, plus I am halfway through the book and haven't been to The Hidden Bear in a minute. And it *was* a good game.

"Fine. One drink and that's it." He slaps me on the shoulder, and I turn around and join the guys to celebrate our win.

✕

One drink has turned into four beers, two shots, and some other things that Jacks handed me. Honestly, it was an accident, but I'm having a good time. I'm sitting in a booth with Jacks, Holt, and this other kid named Erikson who plays offense for Grand Mountain. He's a freshman and has a bright future of playing ahead of him. Some of the other guys, including Ryan, are sitting in a booth behind us. The hockey team is all residing in the same area of the bar. We're all chatting and having a good time. A couple of players are playing darts, some are dancing, and the rest are just chilling in the booths. Most of us are pretty drunk right now, but after the game, it's well deserved.

"I think I'm going to ask her to the banquet," Ryan says to someone at his table. He's talking loud so that I can hear him.

"Who?" Another kid asks. My head can't think of his name right now, I think he is a transfer from somewhere. I haven't talked to him much yet.

"Hadleigh, she's the slut in the short skirts, so she can flaunt her ass to all the guys she's fucked." Ryan says.

I turn my head around so fast I get minor whiplash. What the fuck did he just say about Hadleigh? *My Hadleigh?* God, I want to curb-stomp this kid. He doesn't deserve to breathe the same air as anyone, especially Hadleigh. I want to fuck his face up so hard that he has permanent brain damage.

Wait. I need to calm down. The alcohol is making my brain all fucked. I need to stop having my first reaction to everything Ryan says to be to punch him. I'm not like this, usually. But the way he talks about her just makes me want to fuck his face up a bit. I swear sometimes he just does this within hearing distance from me to get me in trouble.

Hold on. Did he say he was going to ask her to the banquet? I had the exact same idea.

"Did you hear what I said, Grant?" Ryan's looking right at me, and I forgot that I was still turned around to face his direction. Okay, it's time to take the high road. Getting kicked off the hockey team for kicking the shit out of Ryan is not how I want to leave the team.

"I did, actually." I'm keeping my responses to him short and simple from now on. Hopefully, it will deter me from getting too heated and punching him.

"Do you have anything to say to that?" He asks me, trying to provoke me.

He asked the question, and I might as well answer. "Yeah." I get up out of my seat and walk over to his booth. I stand in front of it and look down at him. What a tiny, sad little man. He looks up at me and smirks. Of course, he is. Such a fucking instigator.

"Eventually, you'll show your true colors, you know, the ones that are shining so brightly for everyone right now." I raise my hands and gesture to the people around us. "And she'll *hate* you for it. You don't know her as I do. Hell, you don't understand the female population at all."

"I second that!" Jacks says from our table.

"Thanks, buddy. Anyways, you'll never get her. You'll never have her, at least how you want her. You don't care about her—" he cuts me off.

"Oh, you mean like you care about her?" He stands up to face me. He's a couple of inches shorter than me, so he still looks up at me while talking.

"Yes, actually. You'll never care about her how I do. You will never know what she truly likes because you just like manipulating people into sleeping with you. You don't respect women. Therefore, Hadleigh will never be yours. You could never manipulate her, she's too smart for that, and if you knew her you would know that."

"Since we're friends, according to her, I think it's working so far." He smiles.

"I'm five steps ahead of you, motherfucker. And I'm not even thinking about myself anymore. Just her. It's all about her. You could never measure up to that. So, fuck off and leave her alone." Jacks comes over and leads me back to the table, and we both watch Ryan exit the front door of the bar. Good riddance.

"You really wanted to punch him, didn't you?" Jacks asks me.

"So fucking bad, but I decided to assault him verbally instead. How did I do?" I was still a bit drunk, so I couldn't tell if my words were coherent.

"From where I was sitting, you did well. He got what he deserved. Do you think he'll lay off her?"

"I hope so, but probably not. I think he wants me to beat the shit out of him just to spite me so I can get kicked off the team. I won't stoop to his level, though, not anymore."

"I'm proud of you, man." He tells me with a smile.

"Thanks." I always wanted to be the type of man to make my dad proud. He and my mom were the perfect couple. I remember hearing my dad talk about the moment he finally knew he was ready to settle down and be the man he could always be for my mom. I think that's how I feel right now. I want to be the kind of guy she deserves. The kind of guy she could love. This feels like the first step. The first step to becoming good enough for her. I feel a bit clearer now. I see my path laid out in front of me. I don't know if it's the alcohol talking, but I think my dad played a part in helping me. I think he will always be with me, guiding me in the right direction.

Message received, Dad. I won't let my fear of failing her get in the way of something that could be great. I just hope she feels the same way.

Jacks excuses himself to get another drink, and someone taps me on the shoulder, and before I realize it, they sit opposite me in the booth. I don't know who this kid is, but he looks like he could kick my ass. He's just staring at me—the glare alone could cut me.

"I'm Oliver." He holds his hand out to shake it, and I do. I'm still scared of him. He has cold hands.

"Grant." We sit silently for a few seconds before I ask him, "Who are you?"

"Hadleigh's older brother." Oh.

Oh. Shit.

"It's nice to meet you. Hadleigh told me you went here."

"I do."

More silence. "You're a criminal justice major like Paige, right?" I say, trying to move this conversation forward.

"How do you know Paige?" He looks murderous right now. I'm so fucked.

"I—I met her when I went to the library once to find your sister. They were all sitting at a table together." This kid is making me so nervous. If he's going to kill me, I hope it's quick and not slow and painful. He seems like the type to do slow and painful. "Did you need something from me?"

"I heard what you said. Earlier. To that Ryan kid."

Oh fuck. Okay. Yeah. I'm definitely getting murdered tonight. "Oh, that, well—"

"You're a good guy, Grant." Oh. That's not where I thought this was going, but he continues. "I know all about what's been going on with you and my sister, and at first, I was pissed."

"Rightfully so. You seem protective of her, so that's valid." I tell him.

"I am. She's a great person and deserves to be happy."

"She does." I agree.

"Before tonight, I thought nobody would ever be good enough for her, especially Ryan. I hate that kid. He gives me bad vibes."

"I don't like him either. He's a dick."

"Yeah, he is." At that, he smiles, or I think it's a smile. It's more like he upturns his lips and that's about it. "I just want to caution you on a few things about my sister, if I may."

"Yeah, go ahead. I'm all ears."

"Do you like her?"

I pause, not expecting the question. "I do."

"Good. I like you, I think you'd be good for her. She needs someone like you. It'll soften her a little bit. But don't force her to open up to you. She'll retreat backward if you try to force Hads to do anything. And maybe give her some space to think the situation through. She's a thinker, always leading with her head and not her heart. But in time, I think her heart will win over. Just don't push it, and you'll be fine." He's staring at me, and I don't think he blinked that entire sentence.

"Thanks. I know she has a hard time trusting people, but I'm going to try my best to prove to her that I'm in this with her. My biggest fear is failing her, and well anyone, I guess. I don't want to fail her." I don't know why I'm laying out my issues to Hadleigh's brother in a dimly lit bar right now, but I didn't think any part of tonight would happen.

"Failure is part of life. It happens, unfortunately. I know about failing people too. It's not easy to forgive yourself. It took me a while to realize how you get back up from it matters more. I failed someone once by not being there for them, not protecting them." He pauses. "The fact that you said all that to Ryan proves to me that you're a good man. Even if you fail—which you won't—but if you did, what matters the most is how you pick yourself up and promise to do better next time. Actions, not just words. My sister deserves that. Someone who will always get back up and be with her. Someone who cares about her."

I really digest what he's saying right now, and he's right. "Thank you for telling me all that. I promise that I will always get back up for Hads. Nothing on this Earth could stop me from standing up for her. My main goal isn't to hurt her. The opposite, actually. I want her to be the happiest she can be, even if it means it's not with me. Her happiness is all I care about."

He's quiet for a minute, then he looks at me and says, "You're a good man, Grant. Believe in that and yourself for once." Then he gets up and walks out the door of the bar.

34

Hadleigh

It's been a week since Grant took care of me and let me wear his damn sweatpants, and I've barely seen him. Maybe he felt weird about what he did and decided that I wasn't worth the effort. Or perhaps he's just avoiding me. Or maybe he's just busy.

I've barely given it any thought.

I'm sitting in criminology, writing down notes, when Paige elbows me. "What?" I whisper to her.

"Why does Ryan keep staring at you?" She nods to where he sits, and sure enough, my eyes meet his. I give a small wave, and he just smiles at me. I've had genuine fun with him every Tuesday night. It's weird. I don't understand why Grant doesn't like him, but maybe Ryan and his personalities clash.

"This concludes our lesson on restorative justice. Remember, projects are due in a few weeks! They better not be late, or you'll automatically get a zero." With that, our professor grabs his things and leaves.

"He really wastes no time in between classes, does he?" Paige laughs.

"Nope." Oliver gets up and stalls for a second, wavering beside Paige and I's table.

"What are you doing?" I ask him. He usually leaves and returns to his apartment since he has no other classes on Thursdays.

"I'm waiting for you guys." He says.

"Awww, Hads, I told you he has a heart." Paige giggles again.

"Paige, shut up and grab your stuff." He grabs her bag off the floor and hands it to her, doing the same thing with mine.

"Ol, do you have a hot date or something? What's the rush?" I question. I've never seen him like this. It's weird.

"Just hurry up. I want to get lunch with you two idiots, and all the good seats in the dining hall will be taken."

"The good seats?" I ask.

"The ones in the corner away from everybody else," Paige answers for him. I look between them and grab my stuff. We make our way out the door when Ryan stops me.

"Hey, Hads, can I talk to you?"

"No." Oliver grabs my arm and starts pulling me towards the stairs.

"Oliver, what's with you? Let go of me!" I'm whisper yelling now. I don't want to cause a scene with my brother's mood.

"Yeah, sorry, Ryan! We're late for a thing!" Paige cheerfully says and grabs my other arm, leading me away. What is with these two today?

"Guys, let go! He just wants to chat. I'll meet you at the dining hall." I shake from the holds they have on me, and they're unmoving—like statues. Oliver looks like my bodyguard, and Paige just looks confused.

"Guys, It's fine. Just go." I tell him.

"No." They both say at the same time. I tilt my head at them and make an annoyed face.

"Okay, then stay here and eavesdrop for all I care.

Whatever!" I turn on my heel and walk back to where Ryan is standing, looking somewhat confused about what just happened, which makes two of us. "Hey, sorry, those two are being weird today. I think the lecture might have rattled them or something. What's up?"

"So, the hockey team has this banquet every year at the end of our season, and I was wondering if you wanted to go with me this year?"

Either Oliver or Paige scoffs behind me, and I ignore it. "Oh, I wasn't expecting that. Um. Sure, just as friends, though." I smile at that last part. I've always made sure Ryan and I never crossed that line and got all weird. I enjoy having him as a friend, and trying to figure out my feelings about Grant has been a big mess. It wouldn't be fair of me to have something with Ryan while still trying to figure my life out.

"I know, Hads. Just as friends. I didn't want to go stag this year, you know?"

"Yeah, I get it! Just text me the details and stuff!"

"Sounds good!" He turns and walks away, and I do the same while keeping my head down, not wanting to make eye contact with either Paige or Oliver right now. We walk in silence, and when we get halfway down the stairs, Oliver finally speaks.

"If he touches you or lays a finger on you, I'm giving Paige the first swing, and then I'm kicking that kid's ass." Paige squeals at that.

"Geez, okay. What do you have against him, Ol?" I'm genuinely curious. He's never been so keen to hit someone before, well not *that* much, anyway.

"I just don't think he deserves you. Rumor has it, anyway."

"Those are rumors for a reason. Who knows if

they're true? Plus, he's been respectful to me the entire time we've been doing our project. So back off." I said that harshly, but Oliver has to realize he can't control me or my decisions. He doesn't know Ryan like I do.

"My gut is never wrong about someone, Hads. He just gives me...icky vibes." Paige and her gut. I trust her, but she just doesn't get it.

"Guys, I understand you're trying to protect me, but I don't need you to. It's my life. I appreciate you both, but let me make my own decisions. Okay?"

They look at each other and then look at me. Paige nods first, and Oliver barely moves his head.

"Good. Thank you. Now let's eat. I'm starving." I say as I turn and walk down the remaining stairs and out the door.

Oliver scoffs at something and looks a bit pale. He's been weird the past few days. Paige has been the same, but Ol has been odd. I would ask him, but I guarantee he won't tell me why. So I just leave him be for now.

✕

I get back to my dorm after that weird lunch with Paige and Oliver. Oliver and I were silent for most of the time, while Paige mostly talked about how Amelia made a new playlist for her to listen to. I open my door and Taylor is sitting at her desk with her textbooks open.

"Getting ahead on studying for finals?" I ask her.

"Nope, I have a paper due next week. When have you known me to get ahead on something?"

"Fair point. How are you? I feel like we keep missing each other lately." Every time I come back, she's leaving, and vice versa. Usually, we would talk at night, but we've both been too tired.

"I'm alright. I'm going on a date this weekend." She says, smiling at me.

"Oh, do tell, with who?" I ask, sitting down on the edge of my bed.

"This kid from my journalistic research class. His name is Alex. He's really cute, and I'm excited. I haven't been on a date in a while."

"Yeah, it's mostly been one-night stands, right?" I ask, knowing the answer.

"Hey! Don't judge!"

"I'm not, nor would I ever! Women deserve to not be shamed for having one-night stands. Men don't get shit on for it. They get high-fived. As a matter of fact," I stand, walk over to her, and high-five her, "I feel better now."

"Thank you. Anyways, it's on Friday night, so don't wait up." She tells me.

"I won't be here Friday night anyway, it's Ella's birthday and she's hosting us at her apartment for dinner and a sleepover. I think she wants us all to drink."

"Oh, good. If my date goes well, it'll be better knowing you won't be walking in on us like that one time."

"I wouldn't have walked in on you guys if you gave me notice or left a note on the door! A bit more heads-up would have been nice. I saw that guy's bare ass, and I haven't unseen it since." That moment was a core memory for Taylor and I's friendship, and we laugh about it now, but it scarred me freshman year. Sometimes I still have nightmares about it.

"I know! I've told you before that there wouldn't be a next time, and there hasn't been!" She tells me, looking back at her textbooks.

"Yes, thankfully. I think I'm going to go take some pictures. Do you want to come with me?" I ask her. I also write myself a note to text my parents later. I usually update them once a day on how things are, but I've forgotten the past few days.

"No, it's okay. I want to get more of this paper done since I will be busy this weekend. Have fun, though!"

"If you want a break to get coffee, text me, and I'll meet you at the library," I say while grabbing the camera equipment I keep under my bed.

"Sounds good. See ya, Hads!" Taylor tells me as she puts her headphones back on.

"Bye, Tay!" I say while shuffling down the hallway of our dorm.

35

Hadleigh

  It's Friday night, and I'm sitting in Paige's car. We're going to Ella's house for her birthday dinner and a sleepover. Amelia's sitting shotgun and is playing music from her playlist titled 'I miss everything' which she described to me as yet another one of her depression playlists.

  Which is exactly how we want to feel before a party. Right.

  I also don't know why we let Paige drive because she's the slowest driver that I've ever seen. I swear Paige is like someone's grandma hidden in a 20-year-old's body.

  "Paige, the speed you're driving combined with the sad-ass music is making time stand still back here." I'm in the backseat with my eyes half closed from how tired I feel.

  "I told Paige I could drive, but she threatened to put sugar in her own gas tank so she could drive. You know she hates when other people are behind the wheel." Amelia tells me.

  "I don't *hate* it. I just prefer to be the one driving. Plus, I'm a safe driver, so both of you hush. We're here." She tells us as she puts the car in park. We all get out and grab the food we brought. Ella insisted on making the entire dinner, but we couldn't let her do that on her birthday, so we all made one dish. I made Pho, which is a noodle soup with beef broth, ginger, onions, and fish sauce. My mom usually makes the broth herself, but I had to improvise since the kitchen in my dorm hall is terrible. I used to eat this all the time at home, and was excited to make it again. Paige made homemade mac and cheese, which one of her hometown friends sent her the recipe for. Apparently, Paige was over for dinner a lot as a kid, and she loved eating it. Amelia brought snacks for the movies we're going to watch all night. She bought Doritos, goldfish crackers, my favorite crinkle-cut chips, all of Ella's favorite candy, and a bottle of white wine.

 We walk up to the second floor of the building to Ella's apartment. She doesn't live far from campus—about fifteen minutes. We knock and she yells at us to come in, so we do. It smells like tacos in here. We look over to where Ella stands in her kitchen, and she has an entire taco bar laid out on her table. There's chicken and steak with an assortment of vegetables and rice and more toppings in a ton of bowls. Ella has also made her famous homemade guacamole and cupcakes. It seems that she is frosting those right now. I swear there are mini churros on top. Ella has an entire part of the table dedicated to drinks, and it looks like she made us all margaritas for tonight.

 I'm so excited.

 Ella's apartment is so very her. Her floor plan is wide open. There's a little hallway with a shoe rack and coat closet when you walk in. That hallway opens into the kitchen and dining room area, connecting with an arched wall to the living room. Her kitchen is small, but it works well enough for her. The dining area has a big table that can comfortably fit around six people and a wine rack filled with wine and other alcoholic beverages. Her living room has two half couches that are brown in color. Her apartment is very neutral-toned basically everywhere. The walls are beige all around, but there are pops of color everywhere. Ella's a plant mom, at least that's how she describes herself. There are plants all over her apartment. She has a neon sign in the front hallway that says 'that bitch' which fits Ella very well. It glows a muted pink when it's on. There are blankets scattered all over her living room. We'll all huddle in the living room tonight and sleep on her couches that pull out with the comfiest blankets. Ella probably has some black market blanket dealer because I've never felt blankets comfier than hers. She has a bookshelf in her living room, next to her TV, and a few in her bedroom. Those are white, and the one in the living room has vines and fairy lights on it.

Ella's birthday is April 4th, so technically we missed it by a few days, but she and Alissa went out for a night on the town since the rest of us were busy. Ella wanted to do something more lowkey for the four of us, so we decided on dinner and getting drunk in the comfort of her apartment. I'm excited for a night of just us since we won't get to have many of these get-togethers next year.

All three of us put down our dishes on the open parts of her counter, and she hugs us all simultaneously. "I'm so happy you're here!" She pulls back and sways a bit. Yeah, she has definitely been drinking already. Good for her.

"Happy birthday, Miss Ella," Amelia says.

"Yes, happy birthday, my girl! I was going to bring balloons that said 22 on them, but I was forbidden." Paige says.

"Happy birthday!" I say, making myself comfortable at the dining room table.

"The taco bar is all ready for us! Let's eat, but first, everyone takes a margarita. We are getting fucked up tonight." Ella practically shoves them in our faces, and we each take one.

"I think Paige is going to be drunk after half of this," Amelia says. She's right. I might be too. I haven't had alcohol in a while.

"That's fine by me. You guys know I only drink around you guys." Paige says while sipping her drink and sitting at the table. We all grab our plates and make our tacos. As does everyone else, I grab a bowl of Pho and a side of Paige's mac and cheese. We sit around the table and discuss the many topics of our lives. We laugh, joke, and fuck around until we're all full of alcohol and good food. By the end of dinner, we're all drunk and giggly. Ella's a master at cooking. I always love what she makes. We help clean up dinner, and eventually, we're sprawled on the couches in her living room with blankets enveloping us. Ella and I are on one of them, and Paige and Amelia are on the other.

"I think we should watch a horror movie!" Paige says, eyes wide.

"Paige, you watch horror movies alone at night in the dark like a psycho. You know I won't watch them with you. Tonight is no different. I say we watch a travel documentary!" Amelia says, slightly slurring the last few words.

"No, no, no. It's Ella's birthday. She should pick what we watch!" I say to them a bit louder because we are all shouting at this point.

"Okay! I'll pick...." She pauses for a second, taking another sip of her margarita. *"John Tucker Must Die!"* Amelia groans.

"We watched that one last time, but it's fun, so I'm fine with that." She takes a sip from the bottle of wine she brought straight from the bottle. She doesn't even have a glass.

"I love this one! It's got so many good cliches in it. Plus, I'm feeling sleepy anyway, so I won't feel bad if I doze off since I've seen it before." Paige says, yawning at the end of her sentence.

"Nobody's allowed to fall asleep on my birthday! We're staying up all night!" Ella yells at us as she queues up the movie. It's only around 10 pm, so I'm not tired yet, but Paige likes to go to sleep early. I know Amelia's awake because she stays up late every single night, often texting our group chat random memes in the early morning hours. The movie starts playing, and we all settle in for a cozy night. Around halfway through it, we get up to get snacks, passing them back and forth. By the end of it, Paige is asleep and sprawled across Amelia while Ames plays with her hair. I don't know when or how it happens, but eventually, we all fall asleep against each other while more movies that I can't name play in the background. I feel drunk and happy while I drift off into sleep.

※

I wake up sprawled on Ella's couch. I look over and see Amelia's curly brown hair underneath a blanket on the other couch, and Ella is quietly sleeping next to me. I hear more crunching and make my way into Ella's kitchen. I spot Paige sitting on the floor eating Doritos in the dark. Ella's kitchen has enough room on the floor that she can sit comfortably. I turn the light on, and she flinches at me. I sit down next to her, and she mindlessly passes me the bag of my favorite chips that are on the counter above us.

"What are you doing in here? It's 5 in the morning, P." I ask her.

"I couldn't sleep, so I came here to snack a bit. Did I wake you? I'm sorry, I wasn't trying to." She says, a bit sadder. She might still be drunk, but I think I am too.

"No, you didn't wake me. Why couldn't you sleep?"

"I had a nightmare, but it's no big deal. It happens a lot, and I'm usually hungry after. Amelia sometimes meets me in our kitchen and snacks with me at home. It's sort of a routine we have." She says.

"What was your nightmare about?" I hear footsteps coming towards us, which I assume are Ella and Amelia. It is. They enter our field of vision and look about as good as I feel. Ella's curly hair is all over the place, and Amelia looks...relatively normal actually. This is probably around the time she goes to bed every night.

"What are you guys doing?" Ella asks as Amelia sits down, having done this before, apparently.

"Paige and I couldn't sleep, so we decided to snack on the floor. Come join us." I say as I pat the spot next to me, and she sits right down and grabs for the chips. We snack in silence for a bit when Ella finally talks.

"Leo stood up for me at work the other day, and I realized that maybe he's a human being and not a demon inside a skin suit." I don't think she realized she called him Leo, but I'm not going to be the one to mention it.

"What?" Amelia says as her eyes get wide. Paige's eyes light up, being the only one in the group who likes to ship people together. It's funny that Paige loves relationships, but since I've known her, she has never been in a serious one.

"I was having a rough day. There were some things going on with my sister and trying to handle the internship, and he helped me out with some things. I was stressed, and he took the blame for a mistake I had made. I realize he might not be as shitty of a person as I thought he was." All of us are stunned. None of us has said a word since she started talking. Ella complimenting Leo is something I thouhgt I'd never hear—in this lifetime at least.

"Wait, I thought you hated him?" I ask.

"I didn't say I changed my mind about him—he's still a shit bitch—but he might have more human DNA in his body than I originally thought." She says.

"*Shit bitch*?" Paige says under her breath.

"Someone please change the subject off of Zimmerman or I'm going to need more alcohol." Ella says to the room.

"Paige, what was your nightmare about?" I ask her straight up and Amelia nudges me with her elbow—shooting me a harsh look.

"It was nothing, just a memory I'd rather not relive." She's talking quietly right now, and I feel bad for bringing it back up. "I know I say it all the time, but you guys really mean a lot to me. My home life was never great, and I always felt left behind as a kid. When I came here and met all of you guys, that changed. Just the fact that you guys will sit on the floor with me and eat snacks makes me want to burst into tears. I used to do this alone when I was younger, but now I'm not alone, so thank you." She says, some tears running down her face. All of us are silent, letting those words sink in.

Ella reaches out to her and holds her hand. "I know the feeling, P. I have a shitty parental situation too. I'm always here for you if you want to talk about it. Ask Hads. I'm a very good listener."

"She really is. Ells gives great advice, too." I say.

Paige looks up at Ella and smiles, her eyes still wet with tears. "Thank you." Ella simply smiles at her and a look of understanding crosses each of their features.

"Anyways, on a lighter note, my next trip has officially been booked! I'm heading to Crater Lake in Oregon. It has one of the deepest lakes in the United States and is on top of the Cascade Mountain Range. I'm very excited about it." She smiles, and I don't think I've ever seen Amelia smile more than when she talks about her travels.

"That sounds fun Ames. When is that?" Paige asks her.

"This summer, probably in July." She tells us.

All of us are swaying a bit, still drunk from the shenanigans from the night before.

"Grant's eyes are blue like a lake." I clamp my hand over my mouth, wondering why that just came tumbling out. The girls all look at me like I just confessed my love for him.

"Are they now?" Amelia asks me.

"I've never noticed that. Please tell us more, Hads." Ella is leading me. She wants me to spill my guts.

"It was just an observation I had. I blame Amelia.

She was the one who was talking about lakes!" I say, yelling at her, and then we all start overlapping with our shouts and arguing. We stay on the kitchen floor until around 9, talking and gossiping about all sorts of things. We all get up and start to make breakfast, with mimosas, of course.

"I cannot handle any more alcohol," I say.

"The only cure for a hangover is more booze. Trust me." Ella says, throwing a kitchen towel at me. Amelia saunters in and grabs one, handing it to Paige and then taking one herself.

Ella continues to make the french toast while I scramble the eggs. Paige is sipping a mimosa while quietly mouthing along to the lyrics, and Amelia turns on her breakfast-making playlist, which consists of upbeat songs that we all sing to in the kitchen. When breakfast is over, we all sit on the living room floor and play board games until Ella politely kicks us out because she needs to take a nap before going out with Alissa tonight. They're going to a concert not too far from campus.

"That works for me. I have plans with Oliver tonight to work on our project for criminology, and I'd rather not be drunk still when we meet." Paige says to us.

"I have plans to blackmail a U.S. Senator tonight, so I should be going as well." We all stare at Amelia as she gathers her stuff. Paige throws her clothes and things in her tote bag that says 'dangerous women read' on it. That one's my favorite of hers. We all gather in a group hug before we head out.

"Thank you guys so much for coming over to celebrate with me. You're the best friends a bitch like me could ask for." We all smile at that and shuffle out her door and into Paige's car.

"Paige, please go over the speed limit this time, or I'm grabbing your wheel and running us into a telephone pole." Amelia says while hooking her phone into Paige's car cord.

"Amelia, I'll delete all the music off your phone! Let me drive how I want!"

Ames puts both her hands up, conceding, and I sit in the back seat and laugh at them.

That was one of my favorite nights we have had together this year. I wish it never ended. In the future, I'm not sure where we'll all be, and I don't know how many more nights we'll have like that one. *Is it odd to miss something that isn't truly gone yet?* I don't think much on that as Amelia starts playing *Good Days* by SZA, and we drive back to campus.

36

Hadleigh

  I'm walking into the library cafe for Ella and I's annual Sunday sit down when I run into my friend Drew. They were walking out of the library while I was walking in.

  "Hey, Hads! How have you been?" They ask me.

  "I've been good, actually! Really busy. Did you see we have a final project and an exam in bio? How stupid is that?" The workload this semester has been awful. I have so many projects and tests I can barely keep up.

  "Yeah, I'm halfway to dropping out at this point. I'll see you later. I have to run to work right now."

  "Sounds good, don't work too hard!" I yell as they walk away.

  "Definitely not!" They say back to me. I settle into our usual booth and wait for Ella. She's usually here before me. Oddly, she's not here now. I check my phone to ensure she didn't text me to cancel when she comes in and sulks into the booth.

  "Is everything okay?" I ask, a bit worried about her.

  "Yes. No. I don't know." She says. I've never seen her look so off before.

  "Do you want to talk about it?"

  "No."

  "Okay, that's fine. I'm always here if you want to talk about anything, though. Just because you're like my older sister doesn't mean you can't come to me with stuff too." At that, she smiles.

"I'm okay, really. I might've had a regretful hookup last night that I wish I could erase from my memory." She tells me quietly.

"Yikes, that doesn't sound fun. Female or male or nonbinary?"

"Unfortunately, male."

"That sounds about right. I'm sorry."

"It's okay. Alissa and I got super fucked up last night, so it was kind of my fault. I had fun until I woke up this morning next to someone I shouldn't have, but it's fine. I'm fine. How are you?"

Before I can answer, Amelia plops down in our booth.

"Hey, guys. What's up?" She makes herself comfortable and looks at us both. When she looks at Ella. "You look like shit."

"She had a rough night." I say to Ames.

She raises her eyebrows. "Clearly."

"Amelia, I can't deal with your emotional warfare shit this morning. What are you doing here?" Ella asks her.

"Oh, right. Paige is working on this project for her investigations class, and she's taken over the apartment. She's playing detective right now. It was a bit scary, so I came to get her a breakfast sandwich and to get me some coffee. She tried to trick me into getting her some, but I'm not handing her a guaranteed panic attack in a cup."

"That's valid."

"Yeah, that makes sense." I agree with them.

"That girl is the last person I ever expected to

be into murder so much. It's quite the dichotomy. She has turned our apartment into a crime scene that she has to investigate. Apparently, she set up some famous murder scene and is trying to figure out what the police could've done better for this project. It's scary how good at this she is."

"I agree. That girl could solve anything if you just give her enough time. She scares me sometimes." Ella says that, and I laugh along with Amelia. Paige is the sunniest person we know, but she has this other side to her that she doesn't show many people. I'd trust that girl handling my murder case. It's weird.

"Paige also told me about a certain conversation that occurred between our little Hads here and Ryan the other day. Care to elaborate on that?" She's looking right at me.

Fuck. I was going to tell Ella anyway, so I might as well just tell them both right now. "Ryan asked me to go with him to the hockey banquet they have every year." Ella's mouth is wide open.

"Okay, Amelia, you're staying for a minute. I'm grabbing us coffee, and we're fully discussing why this is a horrible idea, and you're not telling him yes. Okay?" I don't say a word about that. Amelia starts laughing again—probably knowing I told him yes—and Ella just turns and goes to the counter to get us coffee.

"Paige told me she and Oliver tried to get you out of the situation. Why didn't you go with them? I thought you were trying to figure things out in that big brain of yours with Grant?" Amelia asks me, and she seems genuine. I want to answer her, but I'll wait until Ella returns.

"Amelia, what's new with you? Anything?"

"Not much, just the usual. Changing my major and disappointing my parents for not following the path they wanted me to. It's no big deal. Answer my question."

"Okay, I don't think we have time to unpack all that, but you told them about your major change finally? I'm guessing they didn't take it too well." I say to her. I feel like I've been a bad friend to the girls. I didn't even know Amelia was feeling this way—disappointed that her parents don't get why she wants to study journalism. I've been too wrapped up in my entire situation that I've neglected my friends and their problems.

"No, they didn't, but that doesn't matter. I think it's a better fit for me, but my parents disagree. It really isn't a big deal." Ella comes back, and Amelia scooches in and gives her room to sit down. Ella hands me my coffee and takes a long sip of hers. "What did Ryan do?"

I told her how he cornered me after class and asked me while Paige and Oliver tried to drag me away. I tell them how I already said yes to going to the banquet with Ryan, but just as friends. I also told them about what Paige and Oliver were saying, and how their thoughts about it were nice but I can make my own decisions. "But why does saying yes feel like it's carrying some sort of weight?"

They both look at each other, and Amelia abruptly gets up and grabs her stuff. "I should get back to Paige. She's probably halfway to tearing one of our walls down. I'll see you guys soon." When I look back at Ella, she meets my eyes for a half second and then looks away. What's going on with everyone lately?

"Why did she just leave like that, and why can't

you look me in the eye right now? Is there a stain on my skirt?" I'm so confused. *Why are they being so weird?*

"No, it's just, well, maybe the decision is weighing on you because you have feelings for someone else." She tells me.

"What?"

"It was just an idea."

"You guys don't know my feelings."

"I know we don't."

"Exactly. So stop hypothesizing about them."

"Anyways, we want to help you get ready for it, of course. Just text the group chat what you're wearing. I can do your makeup and hair, and Paige, Amelia, and Alissa can be moral support."

"What makes you think I need moral support?" I ask her, a bit sharply.

"Come on Hads. We're your big sisters. Let us be there for you in the big moments."

"Ells, I don't know if this qualifies as a big moment." I look down at my coffee.

"Even if it's a small moment. Let us be there for you. I won't get to do this next year after I graduate, you know."

Wow, she's good. Guilt tripping me into asking her for help. I have to hand it to her, it's kind of working. "Fine. You guys can help. But unlike last time, nobody will be hiding in the closet."

"Hads please, I've been out of the closet for years. I refuse to hide any more than I already have. So, you have a deal." She smiles at me. I'm thankful that this college has brought us all together. I can't imagine not having them in my life. It's still hard for me to ask for their help sometimes. My brother is great, but I've never had sisters before. Paige, Ella, and Amelia are my non-biological sisters now. I can't imagine not joining the book club during my freshman year. My life would look so different, and that thought scares me. The fact that one or two decisions I make can alter my life so drastically. I think that's what has always scared me about the future, thought I can feel the walls I have up all the time, cracking more and more each day. Because of those three, the guard I've always had up is slowly starting to crumble. THey've proven that no matter how many other people I push away, they'll never go far.

"Thank you, by the way." I say to her.

"For what?"

"For dealing with me and helping me through some tough spots this year. I don't think I ever told you how much I appreciated these weekly coffee dates."

"Hads, I'm your friend. You're not someone I have to deal with. You're someone I truly love spending time with. All of us do. We love you for who you are. You shouldn't have to change anything about yourself to be with someone else. You're perfect and worthy of everything as you are."

Her saying that to me is making me a bit glassy-eyed. I don't normally cry, especially in front of others, but I let one tear fall before I push them back. She wipes it from my face and proceeds to talk about what she and Alissa did last night.

Who knew books could bring me these amazing people into my life?

I sure didn't.

But damn, I got lucky.

37

Hadleigh

"Hads, stay right there, please, babes." I'm sitting in my desk chair while Alissa does my hair and Ella works on my makeup. Paige and Amelia are on my bed discussing a show they have been watching. Something about some gangs from the old days and Cillian Murphy.

Tonight is the night. The banquet. It's only a semi-formal dress code, but Ella would die if any of us went anywhere that's remotely fancy and didn't look our best. I was going to throw on this old dress that I had, but Ella bought me one, saying it was an end-of-the-year graduation present. I can't exactly say no to her—especially since she got my size and measurements correct. I swear she came in here while I was sleeping and measured me.

I have my dress on already. It's a black belted mini dress. The sleeves are mesh, and it has a sweetheart neckline. It's A-line, and Alissa is putting a black bow in my hair to match it. Ella keeps my makeup simple by doing a quick sweep of brown on my lids and black eyeliner. It's not that fancy of an event, so lip gloss and chapstick are where it's at. Plus, it won't get ruined since I'm not kissing anyone tonight.

At least I hope I'm not.

"So, Alissa, what do you do now that you've graduated?" I ask her. I'm genuinely curious because she's been an excellent addition to our little friend group. She and Ella have this fire in them, and it's nice that Ella has another extrovert to go out with and get rowdy.

"I'm a software engineer for this company that analyzes different data sets."

"Wow, so you're like a genius." I'm not that surprised, though. Alissa exudes confidence and academic excellence.

"Sort of. I code a lot of different things and gain insights into our products. The other day I spent hours debugging this one software. It took me forever, but I got it done. I did it all by myself. It felt good."

"So, unlike Paige who plots different murder scenarios in her head, you code things? That's cool as fuck." That was Amelia who said that. She seems interested as well.

"Yeah, well, my parents wanted me to go to school for something different, but it wasn't what I wanted. I was always interested in code and computers ever since I was little. They eventually warmed up to me doing what I wanted, thankfully."

"That's nice." Amelia sulks back a little bit and turns back to Paige.

"Okay, Hadleigh babes, your hair is done!" Alissa fluffs my hair a bit and turns the mirror.

"Liss, I love that bow in her hair. It's so cute!" Ella says as she sprays setting spray on my face. "Okay, Hads, take a look. Ah! This was so fun!" She practically squeals at me.

I stand up, walk over to my long mirror, and look at myself. I look good. My hair is curled and out of my face with the long, black bow. My makeup is simple but accentuates my features nicely. This dress also fits me like a glove. Ella and Alissa did good. I turn around to face them.

Paige is nearly in tears, Amelia has a soft look on her face that I've never seen before. Ella looks like a proud mom, and Alissa is smiling at me. I love these girls so much that it hurts. "Thanks, guys," I say, hoarsely. My throat dry right now for some reason.

"No problem, Hads. We love you!" Paige comes up to me and hugs me.

"Paige, we didn't even help," Amelia says to her.

"Moral support is still helping!"

"Paige, do not get tears on her dress! I will kill you!" Ella says as she pulls her off me. I pull them all in for a group hug.

Paige's hand finds my dress and slips it into the pockets on it. "THE DRESS HAS POCKETS! OH MY GOD!" Ella simply smiles at us. I love them so much.

"I don't know what I did to deserve you all. Thank you for everything."

"We love you so much, Hads, but do not mess up your makeup. You never cry in front of us. This is not the right time." There are a few knocks at the door. Damn, I'm really bad with timing this, aren't I?

"Don't worry. You guys don't have to hide this time. It's okay." I open the door and find Ryan standing there. He looks nice. He's wearing black pants and dress shoes, with a white button-up and a black bow tie. Cute, I guess.

"Oh, hi, everyone. I didn't know you all would be here. You ready to go, Hads?" He looks me up and down, and I feel a bit on the spot right now. This feels weird. Is it just me?

"Yeah, I'm ready. I just have to put my shoes on." I

grab my chunky black pumps and throw them on. They give me a couple of inches, but I haven't worn heels in a while. It's going to take me a minute to get used to them again.

"Ryan, just so you're aware, I already have three perfectly planned how-to-get-away with-murder scenarios in my head. If you hurt her or try anything funny tonight, I will be using them on you, that I can promise you." Paige says that, meaning it to be a threat, but coming from her, it doesn't really sound like one.

"Paige, it's okay, calm down." I say to her. "You guys can let yourself out. Taylor should be home soon, so don't bother locking it."

Ella blows me a kiss, and the rest of them don't move. I close my door behind me, and I swear I hear Paige saying that Grant bought me flowers and Ryan didn't. I brush that off. I wasn't going to expect them. This isn't even a date. It's just a banquet.

Ryan offers me his arm, and I thread mine through his. "Shall we?"

"We shall." We have to drive to this banquet area, so he leads me to his car. He opens my door for me and heats up the car.

"You look great tonight, Hads."

"Thanks. You do too."

My stomach feels nervous, and I feel like throwing up a little bit, but I shove that down as Ryan drives away and heads to our destination.

✕

Grant

Tonight is the night I've been dreading for weeks. Ryan followed through on his threat to ask Hads to be his date, and she accepted. I was going to ask her with a bit more gravitas, but he beat me to it. I was waiting for the right time—like Oliver said—but I was too late.

And now I'm going to the banquet by myself. Well, with Jacks and Claire. It hurts me a bit to see them here together. Don't get me wrong, I'm happy for Jacks, but I wish Hads was beside me tonight. I could've asked my mom to come with me, but I didn't think she would want to make the trip for just one night, so I didn't ask her. Plus, we ended our season kind of shitty. We lost in overtime to this other team that we could've easily beaten. It was an off day for the entire team, but nevertheless, we still did well this year. I'm proud of the team. I just wish I had someone to share it with. The three of us got to the venue early. The banquet is held yearly in the same ballroom in this one restaurant. The round tables, the dance floor, and the buffet are all here —same as last year. Some of the team has trickled in, along with our Coach standing in the corner talking to a bunch of administrators. Jacks pats me on the back, he knows what I'm feeling tonight, but he forced me into my clothes and got me out the door.

I'm wearing all black—like I'm at a funeral. I have a nice button-up and pants on. I even threw a jacket on because I was cold. We head to the table where all the sophomores sit. Coach groups all the class levels together for some reason. Jacks and I sit next to each other, and Claire smiles at me from two seats over.

"How are you doing, Grant?" She asks me. Claire's pretty. She and Jacks make a cute couple. Claire has long blonde hair—curly tonight—and a bunch of freckles on her face. She's wearing this cute pink dress that reminds me of this one sweater Hadleigh was wearing one night. Fuck, don't go there. "I'm alright. I just want to get tonight over with."

"Well, if you want someone to dance with for a song or two, I'll dance with you unless Jacks steals me first. I don't want to see you sulking all night. You deserve to have fun after the season you had." She pats my hand, and I smile at her.

"Thanks, Claire, I appreciate it." I'm sitting facing the door, which I regret because I see Ryan walk in first, and then I see her.

Her.

She looks fucking perfect, and it's killing me that she's here with him. As if she senses I'm looking at her, she turns her gaze onto me. Every time we do this dance—I look at her, and she's looks back at me—the entire world fades away. It's like we're in our own little world. I know she feels it too. *I know it.* But I can't do anything about it—at least not tonight, or maybe ever. She's wearing a classic Hads dress, black with a bow on it, and in her hair I now notice as she averts her gaze from mine. The sleeves are mesh, and I know she's cold because she isn't wearing tights underneath her dress like she always does when she wears skirts. Ryan looks over at me and flashes me a middle finger, and I feel like I'm going to be sick. I excuse myself and go to the bathroom to splash some cold water on my face.

Jacks follows me in. "Are you okay?"

I'm fisting the sinks so hard my knuckles are turning white. "Fine."

"I know it's killing you to have to watch her with him. That doesn't mean it's over for you, though. I saw how you both looked at each other. Neither of you wanted to look away. There's still hope. I have a feeling it will all work out, G."

"I don't want to give myself hope, J. I might just end up disappointed. It's fine. I'm fine." I'm not fine at all. All the memories of our study sessions, ice skating, and those damn stolen moments when I had her are flashing through my mind. I need to get out of my head before I explode. *Does she think about those as much as I do? Did they mean as much to her as they did me?*

"Ryan isn't sitting at our table either. There were too many sophomores, so Coach split us up. Let's go back, okay? Dinner's starting soon." I know he is saying that for my benefit, and I love him for it. It eases my mind a bit, knowing I won't have to watch them together at our table.

I take a deep breath. "Okay."

We head back to the table, and dinner flies by. I spend the entire time trying not to look at where they're sitting. Coach makes a speech I don't listen to and tells us to have a great night of dancing and fun.

Except I don't feel like dancing or doing anything. I'd rather be in my dorm than watch them dance together. Jacks and Claire excuse themselves from the table so they can dance. A slow song just came on. I recognize it. *Like Real People Do* by Hozier. I watch Jacks and Claire dancing to the song and notice Ryan and Hads next to them on the floor.

Fuck me. I can't do this. Here I am, sitting alone at the table while everybody is talking and having fun around me. I need to get out of here.

Except I don't move. I watch Hads. She has no clue how to slow dance, and it's adorable. Ryan is trying to lead without telling her what he's doing. She keeps tripping and stepping on him with her chunky heels. It hits me right in the chest. My heart is pounding right now, and then she looks over at me, and my heart stops.

We should just kiss like real people do.

The song narrates what I wish I could do, and she's staring at me. Hads is looking at me while dancing with Ryan. I don't avert my gaze. I let her know with my eyes that I've been watching her for this entire song. If I could speak to her with just my eyes, I would be saying:

Drop his hand, and dance with me instead.

He wants you, but I need you.

I'm halfway to grabbing you off the dance floor, sweeping you off your feet, and making you mine.

I want to be yours. Please give me a chance to be yours.

Never in my wildest dreams did I see you coming, but I'm so glad you're here. In my life, even if I don't get to have you how I want you.

I love you.

Let me love you how you deserve.

Please.

The song ends, and she and Ryan go off somewhere, but I lose them in the crowd on the dance floor. Claire and Jacks come back over, and Claire offers to dance with me, and I accept. The next song that's playing is *Can I Be Him* by James Arthur, and I want to die more than I did before. "We can wait for another song, Grant. I'm going to grab water. Do you want one?" Claire asks me.

"Uh, sure. That sounds good."

"Babe, do you want one?"

Jacks lifts his head and smiles. "I'll take whatever

you want to get me."

She smiles at him and leaves. That entire interaction makes me want to stick a fork in my eye. He's not doing it on purpose, he's just in love, and I'm not actually mad at him.

"How does it feel getting the top defensive player for the team this year?" Right. Before dinner, Coach gave out awards. Nothing too fancy, just some highlighting the team. Everyone gets one. I got the top defensive player for the team, and Jacks got the one for top blocks this season. We make a good team. I'm glad to have him by my side, on and off the ice.

"It felt good, I guess. I'm proud of how I played this year and glad I am still on the team…" I trail off because the only reason for that is here with someone else. I see her heading for the door from the corner of my eye. Is she leaving?

"Jacks, I'll be right back." I excuse myself and follow her out where she went. I think she's headed for the parking lot. She looked flustered, fuck. What just happened in the fifteen minutes after they left the dance floor?

※

Hadleigh

The song ends and Ryan pulls me off the dance floor. I hope he didn't see how I looked at Grant the entire time we danced. God, I knew I shouldn't have come tonight. Grant is dressed in all black, and when I first saw him, the look on his face hurt me. He looked so melancholy, but I brushed it off because he seemed to be having a decent time with Jacks. My stomach fluttered until I locked eyes with him while dancing, and I couldn't look away from him. His eyes were latched onto mine, and with the song playing in the background, I could barely concentrate on dancing. It was just him. He was the only one I saw for the three minutes that the song played.

    I don't know what's wrong with me. I came here with someone else and have been thinking about Grant the whole time. How he looks, what he's doing. When he got his award tonight, I felt a twinge of sadness seeping through me. He smiled and took a picture with his coach, and as soon as that was done, his smile dropped. It physically hurt me to see him fake smiles like that. He normally smiles with his whole face, but he just moved his mouth this time. Tonight just feels wrong. Everything about it. Ryan leads me into a nearby hallway.

    "Okay, look, I know I'm a crappy dancer, but these heels hurt, and that was the first time I've slow danced since prom senior year." I tell him.

    "You danced amazing, Hads. I don't care about that. You just look so sexy right now I can't handle it." He's leaning in and trying to kiss me. *Abort!*

    "Woah, Ryan. What are you doing?"

    "Do you wanna get out of here? Can we go to my car? God, you're perfect." He's running his hands up and down my dress. He pushes me into the hallway wall, grabs my hands, and puts them above my head.

    "Ryan, stop. We can't leave early. They haven't served dessert yet." I'm so confused. My mind is going a thousand miles a minute. I'm just trying to get him off of me.

    "Please, Hads, God, I want you so bad. Please just

let me have you finally. I've been waiting months for this." *Months?* What the fuck is going on? I feel like I'm going to throw up.

"Ryan, what are you saying right now?" He's trying to kiss my neck, and I push him off a bit with my legs. "Ryan! Stop for a second. What's going on?"

"Baby, I can't stop even if I wanted to. Just let me fuck you. You've pulled me on this string long enough."

"Ryan, we're friends. You agreed to this too."

"I bet if I pushed your panties aside, you'd be wet as hell for me. Us being friends was bullshit, Hads. I know you like me. Stop pretending." He moves his hands down under my dress, and I freeze. What the fuck is going on?

"Ryan, don't. I don't want this or you. Let me go." I shove him off and realize that Grant was right about him. He did just want me for sex. Fuck, this hurts. I can feel tears brimming. How could I be so stupid? Ryan seemed nice, and I fell for it again. I guess he never really wanted to be just friends. I have to get out of here. I need air. Ryan won't get off of me. He has me pinned against the wall, so I take a page out of Ella's book, knee him in the balls, and he falls to the floor.

"Don't fucking touch me or contact me ever again. I'll finish our project by myself." My voice sounds shaky, and I hate it. Tears are falling from my eyes because this happened again. I let someone in that I shouldn't have, and they played me. I feel so stupid right now. I walk towards the exit but must cross the ballroom again to get out. I don't know where Ryan took me, but nobody heard us, which scares me. *What was he going to do if I didn't knee him?* I can't think about that right now. I just need to get out of here.

Out. Out. Out.

I get out the doors and into the parking lot. I'm breathing heavily and crying in public. God I hate this, I grab my phone from the pocket of my dress. I'm about to text the girls to come to pick me up when someone touches my shoulder. I flinch, thinking it's Ryan, but a familiar face looks down at me when I turn around. He notices the tears on my face and tries to wipe them off, but I back away from him too. I'm too on edge right now. I don't want anyone touching me.

I'm the one who speaks first. "You were right." He doesn't say anything to that, but his face shows me that he knows what I'm talking about.

"I didn't want you to find out this way. Did he hurt you?" He's searching my face. "Hads, did he hurt you? Because I'll hurt him right back, just say the word."

"I'm sorry I didn't listen to you." I'm still crying. I feel exposed and vulnerable, not just because I'm in public but because I'm still crying. In half an hour, I've cracked and fallen apart. I feel wide open and on display for the entire world to see how I fucked up again. Grant being the only one that came to see the show—me breaking apart after not listening to his warnings.

"Baby, please don't apologize right now. You didn't do anything wrong." He steps closer to me, and I take another step back. I don't want anyone's pity right now—especially his. He holds out his jacket, and I realize I'm shaking, but I don't feel cold. I take his jacket and put it on, hoping to stop the shaking.

"Just stop, please. I—I just need a minute. So, say I told you so, and go away." I don't want him to leave me. I just feel so off-kilter that I'm pushing him away. It's what I always do. I'm never going to be able to stop doing that. It's just too easy. Letting him in right now would cause more harm then good—at least that's what my brain tells me right now. I look at my phone and text the girls an SOS to come to get me. I send them my location.

Ella: Are you okay?
Paige: I'm thinking of scenario number 3 for Ryan. It's the most painful.
Amelia: Paige, I'm helping with that.
Ella: We're on the way.

"Why do you want me to rub this in so badly? Hads, I'm not happy about this. It makes me fucking sick seeing you cry right now. Why do you want me to push the knife in deeper?"

"Because it's easier! It's easier than admitting that I made a mistake and trusting someone when I shouldn't have. It's easier than admitting it fucking happened again! That someone just used me for their own personal pleasure!" I'm sobbing at this point. I feel so angry at myself, at Ryan. Kyle. It all just fucking hurts. I thought I could move forward, but this proves I'll always be back in the same position—used and thrown away. "I can't think straight right now. Please just go back inside and leave me alone!" I'm full-on yelling at him.

"I won't." He says, unmoving.

I scoff. "You won't?"

"No."

"Grant, just leave! Why won't you just leave!"

"BECAUSE I LOVE YOU!" He shouts.

He what?

38

Grant

Considering what just happened, I'm kicking myself for blurting out that I love her in the middle of this parking lot. This is *not* how I wanted this to go. Fuck. I guess it's too late now.

"What did you just say?" She asks me. God, she looks so vulnerable right now, and all I want to do is put the pieces back together and tell her she's going to be fine. Because she's Hadleigh fucking Baker, and she shouldn't blame herself for Ryan being the worst person on the planet.

Speaking of Ryan, I've filed him away for later, but I'll kill that guy for what he did. I don't know the details yet, but maybe he'll tell me when I'm beating the shit out of him.

"I said I love you." I admit to her. She's standing there in my jacket, looking at me with tears in her eyes. I want to reach out and wipe them off, but she backed away last time. She's still in shock from whatever happened, and it's killing me not being able to touch her or hold her how I want to, but I don't want to make her uncomfortable.

"No, you don't." Is she trying to convince herself or me?

"I do. I—I love you, Hadleigh, so much." My voice is shaky, and I take a breath before speaking again.

"Why?"

"That's a stupid question." I say as I inch closer to her.

"No, it's not. You could have anybody you want. Why me?" She's still crying, and her voice is strained. I wipe a few tears from her face.

"Because when I'm with you, it stops. All of it. You're like…" I choose my words carefully because I'm really bad with metaphors and shit, but I need her to know how much I love her. "You're like the spring. Before you, I was in this state of just being. I was stuck in this never-ending winter. I was so cold and didn't know if I would ever get out of it. And then you came along. Our banter, the games we played, it melted every bad thing around me until all I saw was you." She's crying more now. I don't know if that's good or bad, but I keep going. "I wanted anything I could get from you. You made me feel all these new things, and I know you hated me, but I didn't care. I didn't care because if I had just a little bit of your heart, that was good enough for me. Hadleigh, God, you made me crazy, and you still do. I was going to ask you to come with me tonight, but Ryan wanted to beat me at this fictional game he's playing with me, and he used you to do that. I crashed your fucking date with him a couple of weeks ago because I couldn't stand the fact that he was using you, and I just wanted to be there to protect you. I'm so fucking sorry that he hurt you. I should've been the one to ask you to come with me, not him. I wanted to be the one dancing with you tonight. I didn't know if you felt the same way, so I was holding off to give you time to figure your mind out."

She looks rooted to the ground right now, her face is blank, and I'm scared. I just threw a lot of information at her, and I'm afraid. I'm afraid she'll laugh in my face, but I know she wouldn't do that. I'm breathing so heavily right now, but I take a calming breath before continuing.

"Hadleigh, I know this was a terrible time to tell you this, but I couldn't hold it in any longer. I *love* you, and it scares me because I feel like I might fail you at some point. Hell, I probably will if we give this a shot. Fuck, I'm horrible with words, baby, but my point is that I love you, and I don't want to let you go anytime soon. You're my green light. I've been reaching for you this whole time, unable to get to you. I want to be yours. Because every insecurity of mine fades when I'm with you. I want to banter and argue with you. I want you to hit me with that damn ruler you love so much and let me know when I'm being an idiot." I chuckle and notice that my face is wet. A few tears sprung out from my eyes while I was talking and pacing in front of her. She's still in the same spot, eyes wide, and I turn around and walk back inside. I've always laid all of my feelings out on the table, only for her to shrink back down. I hope this will help her realize that she wants me and wants to chase me down and prove herself wrong. Or this could be another big failure on my part.

Come get me, Hads.

※

Hadleigh

My feet won't move. Roots from the nearby trees have grown around them, and I need an axe to get them out. I'm feeling shocked and confused right now. Shocked about the whole Ryan situation and confused at everything Grant just said. He confesses all that and then turns and walks away. No. I don't think so.

"Where do you get off saying all that and then just waking away?" He stops walking, and I run straight into him. He catches my waist, lifts me up, and sets me on a nearby bench. He leans down and starts to undo the clasp on my shoes. I'm having a flashback to when he undid my skates for me.

"Why are you taking my shoes off? Are you afraid my height would give me more of an advantage for me to claw your eyes out?"

"I'm taking your shoes off because you looked uncomfortable wearing them. And if you tried to claw my eyes out, I'd let you." He looks at me when he says that, and my stomach somersaults. Neither of us talks while he removes my other shoe and sets it next to me on the bench. He's still kneeling before me, and now I'm looking down at him, only slightly. I want to run away from all of this. I don't think I can do this. The feelings in my head and heart are scaring me right now, and it just hits me—the words he just said.

"You love me." I basically whisper that as if it's a secret. As if he didn't just scream it to the world. He meets my eyes, and I brush a tear off his cheek, and he does the same to me.

"I do. So much." He admits in a low whisper.

"That scares me."

"I know, baby, it's okay." He gets up and sits next to me, his hand going to my back. "Can I?" I nod at him, and he starts rubbing my back. It's comforting. I feel safe in his presence right now. "Hads, you don't have to say anything back right now. I know your mind is going crazy at the moment."

I take a deep breath. That validation comforts me. I don't want to say anything I don't mean because that's not fair to Grant.

"I understand you might need some time to digest everything and heal from what happened tonight.. I'll wait as long as you need, and even if you figure out that you don't feel the same way I do, I'm not going anywhere. I'll always be here for you if you want me to be. You have my word." His hand is still rubbing my back, as a car pulls up. Ella hops out along with Paige and Amelia. They spot me and run over to where we are. I stand up, and Paige reaches her arms out and hugs me.

"Are you okay?" She asks me, concern in her voice. I've never been so happy for her presence. Amelia stands by her and catches my hand, squeezing it. Letting me know she's here for me too. Ella bypasses me and goes up to Grant.

"Where is he?" Her voice sounds cold and distant. Damn, she's scaring me right now.

"Inside."

"Thank you." She tries to get by him, but Grant puts his arm out.

"I'll take care of him. Just make sure Hads is okay. She needs you right now." She looks at him, reaches out, touches his arm, and turns around. She searches my face and hugs me so tight I can't breathe, and I let her. "Are you ready to go? Are you okay?"

"I'm okay, I think. Just a bit shaky." I tell her, tears still falling, a bit slower now.

"Did you leave anything inside? I can go grab it." Amelia offers.

"No, I just had everything in my pockets. I don't need to go back inside." I say as Ella nods toward her car, and as I start walking, the girls form a semi-circle around me. Protecting me, like they're my bodyguards. I realize I'm still wearing Grant's jacket as it brushes against my skin. "Give me one second." I run to where Grant is. He's on the steps to the building, about to head back inside, when I grab his arm, and he turns around.

"What is it?" I hold out his jacket. "Keep it."

"I'm not cold anymore. Take it, please." I tell him, my voice breaking.

"No. It looks better on you, anyway. I'll be fine." He smiles at me, a genuine smile, leans down, and kisses my cheek. "Was that okay?" My face feels hot all of a sudden. I nod.

"Yeah." I smile at him. I'm still a mess, but the comfort feels nice, even if I'm confused and off-kilter.

"Get home safe. I'll see you soon." He turns around and walks into the building and out of my sight. I stand at the entrance for a moment, turn around, and run back to my girls. They're leaning against Ella's car, and they perk up when they see me coming back. Amelia opens the door for me, and I shuffle into the back seat. Paige follows me. Amelia's riding shotgun, and Ella starts the car. Paige looks at me and asks me if I'm okay again. I don't know if it's the heightened emotions from the past hour or what, but I burst into tears. Paige shuffles over, holds me in her embrace, and lets me cry. They don't judge me for crying. They don't say a word as we drive back to campus. Paige just holds me while I cry all over her shirt. *Ribs* by Lorde is playing quietly on the speaker, but my sobs are louder than it.

"Thank you for coming to get me." I say through tears.

"Anytime you need us, we're there, Hads. Do you

want me to call Oliver?" Paige asks.

"No, I'll talk to him at some point." I don't need his cold stares right now. Just these three people's warmth around me. The car goes quiet.

"Hads, you don't have to tell us what happened yet. Just feel what you're feeling and tell us when you're ready," Ella says, and I nod. I slouch back into Paige's embrace and cry more.

As long as I have them, I'll never be alone again. But my heart feels empty all of a sudden. It might have finally iced over, never to be thawed again.

39

Hadleigh

It's been a week since the banquet. I've gone to class, I've stayed on my normal routine, and it has *sucked*. I feel like a shell of who I once was. What Ryan did the other night changed me. After I finished crying in the back of Ella's car, I stayed the night at Paige and Amelia's apartment. Paige brought out a bunch of blankets, and we all had a sleepover in their living room. We stayed up all night. They made me laugh, we ate snacks and watched movies, and I passed out in Ella's lap as she combed my hair and took off my makeup for me. When we woke up, Amelia made waffles, and we sat at the table and had breakfast. They didn't ask me what happened, and I didn't tell them because I didn't want to say it out loud.

I couldn't.

Ella asked on the way home if I needed to go to the hospital, and I said no. I didn't need to, but I might have ended up there if I hadn't stopped it when I did.

That fucking terrified me.

I last talked to my brother a week ago, and my parent's text messages to me have gone unanswered. I didn't want them to worry about me, but they called me yesterday, and I talked to them for a bit, keeping my tone as light as possible. Ella's meeting me at the library cafe for our usual Sunday coffee date. We canceled book club Wednesday too, and though I was sad I wouldn't see the girls, they brought over ice cream and we had a movie night. It was nice being with them and not having to talk about anything, but I'm ready now.

Ella comes back to the booth with my coffee. "You can start whenever you're ready."

I tell her everything that happened. With Ryan. With Grant. I spare no details. I go over everything that happened, remained as detached as possible. By the end of it, she looks like she's ready to kill someone. "You mean to tell me all that happened with Ryan, and then Grant confessed his love for you all in one night?"

"All in one hour, actually."

"Jesus Christ."

"Yeah." I don't know what else to say. Admitting that out loud has definitely helped the guilt off my shoulders, but now I just feel empty.

"Hads, this was not your fault by any means. I need you to know that." She tells me.

"Why does it feel like my fault, though? Why does it feel like I'm the one to blame here?"

"Guilt is a weird thing, and you haven't fully healed from what happened in high school. You have these trust issues that run deep, and when you finally thought you could trust again and open yourself back up, it got broken again. It's difficult to open yourself back up again, but you did it. Now, you just have to forgive yourself for trying to see the best in someone that didn't deserve it. It's not on you, babes. I promise."

"I know it's not. My brain just doesn't agree with me. I just hate that I was dumb enough to fall for his stupid games when Grant was in my face telling me the entire time that Ryan sucked. I didn't listen to him because I'm stubborn. I wanted to prove Grant wrong, and I got hurt."

"To be honest, Hads, yes, he did try to tell you the whole time, but I think he knew words weren't enough to show you how fucked up Ryan was. He seemed heartbroken in the parking lot at what happened and you didn't even tell him details."

"I know. I wanted to tell him, but everything was a mess, and I couldn't get the words out."

"He didn't need to know then and he knew that. He was only worried about you, Hads. He only wanted you to be okay."

"I know. I just feel so broken now. I feel so worthless. I feel like I always let the wrong people in, and I'm scared to open my heart up again. If I get hurt or betrayed one more time, I don't think I could return from that. I think my heart will officially split and fall out of my body."

Ella scooches closer to me in the booth, wraps me in her arms, and wipes my tears. I didn't even notice I was crying. I feel like Paige lately—I'm always crying. Someone tapped me on the side the other day, and I thought I was going to have a panic attack at just that small accidental touch. I've been jumpy and just sad—so fucking sad all the time. I thought I was stronger than this.

"Hads, you could consider talking to someone about this. A professional, maybe? It doesn't have to be multiple sessions if you don't want it to be. You could just do one. Have you thought about reporting Ryan to campus police?"

"It crossed my mind. I walked into criminology with Paige the other day, and I couldn't even sit there knowing I was in the same room as him. Paige made up this excuse to get us out of there, and we went to the bathroom, and I broke down again. My brother tried to follow us, but Paige yelled at him, and he left. He looked upset, and I felt bad. Oliver is a fixer. He likes to fix things. I just didn't know how to tell him I didn't know if I could be fixed yet."

"Hads, I think it's a good idea. He's not someone who should be freely walking around, but I'll support you in whatever you decide. That includes whatever you feel is best going forward with Grant. Don't rush your feelings. Take the time to think about everything he said and has done for you. The girls and I will support you in anything you do, but just take your time. Be nice to yourself for the next few days. It's okay to skip class and just sit in your room and do what you want to do. That doesn't make you a failure."

I'm crying at her support. She's next to me, rubbing circles on my hand. Comforting me. "Thank you. For always being there for me. For jumping in your car and coming to get me when I needed you guys."

"Of course. It helped that we blasted *Getaway Car* by Taylor Swift the whole way, and I might've gone twenty over the speed limit." I laugh, and she smiles.

"I think I like him, Ells."

"You think? You're going to have to do better than that. You need to be sure. Like I said, take your time. He doesn't mind waiting. I think that boy would wait forever for you if it meant he got you for just one day. But I think you know that's not fair to him, which is why you need to be sure." I smile at that—Ella's right again, as always.

"I'll think about it for a bit. And thank you again. I feel like I've been saying that a lot, but I mean it."

"I know, babe. Just let me know what you decide to do about Ryan. I'll go with you to campus police or therapy if you decide that route."

"Thanks. I'm going to sit here for a few and read." She gets out of the booth, and I do, too—to hug her.

"I love you, H. Be patient with yourself, okay?"

"Okay." I nod at her, and she walks out the library's front doors while I sit back in the booth.

I know it's going to take time. Healing requires a bit of brokenness first. I know that. I'm in that right now. Paige would tell me to let it hurt and then let it go, so that's what I'm going to do. It hurts like hell right now, and when I'm ready to let it go, I will. I'll let part of it float off into space and be taken away from me, but there will always be a piece of it that stays with me. A piece of it to remind me of these feelings and how I got through it.

I can do this. I'm letting myself feel for once, and that's okay. It doesn't make me weak or vulnerable. It just makes me human. I pick my book up and begin reading where I left off.

Life can be beautiful again, and I'm going to let it.

40

Grant

It's been around two weeks since everything happened. The first few days, I felt okay. I knew it would take her time to figure everything out, and that's okay. I respect that. I just *hate* playing the waiting game. I could either be waiting around for the best news of my life or news that would hurt so bad I'd want to run my car off a cliff. But either way she decides, I know I'll support her decision. Jacks is trying to keep me positive. We have this whiteboard on our dorm door on which he keeps writing inspirational messages. I hate to admit that they make me feel better.

I'm sitting in my bed, in sweatpants, when Jacks comes in. He sees the state that I'm in and hops onto my bed. "You look like shit."

"What happened to being nice to me while I'm down?" I ask.

"Well, downtime is over. Take a fucking shower, Grant."

"Hey, fuck you. At least you have someone to take a shower for. I'm sitting here dying a slow death, most likely. The longer it takes her to decide, the worse it's looking for me."

"You don't know that. Don't jump to conclusions." He throws my towel at me.

"Well, what the fuck do I do? What do I do if she realizes I will never be enough for her? What if she gets bored of me in the future? The what-ifs are running through my head and won't stop!" I'm yelling and pacing around the room. Jacks is sitting at his desk, just watching me.

"Where do I go, Jacks? I feel lost, without a map, without her. I feel so lost. I feel like a kite with no strings attached, just floating freely into the atmosphere. The only thing running through my mind has been her since I walked away from her on those goddamn steps the other day! I just—I don't—" He cuts me off by grabbing me and hugging me. I'm crying at this point. I'm so afraid that I gave my all to her and will still fail in the end. I just hope I haven't failed her. That hurts me more than failing myself. I never knew I could love someone this much. But with Hads, everything feels dialed up tenfold.

"What if she never realizes how she feels? What should I do? Am I just supposed to let her move on to someone else while I watch from a distance? Jacks, what do I do? Please tell me what to do."

"I can't. You just have to hope that this works out. I think it will. I've told you many times that how she looks at you isn't how you look at a friend. She just needs time, and that's okay. Whatever happened with Ryan had to have shaken her a lot for this to affect her so much."

"I told you not to say his name around me." I shoot him a glare.

"I know. I'm sorry. I'm just saying that we don't know what happened in that hallway."

I stop and think for a moment. He's right. We don't. "We could maybe find out, couldn't we?"

"Oh, I really don't like that face you're making

right now. What's going on in your head?"

"We could confront him. Make him tell us what happened. A douche like Ry—like him would want to rub it in, and I don't know, be a dick about it like everything else."

"What should we do then?" Jacks asks me.

"Do you know where he is?"

"It's Saturday. He's probably at the gym or something."

"Let's go find him then."

"Alright, let's go." I grab the keys and am about to head out the door.

"Okay, maybe I should shower first." I say.

"Yeah, that's a good idea."

※

We go to his dorm, the dining hall, and then the gym. We find him in the gym, and Jacks smiles slightly because he suggested we come here first, but I wanted to try his dorm.

Whatever.

He's lifting weights, and Jacks shoves his spotter away and stands to spot him. Ryan stalls for a second and realizes that Jacks is over him now. I don't think he's seen me yet.

"Are you only benching 95 right now? What the fuck? I could lift that with one hand, and you sure are breaking a sweat." I say to him.

"Grant, come on, let's go easy on him. He needs a spotter for benching that little weight, be nice." Jacks says to me. When Ryan heard me speak, he faltered a bit, the bar starting to shake.

"I'm on set number four, might I add. What are

you two doing here?" He's struggling to put the bar back on the rack, and the bar is stalled against his chest. Neither of us moves to help him.

"We just wanted to ask you about what happened at the banquet. You clearly did something to someone we both care about and I want to know what happened." I've never seen Jacks act like this before. He's actually good at this. Is this interrogating? Are we interrogating?

"Little help here guys?" Ryan's struggling right now, and I can't help but laugh. He's struggling with 95 pounds. Pathetic.

"You help us first. What did you do to Hadleigh." I say. Trying to keep my voice as neutral as possible, but my voice cracked a bit saying her name. The worst has gone through my mind on repeat. If he says anything remotely like I think he will, I might explode on him.

"Yes, and we want details, none of this cheap shit. We'll know if you're lying too." Jacks adds.

"Oh yeah?" He says, out of breath and turning red. I don't feel bad. It's kind of fun to watch him struggle.

"Yeah. Start talking, or that bar is going to impale you. I don't have all day." I say as I push it down on his chest.

"Get the bar off me and I'll tell you!" He shouts, and Jacks lifts the bar off him, using three fingers. He gently places it back on the rack. Ryan stands up and goes over to his water bottle. He takes a long sip and then speaks.

"That girl dragged me along for months, wearing those outfits and laughing at my jokes. She was practically begging me to do something about it. She insisted we were just friends, but everyone knows that when a girl says that, she wants it to be more. So, I tried to make a move the night of the banquet, and the bitch told me to stop! I told her stopping wasn't an option after she strung me along for the entire semester, and then she kicked me in the balls and ran."

"She kicked you in the balls?" Jacks questions with a chuckle.

That's my girl. "So you're saying you assaulted her? She said no, and you continued. That's fucking assault you fucking prick."

"It's not assault. I didn't do anything she wasn't asking for, okay? Just leave me alone." He tells us.

"Why don't you leave every person alone within a one-hundred-mile radius?" Jacks says.

"I don't know if you know this, so let me educate you. If a girl says no, you fucking stop. If she's hesitant, you fucking stop. If she's stiff as a board and isn't having a good time, you fucking stop. Have you not heard of fucking consent before, or do you only like having sex when it's illegal?" I'm fuming. I'm seeing nothing but red right now. I want to grab a dumbbell and beat his face in. How dare he do that to her—touching her when she didn't want him to. My heart is aching right now. If I could run to her right now and hug her tight, I would. But first, I have to deal with the situation at hand.

"It's not fucking illegal if she was asking for it." He spits at Jacks and me.

"That's it—" I swing my fist back, ready to hit him, but Jacks beats me to it. Ryan's jaw makes a cracking sound, and Ryan hits the floor with a thump. "Did you just knock him out?"

"It's not knocking him out if he was asking for

it." Jacks throws a smile in my direction. "Sorry, he was getting on my nerves. If he were saying this about Claire, I would've let the 95 pound bar crack his chest open."

"Thanks, J. You're a good friend."

"I know. Do you feel better?"

"No, actually, I don't." I can't believe he did that. He fucking assaulted her. He should be in prison for what he did. There's no way I can walk around this campus feeling safe, knowing that she's safe, with him still around.

"Didn't Leo say that his sister was good with software and coding and shit?" I ask Jacks. Leo is friends with our captain—Holt—so he always hangs around, especially when we go out.

"Yeah, why?"

"Do you think she can hack security cameras and get the footage from that hallway?"

He smiles at me. "I like where this is going. Ask him for her number."

I pull my phone out, stopping the voice recording I was taking, and send the text. "I just did. I'm waiting for a response."

"Ah, your favorite game." He laughs as we walk out the door to the gym.

"That's hilarious, J, really funny," I say, clearly not laughing.

"Ah, come on. As I said, it's all going to work out. Now I'm going to sit on this comfy chair while you go get me ice for my hand—which really fucking hurts, by the way." I shoot him a stare. "Please?" He says.

"I'll be right back, don't lose any fingers while I'm gone."

"No promises."

I pull my phone back out and make sure the voice-recorded confession I took is still there. It is, and I exhale. I knew recording it could be dicey, but I needed to do it. The more evidence, the better right? Plus, I don't want this all to fall on Hads. She's been through enough.

This is the least I could do for her.

41

Hadleigh

"Okay, since it's just about the end of April, I brought the printout of my stats for the first third of this year. It's organized from most liked to least liked. There are many other categories as well." I stop dead in my tracks. I was walking into book club like any regular Wednesday night, when I see my three best friends sitting in a circle with some snacks on the middle table. They all turn and look at me at the same time. Amelia gets up and walks toward me.

"Book club tonight is turning into girls night," Amelia says, grabbing my arm and leading me to the empty chair by them.

"What's going on, you guys?" I set my stuff down next to my chair

"We're worried about you." Paige says.

"Worried? Why?" *I'm so confused.*

"About Grant and the entire situation at the banquet," Ella says. "Processing this is going to take time. We want you to be able to start healing because we care about your mental well-being. We just want to help. So we figured we could start with some quality time."

"Okay...I appreciate the concern. I get where you're coming from, but I'm fine. Give it a few weeks, and I'll be back to normal." I say to them.

"It's okay to not be okay. It is so okay to not be

okay, Hads. You do not have to be on all the time. You don't have to put this face on every day and pretend like everything is fine." Paige says.

"I know we talked about this on Sunday, but in no way was this your fault. You did nothing wrong, Hads." Ella tells me again.

"I know.... but I'm so *scared.*" I admit to them. They all get up and crouch around where I'm sitting. "I've been trying my hardest to move forward, but I can't. I feel stuck. I'm scared to open myself back up because I can't handle getting hurt again. It was easy with you guys, we kind of just fell into this friendship. It was so effortless with you guys like we have been friends for our entire lives. But with someone like—" I stop myself.

"Like Grant?" Paige asks me. Amelia has moved to stand to my right, and Ella's still crouching in front of me.

"Okay, first things first, I think therapy would help, Hads. It helps to talk to someone about these things." Ella says.

"I think you're right. I don't know why therapy is such a hard step for me." I sniffle. A few tears have escaped.

"It's scary to admit that you need help with something, but it's okay to talk through your feelings," Ella reminds me.

"Therapy can help rewrite your brain to realize that none of this was your fault. It doesn't work for everyone, but I think it could help you. It will help you work through your feelings, which is the most important aspect." Paige says as she grabs my hand and squeezes it. "It was *not* your fault. But no matter how often we say that, your smart brain won't believe us. Therapy has helped me in the past and even now. It's a scary step, but we'll be right alongside you, supporting you in any decision you make."

I think through what she's saying, and she's right. I don't believe them, but I want to. "Okay. I'll try it." They all smile at me. "What do I do about the Grant situation?" I say, wiping my tears.

"Graaaant!" Paige sings his name.

"Ella told us what he said to you. The big L word..." Amelia smiles at me.

"Ella, seriously?" I say to her. *I told her that in confidence!*

"Technically, you two don't have attorney-client privilege, and you're not protected by HIPPA, so..." Paige is giggling.

"I had to! Those two are scary, and they could tell I was lying when they asked about what I knew!" Ella exclaims.

"Did you guys threaten her?" I turn to look between Amelia and Paige. Paige shrugs, and Amelia smirks. I guess there's my answer.

Paige jumps up from kneeling and starts pacing the room as if she's giving a big speech. "Hads, look, I've known that you were in love with Grant the entire time, and I've been waiting for you to play catch up, but I'll have to lay this out for you. Ever since you went ice skating with Grant, you've loved him. You just pushed him away because it was what you're used to. Now, did you or did you not make out with him that night?" She stops pacing and waits for me to answer.

I look between Ella and Amelia. "Is this an episode of *Law and Order*? You guys are allowing this?"

"Yup." They say in unison.

"ANSWER THE QUESTION!" Paige says loudly while also banging on the table.

"Yes, yes, we did kiss a little bit. It was nice." I say quickly. Paige is scaring me right now.

"Then, did you or did you not tell him you wanted to remain friends with him?" Paige asks.

"I did, yes."

"Ha! I've caught you red-handed here and you don't even know it!" Amelia snickers at that, and Ella laughs too. What the fuck is wrong with my friends?

"What?" I say, still confused.

"That's your pattern. Every time you get close to someone, you push them away. You get close and then retreat—keeping them at arm's length. You wanted him as a friend because it was also the safe option. BAM! I rest my case." She sits down, rather dramatically I might add.

"Okay, well, that's partially true. Paige got us halfway to the point we were trying to make, but the main thing we're trying to say is that you love him too, and you should be together and all that other romantic crap." Amelia says as she walks back to her seat and plops down next to Paige. They fistbump.

"Okay, don't listen to either of them, even though they're relatively right. Look, you don't need to be afraid to open your heart up to him, Hads. He's not like the rest of them, and I think deep down, you know that. Deep down, you know how you feel about him. You're just scared to take that final leap because taking that leap would mean that you would be opening yourself up to getting hurt again, and you don't want to do that. I understand that recent events only make this seem scarier, but Grant's a good guy. He taught you to skate and brought you flowers even though it wasn't a date. He took care of you while you were sick—"

"How did you know about that?" I ask her.

"I saw you wearing sweatpants one day that said 'Grand Mountain Hockey' on them. I assume he gave them to you after he saw us at book club because they were hanging out of his bag." Paige tells me.

"He has done so much for you because he *wants* to make you happy. He wants to see you happy and be the one to ensure you are." Ella tells me, and I know she's right. My judgment just feels so impaired now.

"But why me? I just—I don't understand. He could have anyone else that doesn't argue with him every other sentence. We hate each other!" I say, deflecting yet again. All the things they're saying are thoughts that have been at the back of my mind for weeks. I just didn't want to believe it. I didn't want to open myself back up. I wanted to stay in my box, locked up safe and sound where nothing could hurt me.

"Hads, girl, he doesn't want anyone else. And you guys stopped hating each other about halfway through the year." Amelia tells me.

I stand up and start pacing. "Can you guys make me a chart or something? I feel weird right now."

"Weird, how?" Amelia asks me.

"I don't know. My stomach feels off."

"Love." Paige says.

"What?"

"You're feeling the love. Those butterflies everyone talks about." Ella tells me.

"Hads, bitch, you're down bad," Amelia says while Paige giggles.

"But what if—"

"Hads," Ella says. The room goes quiet, and I can hear myself thinking.

Fuck. She's right. How did I not see this before? I was too tired fighting off my thoughts that I didn't see him how he really was. I saw him in the safe way my brain wanted me to see. He *loves* me. Grant loves me. He straight up told me himself in the middle of a fucking parking lot, and I just let him walk away, thinking that was for the best. Shit, I need to stop being scared of being happy and tell him.

"You're right. All of you are right. Shit! I don't want to wake up one day in the future and regret not even trying because I was scared. I want to wake up one day next to him, smiling and arguing with him about everything because I don't get scared when I argue with him. I want it with him. Fuck, why didn't you guys tell me that!" I say, pacing and yelling.

"We tried to, many times actually," Ella says.

"Isn't that what we were just doing? Oh, she's joking." Amelia rolls her eyes.

"Finally! It's about damn time, Hads! I called this from the beginning!" Paige is yelling at me, grabbing my bag, and shoving it toward me. "Go find him. You need to tell him."

"Right now? It's late. I don't even know where he is. Plus, I might need to write on some index cards so that I remember what to say and—"

"Index cards? Hads, no, you will not sit on this big realization. You go find that man and tell him right now!" Ella exclaims.

"I don't know where he is!" I yell. This is a very nerve-racking situation. Who knew a bunch of romance book lovers would be this passionate about real-life love? I certainly never would've guessed that...

"Try his dorm first! He lives with Jacks in Temple!" Paige yells.

"I don't have time to ask how you know that, but Paige, that's a good idea. Okay, I have to go confess my love or whatever. I love you guys!" I pull them all in for a group hug, and we smile when I pull away.

"Good luck," they all say to me, but I don't have time to respond because I'm running out the doors and into the night air towards where Grant hopefully is. I'm severely out of shape and hate running, but I get to his building in five minutes, swipe in, and run straight into Jacks.

"Woah, Hads, where's the fire?" He asks me.

"There isn't one. Where's Grant? Is he in your room?" I move past him, and he catches my arm. When I turn my head, he's smiling at me. "What?"

"Why do you want to know where Grant is?"

"You're really going to make me say it to you right now?"

"Oh, absolutely." He's still smiling, even wider now. I know he knows why.

I take a deep breath and release from his hold. "I love him, and I need to tell him that, so where is he? This is kind of an urgent situation."

"I knew it. Ugh, this is great news. He's been sulking around our room for what seems like months now. Thank God."

"Can you just tell me where he is? I'm not against kicking you in exchange for information."

"I'm not opposed to the ruler if you have that on hand."

"Ha, ha, funny. Just tell me." I say to him.

"He's at the rink."

"Aren't you guys done with practices, though?"

"He goes there to clear his head sometimes. He's been there a lot lately." That hits me right in the chest, but at least I know where he is now.

"Thank you, Jacks."

"No problem, Hads. I'm happy you finally came to your senses." He smiles when he says that.

"Yeah, yeah, everyone knew but me, whatever. Bye! Thank you!" I say as I run out of Temple and head straight for the rink. God, why do people run for fun? I should have Paige add running to her list of torture techniques. I feel sweaty, gross, and not presentable, but I don't care.

I just need to get to him.

I need to see him.

I need him as he needs me.

I almost run straight into the rink doors. I pull the door open and go straight to where we were last time we were in here. I'm going into this conversation unprepared and not knowing what I'm gonna say say. How do people do this? Just declare their love with no preparation or index cards? It's barbaric. It's not hard to spot him since he's the only person here. Granted, it's a Wednesday night at 9 PM, so that doesn't surprise me. I don't even bother putting skates on because that will take too much time, so I open the rink door and start shuffling toward him. He's skating with his back to me.

"Grant!" He turns around, his eyes wide open, and he looks so caught off guard right now. Perfect, just how I wanted him.

"Hads, what the hell are you doing? You don't

have skates on!" He reaches me in four long strides and steadies me on the ice. He tries to pick me up, but I hold my hand up, and he stops.

"Don't pick me up. I have something to say to you, and I'm afraid if we move, I might forget it."

"Okay. Go ahead." His face looks skeptical. He looks scared at what I'm about to say.

"Grant, you drive me insane about 75 percent of the time I'm with you. You're loud, you play a sport that I don't understand that well, and you actually *enjoy* arguing with me. It's weird, and it drives me crazy. The other 25 percent of the time, you make me laugh like I've never laughed before, and you make me smile." He looks half confused and half terrified. This is actually kind of fun. "But the only thing I know is that I love you 100 percent of the time. I don't know when it happened, I don't know *how* it happened, frankly, but I'm in love with you. That's a fact. I love you, Grant, and you love me, or you did, at least. I just ran all over campus looking for you to tell you this, and I know I made you wait a long time. But I love you, Grant. I do. I love you more than I think I've loved anybody. Including charts, and I really do love charts. Anyways, my point is, I love —"

He cuts me off by kissing me, and I practically melt into his arms. I'm not only coming off the high from running all over campus but also the adrenaline of what I just said. My heart races as he kisses me deeper. He pulls away and touches his forehead to mine. "It took you long enough."

"Hey! I wasn't the one who blurted it out at the worst possible time. That was you!"

"Don't put this all on me. I can't control my

mouth sometimes. It just happened, and I don't regret it one bit." He smiles at me.

"It's all your fault, actually. Your stupid smile and your stupid personality reeled me in like a siren luring a pirate to their death." I cross my arms at him.

"Does that make me the mermaid in this scenario? Because I have a mermaid tail back home that —" This time, I cut *him* off by kissing him. He's shocked for a moment because I've never done that, and then he responds by cupping my face and pulling me closer to him. When we pull away, we're breathing heavily, and he scoops me up and brings me to the bench he sat me on last time we were here.

"What does loving me feel like?" He asks me.

"What?"

"Oh, come on. I gave you so many metaphors in my big confession speech, and I didn't hear you give any. That means I beat you. Grant one, Hades zero." Is he serious right now?

"You cannot *beat* me at confessing our love for each other. That's just not a thing." I say to him.

"All I'm hearing right now are excuses. You really are a sore loser, aren't you?" He asks me.

"Fine! Fine, my God, leave it to you to infuriate me when I just confessed my love for you."

"I'm just saying mine was way better. I compared you to the damn green light from Gatsby, so…" He shrugs his shoulders at that.

I take a deep breath, and for the second time tonight, I don't think. I just speak. "Loving you feels like losing myself in my favorite book. It feels like listening to my favorite audiobooks on repeat. It feels like being in an art museum while it's raining and hearing the rain tap on the roof. Loving you feels like realizing I'm not scared of all the tough things with you. I want all of it. As long as you're by my side, I don't feel scared." His eyes are getting teary, and I can feel mine loading up. "Grant, if you cry, I'm going to cry. Please don't."

"Loving me feels like losing yourself in your favorite book? That's kind of funny, actually." He leans over and reaches for something inside his bag. He pulls out…a book? He hands it to me, and I realize it's one of my favorites from this year. The one he saw me carrying around all the time. It has a bunch of colored tabs sticking out of it.

"Did you steal my book? What did you do to it?" I ask him.

"No, Christ, Hads, I didn't steal it. Of course, that's your first thought. I bought it, read it, and annotated it for you. I stole some tabs from your room when you were sick and got some pens and shit from Amazon." I flip through it, and sure enough, his handwriting is all over the pages, and one of my favorite quotes is highlighted.

"You did this for me?"

He smiles at me. "Of course I did. I was going to use this to ask you to go to the banquet with me. I know you love reading, and I wanted to show you how much I was willing to do for you. Actions not just words, you know? Brendan and Jacks helped me come up with the idea. Is it okay? Do you like it?" He looks and sounds nervous.

"It's perfect." I say as I launch myself onto him. He wobbles a bit as I slip my arms around him and hug him tight. I never want to let him go. "Did you like the book?" I ask him, smiling so hard that my cheeks hurt.

"I actually really enjoyed it. I was *not* expecting that one spicy scene, though. I think I might be into reading now." His cheeks turn red, and I laugh. I'm still on his lap, the book next to us, and he's rubbing my back.

"I need you to chart your top five favorite moments from the book to discuss this deeper."

"Hads, I'll do anything you want me to. Just say the word."

"Please," I say.

He smiles at me and leans in, and kisses me again. It feels like all the happiness is coming back into my body. I'm feelings things again, and I've never been happier to have so many emotions rushing through me. It feels like knowing I deserve to feel like this. It feels like I never want to let him go. He pulls away, and I smile at him again. I want to live with this feeling forever.

"Can I skate with you?" I ask.

"Absolutely, baby."

42

Grant

It's May, and finals week is in full swing. My girlfriend and I have been studying nonstop, and she even made me more flashcards for my final exam. I feel good and very well prepared. Hads made sure of that. We've been spending a lot of time in the library, working on different papers and assignments. We sit in our old tutoring room, and I often lose myself in the memories of every session we had months ago. She still smacks me with her ruler, and I return to focusing, just like the good old days. We've also been having a weekly date night, which was my idea. I took her to this old-school printing shop, and we were able to print out a bunch of charts for her. I even have one in my dorm. It's a ranked chart of all the things she loves about me. I hung it over my bed.

That's not the only good thing that happened as the semester concluded. Campus police were sent an anonymous video and a USB with a voiced confession of Ryan assaulting Hads in the hallway. It included volume and was clear as day. You could hear Ryan saying everything he did. Hads was called to the Dean's office and told them what happened after they watched the video. Her story matched perfectly, and then they kicked Ryan off the hockey team and out of school. Alissa offered for me to listen to it, but I didn't want to. Hads told me everything he did one night anyway.

After I threatened to kill him a thousand times, she promised me she was okay. She also had her first therapy appointment the other day. Ella and I went too and waited for her in the car. She's been going once a week now.

    I'm insanely proud of her.

    I'm walking into my last final exam—my literature one—and I sit at my desk. I got here early and brought my flashcards to review them one last time before taking the test. I have to write four essays and answer other questions, but I'm not nervous. I'm flipping through the flashcards when I see a new one I never noticed. She must have slipped it into the pile at the library before this. I look at it, and it says 'From Hads' on the front. I turn it over and read what's on the back. Thirteen little words that mean more to me than she could ever know.

    'You're not a failure as long as you try your best. I believe in you. -H'

    I hold the tears back because what did I do to deserve this girl? She continues to amaze me every single day. I'll never get tired of her. She understands and loves every part of me—even the ones I don't like.

    My professor comes in and the class grows silent. We're all spread out so we don't cheat, although I don't know how you can cheat on essays, but whatever. I shove my flashcards back into my bag and grab my pencil. I take a deep breath as Collins hands me the test. I open it up and begin.

    I can do this.

I hand my test in and head out the door. I was one of the last people in there because I was writing so damn much. I may have gone overboard, but I would rather have done too much than not enough. I think I did well, and I can't wait to tell Hads that I feel confident about this test. I stop to grab my phone from my bag to text Hads that I can meet her back at our spot in the library when I see a familiar pair of boots in my eye-line.

I look up, and there she is—my beautiful girlfriend—standing right in front of me. Hads is wearing her signature black skirt and forest green sweater combination, but she has my jacket on—the one I told her to keep from the banquet. It still looks better on her than me, and I never want it back. She gives me a cute half-wave, and I walk over to her and kiss her. She's startled, mostly because she hates public displays of affection, but she relaxes a bit, and I pull away.

"What are you doing here?" I ask her. We planned to meet back at the library so I could help her write a paper, and by helping her, I mean distracting her while she shoots me glares and threatens me the entire time.

"I wanted to see you after your test. I got nervous when you didn't come out until now. Were you the last one in there? How do you think it went? Did you remember the thing I told you last night about—" I cut her off with a kiss again. She tends to ramble when she's feeling nervous, and this is the only way I know how to relax her, among *other* things.

"You were worried about me?" I ask her.

"No. Shut up. How do you think you did?" I grab her hand, and we walk to the exit of our building. I hold the door for her, and she exits, grabbing my hand again when we get onto the sidewalk.

"I think I did really well. Thanks to you and your amazing flashcards and study techniques. I'm definitely sure that I passed."

"I'm really proud of you, boyfriend." She tells me.

"You are?" I stop her where we are and turn her to face me.

"So proud." She beams at me. I kiss her again.

"Thank you, girlfriend." I smile against her lips, and feel her smile too.

I want to replay every moment of how we got here because some part of me still doesn't believe I got this lucky with this girl. I know I can't repeat the past, but I sometimes wish to watch it again. It's been a long journey to get here, but we did it, and I couldn't be happier. Loving her and being loved by her is something I want to do forever. But I wouldn't change anything because she has me tied around her finger, and I never want to be undone from Hads. I grab her hand again, and we start walking toward the library, hoping to lose ourselves in the next chapter of our story.

43

Hadleigh

It's the end of May, and summer is right around the corner. Grant and I are walking into a restaurant where Ella has invited us all for her after-graduation dinner. We were all instructed to dress up—Ella was very specific—because we're eating at a semi-fancy place. It's a cidery that Ella and Alissa both love, so naturally, this is where she chose to have her party. Grant's wearing a blue button-up shirt and brown loafers with beige pants. He looks dashing, as always. His sunglasses are on his eyes since it's so sunny out. I opted for a flowy white dress with blue flowers on it. I also have sunglasses on, along with a big floppy hat. I'm wearing strappy sandals that Grant bought me the other day. I said they were cute at the store, and a week later, I went to hang out with him, and he had bought and wrapped them for me. We walk into the outdoor seating area and look around through the row of picnic tables when I see Ella and Alissa taking shots already. They're the only ones here so far, besides us. Ella looks up at me and runs over to me.

"You look stunning! Ah! Grant! You look wonderful as well." Yeah, she's definitely drunk already. Good for her. She's done with college. She deserves to let loose. More than normal, at least. She pulls me in for a hug, and Alissa comes over too.

"We went ahead and started the party before

everyone got here. I hope nobody minds, but Ells and I are already smashed." She smiles at that, and I hug her. Alissa has become one of Ella's best friends, and in turn, she has lowkey become an honorary member of our book club. She's a delight to have around, especially since she helped me so much this semester.

"I noticed. Let's go sit down and wait for Paige and Ames." I motion them back to the table, and Grant's hand is on the small of my back, guiding me over. While walking over, he leans down and whispers in my ear.

"You do look stunning." My face gets hot, and I look back up at him.

"You look wonderful as well," I say as I quickly kiss his cheek. Grant and I both passed all of our finals. Grant even got an A in his literature class. He was so excited when his grades came back. I wish I had taken a picture of the smile on his face. It could have lit up an entire room. Every single day, I'm more proud of him than the last.

We all sit down at the tables. Ella and Alissa pushed two picnic tables together so we could fit everyone. It's just the girls and Grant. Ella will have a party with her family soon, but she wanted to do something special with just us.

"So, Grant, what are your plans for the summer?" Ella asks him. Alissa winks at me, a subtle way of letting me know that I did well with Grant and that she approves.

"I'm not sure yet. Hads and I have some plans in the works. I might spend part of the summer at her house, and she might spend half at mine, but we still have some kinks to work out." He smiles over at me and winks. I'm so excited to spend the summer with him. I can't wait for him to meet my family and vice versa. He talks about his mom a lot, and I'm simultaneously nervous and excited to meet her. I've never met a boyfriend's parents before, and I told Grant I needed him to make me flashcards about all his family members so I could know a bit about them.

"Kinks, you say?" Alissa says, and everyone laughs.

"Guys, over here!" Ella yells at who I only assume are Paige and Amelia since they are the only other people coming today. Paige is wearing ripped jeans, a black crop top, and a white flowy button-down that she leaves open. Her blonde curly hair is long and flowy as ever. Amelia has opted for a short, light pink dress with flower patterns. Her brown hair is pulled back in a cute half-up look. Ella, the main event, wears light-wash jeans with a cropped black shirt and vans. Her red-brown hair is straight, while Alissa's dark brown hair is wavy. Alissa has opted for black jeans and a light purple shirt. We all look adorable.

Paige and Amelia hug everyone, and we all sit at the picnic tables. "I can't believe you've graduated, Ella. That's so crazy to me." Paige says.

"I still can't wrap my head around the fact that I won't see you around campus. It's weird, and I hate it." Amelia says.

"She'll still be at book club. Hopefully, if not, she can just Facetime when we get together on Wednesdays." I say.

"Alissa, can I ask you a few questions?" Grant asks her.

"Sure, babes, you can buy me a drink," Alissa says to him.

"I'm 20."

"Oh shit, right, the drinking age is 21 in the U.S. Whoops! Whatever, let's go over here. We can have a chat." I'm sure he will ask her about the whole thing with Ryan. Alissa helped him out big time, and I know he still worries about it. I tell him he doesn't need to, but he'll never stop worrying about me. I can't believe I was ever afraid to be loved by him. His love is the only one I want. I'm sure of that now.

"So Ella, Ames told me you have had a few interviews. How have those gone?" Paige asks her. Ella is shaking her head a bit.

"I've had interviews but no bites yet. I'm only looking for something entry-level. I know it'll take time to get to my dream job." She seems confident, and I do not doubt that she will reach all her goals one day. If someone is going to crawl their way to the top and rightfully earn their spot, it'll be her. She turns to look at Paige and Amelia. "How does it feel to be seniors in college, you two? That must be a bit scary. I know I was afraid. The beginning of the end."

"It's weird, and I don't want to talk about it. I might cry." Paige says.

"It feels like I'm waiting for another shoe to drop. I just don't know when or where it's going to happen," Amelia says.

"That...makes sense. I think." I say to them. "It's weird to think that after next year, I'll be the only one left on the campus of the four of us. It's going to be weird without you guys and my brother there. He also graduates next year." I say. The tears are coming a bit now. I used to think the future was scary—and it still is—but imagining them not there with me for my last year makes me never want to grow up.

Paige gives me a side hug. "We'll always be close. I don't think any of us plan to go that far. Plus, we're all always one phone call or SOS text away." She smiles at me.

"Plus, you're not going to be totally alone." Amelia flicks her head over to where Alissa and Grant are standing. I look at Grant, and he meets my eyes as if he can always sense when I'm looking at him. He shoots me a wink and continues with his conversation. My stomach flutters.

"Yeah, you're right. I won't be completely alone." I smile again. I feel...happy. Truly happy. How did I forget that I won't be alone now that I have him? Grant walks back over to us, with Alissa not far behind him.

"You okay?" He asks me.

"I'm amazing," I say back to him.

"Grant, would you mind taking our picture?" Ella asks him.

"I don't mind. Just hand me a phone and tell me what angles you want." He says.

We all get up from the table and form a line. We interlock our hands behind our backs and smile at the camera. I'm glad this moment is being captured. It's the last time all of us will be together before we go our separate ways. Paige is going home to New York for the summer. Amelia is heading back to her hometown as well. Ella has her job search ahead of her, and Alissa is going back to England with her brother for a bit. Grant and I are heading to either his or my house first, on opposite sides of the country. We're all splitting up for now. I know it won't last forever, but I wish I could stay here. At this moment, with my friends beside me and my boyfriend behind the camera, he looks at me like I'm the only person in the world he sees. I desperately want to grasp onto this feeling and never let it go.

I'm excited about the future with Grant. But I'm even more excited knowing that our little book club will follow us no matter what. I believe these girls will be beside me for the rest of my life. Grant too. I just have a gut feeling, as Paige would say.

"Everyone say book club!" Grant says, the flash protruding from Ella's phone.

None of us says a word. We all know that this moment is too special for words. But after the picture is taken, we sit, eat good food, and laugh.

The little moments before the big jumps are often remembered the most, and because we took that picture, we can replay this memory again. Remembering how we felt, how we laughed until our ribs hurt, and how I feel when I look at these wonderful people around me. I read that moments of transition are often the loneliest, but I feel more supported than ever. These people around me will never make me feel alone in a crowded room. Grant sticks his tongue out to me as we walk back to his car.

"I hate you," I say with a laugh.

"I love you too," he tells me. He opens the car door for me, and I slide in. I watch the rest of us trickle out of the cidery. Paige and Amelia are walking with their arms linked together and laughing about something. Amelia's drunk, and Paige is leading her back to her car. Alissa is hugging some guy that Ella is shooting daggers at. Alissa must have called Leo to pick them up since both were drinking. Alissa is coaxing Ella into the backseat with her. I cannot wait for the day I find out about Ella and Leo.

Grant slides into the car and kisses me on the cheek. "That was really fun. I always love hanging out with the girls."

"Me too." I say with a smile. My cheeks hurt from smiling and laughing so much.

Grant turns his car on and looks over at me. "Are you ready to go?"

"I'm ready."

I'm ready to see all the world has to offer me. I'm ready for everything. The good, the bad, and all the love that comes with it.

EPILOGUE

Hadleigh

  I'm sitting beside Grant on Amelia's couch. Junior year has just started, and Amelia invited us to watch this travel documentary with her. It's Saturday—so classes aren't in session—so naturally, we said yes. I love having Amelia all to myself, and I desperately wanted to hear about the concert she went to this summer. She had been looking forward to it for a while and I want to hear how it went. Grant has tagged along because Amelia and Grant have both realized that they both enjoy watching National Geographic. Apparently, when Grant was a kid, he and his dad would watch them, and now as he's older, they comfort him. I love hearing Grant talk about his dad. He seemed like a wonderful man. It's easy to tell where Grant got it from.

  Grant and I spent the summer between our two homes. He came back to California with Oliver and me, and I went with him to Vermont. I was initially scared at how Oliver would react, but when they saw each other for the first time, they shook hands and did some weird dude thing, as if they had met each other before. I was skeptical, and neither of them would tell me about it. Whatever. If they like each other and Oliver won't kill him, that's all that matters.

  Both of my parents loved him, especially when we showed Grant all of the traditions we do. He was so excited to learn more about my culture. It was adorable and made me fall deeper in love with him. Grant and Oliver often went to the beach, Oliver tried to teach him how to surf, which didn't work because Oliver is terrible at it too, but lots of laughs were shed. Especially by me, watching them from the sand. Since then, I've been taking many pictures and printing them out to hang all around my room.

    Grant showed me around his hometown. It was small compared to mine, but he took me on a tour of all his favorite spots. The rink his dad used to practice on with him, his old job at this ice cream place, and he even took me to where his dad was buried to introduce me to him. It was a beautiful moment, and he told me his dad would approve. As long as Grant was happy, that's all he ever cared about. I cried a bit after that, and so did he. I don't know how he does it, but he easily brings out my emotions. I'm thankful every day that I wasn't too scared to admit how I really felt. We went ice skating too, and I had a lot of fun with him this summer.

    But now back to school is here. It's nice to have some structure again. Jacks and Grant just moved into an apartment near Paige and Amelia, so we've all been getting together. We all do study sessions in the library and have dinner together some nights. Jacks brings Claire to those sometimes too. They're still going strong. I'm still living with my roommate Taylor—we have an apartment with two other girls—and it's been fun meeting new people. My brother even comes to our dinner nights occasionally. He and Paige had a meeting this morning. They're both co-chairs of the criminal justice club on campus now that the other seniors have graduated, and they're trying to fundraise or something. I stopped listening after Oliver grunted for the third time.

Life is good. Amelia comes over and sits on the loveseat while handing us popcorn. "Thanks for watching this one with me. Paige has been so busy she told me to just watch this one by myself. But since Grant likes them too, I figured you guys would watch it with me."

"Amelia, I feel like you and I don't get much time together. Plus, I like watching Grant's eyes light up like yours when you watch these. And just so you know, I'll always support you and your dreams. I think you could make it to National Geographic one day." I lean over, grab her hand, and squeeze it. She gives me a sad look that doesn't last long until she pulls away.

"Okay, it's starting now." She turns the volume up. About thirty minutes into the documentary, Paige and my brother burst through the front door. Paige has tears streaming down her face, and doesn't say a word as she goes to the kitchen sink and starts scrubbing her hands. I can see her shaking from here. Oliver tries to go to where she is, but Grant stands up and reaches him before he can.

"Dude, back up, give her some space," Grant says to Oliver, and my brother doesn't say a word. *What the hell is going on?* Oliver nods and steps back while Grant stands beside him. Amelia and I get up at this point.

"What did you do to Paige? She looks scared." I ask him. Amelia motions for Paige to stop scrubbing what looks like ink off her hands, but Paige swats her away. She still hasn't said a word.

"Only took your brother four years to get on Paige's nerves. What did it this time? The grunts or the evil stares?" Amelia says as she shuts off the water. Paige immediately turns it back on.

"Guys, I didn't do anything. Something happened." Oliver says to the room. Paige halts when he says that. Tears still stream steadily down her face, and her hands are red from all the scrubbing she did.

Grant shuts the front door, and it's a bit loud. Paige flinches where she stands, and Oliver goes over to her. In a complete twist that nobody—even me—could've seen coming, my brother hugs Paige. She relaxes a bit, and I swear the world has flipped on its axis because my brother just hugged someone willingly.

"Cut the bullshit and start talking," Grant says to them. He looks a bit scared, and I feel nervous. This all seems shady, and I don't like it.

"Oliver, what happened to Paige?" I ask him. More stern now because I want answers since my friend is crying and shaking. He lets go of her and looks at me.

"What's to say something didn't happen to me too?" He asks, speaking a bit louder now.

"Oliver, you have one facial expression—the one you're wearing right now." Grant says. "Just tell us what happened to Paige."

"Guys, I'm right here, and I'm fine, I swear." Paige finally speaks. We all fall quiet. She smiles, but it's not real. She almost looks unrecognizable.

"P, you're not. You're shaking and still crying. Something must have happened." Amelia says. "You don't get like this for no reason. Let's just sit down, and we can talk about it."

"Wait, back up. Has Paige been like this before?" Amelia shakes her head at me, and I drop it. That conversation is for another time.

"Oliver, fucking say something," Grant snaps at

him. Oliver looks over at Paige, and she looks back at him. There's this weird charged energy in here. What could they possibly say that would make Paige like this?

"The dean of students is dead and Paige found the body. He was murdered." Oliver finally says, and we all go silent. "We just came from the police station. We had to answer questions, and they fingerprinted us." I look down at Ol's hands, and sure enough, his fingers are all inked like Paige's. Nobody speaks for a solid few minutes. We all just stand there. Sure, Paige likes true crime and has seen pictures of dead bodies all the time, but seeing someone dead? That must've been terrifying.

"Paige, Oliver, do you guys need anything?" Grant asks, looking between them both. The two of them are still looking at each other.

"Paige, no." That's all Oliver says to her.

"Why not?"

"It's dangerous." He tells her.

"Fine."

"Okay, that was a wonderful conversation that none of us had the context to. I'm going to call Ella. This is an emergency, and we need everyone here." Amelia says as she exits the room to grab her phone.

"The school just sent out an email. A shelter-in-place. Holy shit." Grant says.

Junior year is going to be more hectic than I thought.

EXTENDED EPILOGUE

Grant
Three Years Later

"Did you really need to blindfold me for this? I thought we were just going to dinner?"
My beautiful girlfriend asks me as I escort her to her surprise. Today is our third anniversary. Three years of love and living a beautiful life together. We recently bought an apartment in Virginia near the school I'm coaching at, and where Hads works as a scientist for a pharmaceutical company.

After graduation, we moved in together, and it's been nothing but love and stupid little arguments that always end with us on the floor together, laughing and holding each other. Hads has become more comfortable and less tense over the years. She tells me it's because of me, but I think she's so happy that everything melts away.

"The blindfold was necessary since you keep asking me questions about the surprise. It's bad enough you can tell from my face when I'm lying, but for this, I want you to be completely shocked. I want to see that look on your face."

"Grant, if you're pregnant, just tell me now. I can handle it." She says to me.

"Aw, baby, don't spoil it. How did you guess that so easily?" I feign heartbreak, and she giggles at me, still blindfolded.

Little does she know, I'm leading her into a building—one that we know very well. It's a Saturday afternoon in the middle of May. Nobody should be in here, and I paid one of the security guards to keep everyone away from this area. I spent so much time putting this together with the girl's help. Hads and the rest of the former book club still talk almost constantly. All of us have created our own little family with each other. We get together on holidays, and the girls still have book club once a week. Every Wednesday night, just like always.

I asked Oliver to help me pick out a ring for Hads. I also asked him and her dad for their blessings, which they gave me, along with hugs. They were excited to welcome me into their family officially. The ring box in my jacket pocket has been weighing a hole in my body. I've had the ring for a year, but life got in the way, and I never found the right time to do this.

Not anymore. My girl deserves the best proposal on the planet.

Hads and I are 23 this year, and I knew it was time. I knew from the moment she confessed her love to me on that ice rink that I was going to spend the rest of my life with her, and what a life I couldn't wait to live—officially.

"Okay, I'm opening the door in front of you, and there are three steps up after this." I say to her.

"Grant, where are we? It's chilly in here."

I wouldn't know what it feels like because I've been sweaty and itchy all day. I didn't think I would be this nervous. "I finally brought you back to the Underworld, sorry."

"Ha, ha, very funny."

I open the door for her and lead her to the spot. "Okay, stand there and don't move." I shuffle a few steps over and get in my spot.

"You can take the blindfold off now," I say to her.

She takes it off, and her face looks as shocked as ever. We're back in the exact spot where I ran into her for the first time when I needed her to tutor me. All around us, all my favorite pictures of us are hanging from strings from the ceiling. Pictures from hockey games during senior year, our dates throughout the years, her wearing my jersey. All of my favorite moments that I've spent with her. Some strings are blank, signifying that we have many more memories to create together in the future.

"Wh—what is this?"

"The spot where I first laid my eyes on you. The spot where it all started. You and me."

"I know that, but what are we doing here?" She's looking around at the pictures that hang, and tears start to fill her eyes. She starts to walk towards me a bit.

"Hold up. You're not allowed to move from that spot." I say as I start to walk toward her.

"When have I ever listened to you before?" She challenges me.

"True, but please, just this once?"

She looks at me, "Okay. Only because you said please."

I reach where she's standing, and I take a deep breath. I drop to one knee and look up at her. Tears are brimming in her eyes, and I know she's trying her best not to start crying. I open the ring box and start talking.

"Hadleigh Baker. You are the most extraordinary

person I have had the chance to love these past three years. I've known for a while that I have wanted to spend the rest of my life with you, but I wanted this planned to perfection because you deserve nothing less than that. We may have started out hating each other, but all of that has turned into love. The moments around us remind me that everything up to this point was beautiful, but I cannot wait for the memories that we create in the future, and I want all my future moments to be with you. Will you marry me?" I'm crying at this point, and I don't know why I'm still afraid she will say no. And then she says one word that changes everything.

"*Yes.*" Tears are spilling from her eyes. I place the ring on her finger—it fits perfectly—and I wrap her up in my arms. I kiss her, pick her up, and spin her around. The strings with the photos get caught up in us as I do that.

"I love you so much," I say to her.

"I love you too, fiancé." She says back to me.

We kiss a bit longer in the same spot we first met, and this moment feels full circle. I want it to last forever. I reach behind me and hand her a small gift.

"What's this?"

"Open it," I say to her.

She does, and sheds a few more tears after she realizes what it is. *The Great Gatsby* is annotated and tabbed—just for her. It felt fitting since this book is the reason we met and got closer.

"This is perfect." She says as she flips through the pages. I drew a bunch of annotations, including the famous green light I once compared her to. With the help of Amelia, she's the best at annotating books. I was able to step up my annotated book game, finally. It was fun, even though I'm not the best at drawing.

Little does she know there's one more surprise at the restaurant. All the girls and her whole family are waiting for her. I invited Jacks and Claire too, who also just got engaged. I know I was scared, but I think I knew she would say yes, so I invited them to meet us after I proposed. We walk out of the building, hand in hand, and head towards the car we came in and our future.

I can't wait to do it all with her.

ACKNOWLEDGMENTS

Thank you to Hannah, Lexi, and Grayson. This book is based on my friendship with you guys, and I wouldn't have it any other way. I'm convinced we're all platonic soulmates. Thank you for inspiring me to write this book. I could not have done it without your endless support. To Hannah, who is literally Hads in real life. Thank you for being the sun, moon, and stars. I adore you so endlessly, and thank you for designing the most beautiful cover for this book. I love you! To Lexi, who edited this entire book for me. You are quite literally one of my favorite people on the planet. Thank you for dealing with my emotional escapades and always being there for me, especially when I don't believe in myself. I love you! And to Grayson. Thank you for being as delusional as I am when talking about these characters. I love your brain, your mind, and everything in between. The same personism is strong in us. Thank you all for showing me what platonic love is like and for being the best friends a girl could ask for. I love you. I love you. I love you!

Thank you to Amy, Drew, and Maine for being the best friends and beta readers I could ask for. I value your opinions, and the fact that you all got to read this and experience this world I created first makes my heart feel so full. The endless support from you guys kept me going, and I love you all so so much!

Thank you to Alyssa Williams. Your friendship has kept me going since we were two years old, and I wouldn't have it any other way. Thank you for being by my side through thick and thin and always being my biggest cheerleader. Your friendship means so much to me, and I genuinely have no words to express how much I love you. Thank you for being the strawberry acai refresher to my pink drink. I love you!

Thank you to my boyfriend, Josh, for not laughing in my face when I told you I wanted to write a romance book. Feeling the love you give me always is no match for any romance book. Yours exceeds all of them. Thank you for allowing me to chase my dreams and for always supporting me. Thank you for showing me what real true love looks like. I love you.

Thank you to Eva. Your endless support and excitement for this book have fueled me during this process. Thank you for creating the best playlist for me to listen to while writing.

Thank you to Andrew for helping with some of the dialogue. It was so much fun listening to you come up with ideas, only for Lexi and me to laugh at you. I appreciate your support and help, even if you like to make fun of me.

Thank you to my Mom for always letting me know that I can do anything I set my mind to. Thank you for teaching me everything I needed about life and doing it all as a single parent. I want to be like you when I grow up.

Thank you to my brother, who didn't even know he was helping me with this book. Thank you for helping me with the more technical elements of hockey and for answering my random questions about it all the time.

Thank you to everyone in the booksta community who has been excited and in my DMs telling me how much they love the book already. I am so thankful I decided to make an account to showcase my love for reading, and now here we are! Thank you for being on this insane journey with me and always showing me support and love. I love you all more than you know!

Finally, to my younger self, who always dreamed of holding her book in her hands. We did it! I wish you could see us now and see who we have become. I'm so proud of you for finally using your voice after it had been stifled all those years. I love you, and I'm proud of you. Always.

BOOKS BY THIS AUTHOR

Replaying The Game

Grand Mountain #1

Redefining The Rules

Grand Mountain #1.5

Reconsidering The Facts

Grand Mountain #2

Reconciling With The Rival

Grand Mountain #3

Rewriting The Stars

Grand Mountain #4

ABOUT THE AUTHOR

Emily Tudor creates characters and stories about platonic and romantic love for anyone and everyone. She lives in the state of New York and loves listening to music and creating stories. She loves Marvel movies, the song *mirrorball* by Taylor Swift and buying too many books when she already has many to be read at home. This is her debut novel.

You can find her on Instagram at:
@authoremilytudor
@emil.yslibrary